Joshua's Secret

Tania Park

ISBN: 978-0-6455254-8-9 (Paperback)
ISBN: 978-0-6455254-9-6 (e-book)

A catalogue record for this book is available from the National Library of Australia

Tania Park Publishing.
For all enquiries contact:
goldpark3@gmail.com

Tania Park

Joshua's Secret

Other Titles by Author

The Only Way I Know: 2011 - Biography
Mistaken: 2015 – Crime/mystery/romance
Retribution: 2015 – Crime/mystery
Blind Justice: 2016 – Crime/mystery
Commended 2016 Christina Stead National Literary Awards.
Road Trip: 2016 – Adventure/mystery
The Swan: 2018 Crime/mystery/romance
Finalist 2020 The Wishing Shelf International Awards.
Stalked: 2019: Psychological Thriller
Long listed 2020 Davitt Awards.
Double Cross: 2020 – White collar crime
Long listed 2021 Davitt Awards
The Chest: 2021 – Mystery/crime
Beloved Intruder: 2022 – Romance
Third place – Romance Writers of Australia – Sapphire Award.
Workshop Workings: 2023 – Collection of Winning short stories and poems created in writing workshops.
Redemption – 2024 – Crime/mystery
Jilted in Greece – 2024 – Romance/Adventure
The Price of Freedom – 2024 – Romance/Adventure

Joshua's Secret

Scared and grumpy, Joshua stared through the side window unable to recognise any of the places or buildings they passed, which turned his tummy into a washing machine. 'Daddy, why do we have to move house?'

His dad peered at him in the rear-vision mirror. 'Haven't we talked about this? A zillion times?'

'Sure but I don't want to change schools. I'll have no friends. Who can I play with?'

'You'll make new friends the same way you did when you first went to Kindy. It took you two days to become best buddies with Ben.'

'I'll never be able to play with him again.'

'You can visit every holidays.'

'Now I can't talk to Nanna and Poppy and…'

'We'll visit them lots. It's only a two hour drive. You will spend all the holidays with them. Our furniture is already in our new house.'

'I like our old house.'

'It's been sold. The family has already moved in. You met them, played with the kids.'

'I know.' Joshua dropped his head and closed his eyes because they were all scratchy. He lifted his feet and put them on the edge of the seat but it meant his knees came close his chin. To get comfortable he wrapped his arms around his knees and wriggled back in the booster seat. Too bad if his sneakers were on the seat. He didn't care and Daddy couldn't see them.

'I start work on Monday in the new business. You agreed to all of this, remember?'

Joshua sighed. 'I remember.' It wasn't the only thing he remembered. He could never forget the horrible *screech* and *bang* when another car crashed into them when he was only four. Nor the way Mummy screamed and screamed and screamed. Nor the silence when she stopped and whispered to him. *Don't be scared. Everything will be okay. Daddy will come.* Nor would he forget the blood on her head, and on the crunched in door and window, and on the front seat. The *squeal* of so many sirens. The police cars. The blue and red lights which never stopped flashing. The ambulance. The way they held his head so he couldn't see Mummy when they took her out of the wrecked car and put her on a stretcher.

He fisted the tears from his eyes, sniffed and turned towards the window so Daddy wouldn't notice. It was the last time he saw Mummy.

Even though he was now six, he remembered it all. Mummy was supposed to be up in the sky looking down on him all the time to make sure he was okay. She still loved him. Everyone said the same. Nanna, Poppy, the doctor and the lady he had gone to every week to talk about anything he wanted. Daddy had come too but he was always sad. A couple of times Daddy had cried, although he pretended he had sore eyes but Joshua knew. He wasn't dumb. And he knew Mummy couldn't be up in the sky when she was buried under the ground the same way Kittycat was buried? In a hole. With dirt over her.

The one thing he had trouble remembering was Mummy's face and he was too scared to tell Daddy in case it made him sadder. There was a photo of her next to Daddy's bed. Joshua snuck in there to have a peek so he wouldn't forget what she looked like. He'd also forgotten what her cuddles felt like because now Daddy was the one who gave him lots of cuddles and kisses. So did Nanna and Poppy. But there were never any Mummy cuddles.

He still didn't want to change schools. Nanna said the old house had too many sad memories for Daddy. When he met up with Mummy's friends in town they wouldn't talk to him anymore, which made him sad. So, to make Daddy happy, Joshua agreed to the move, but he didn't like it.

'You okay? We'll be there soon. You'll love the house. There's a big yard with shady trees where we can kick the footy around. I set up your bedroom the same but you've got tons more room for your toys. There's also a desk with a chair in your room now.'

'Okay.' Joshua sighed again and stared down at his fingers which had got all twisted together. When his feet slid off the seat and dangled down he had to wriggle again because the seat belt pressed too hard. It was itchy, so he shoved his fingers under the strap and scratched.

Dumb new house, dumb new school and a new job for Daddy. He'd get better pay, he said. Joshua didn't care because he'd have no friends and no Mummy.

Maybe… a brilliant idea came. He grinned. Yeah, he could, but he had to keep it as a secret.

A blessed silence surrounded her. It was a relief to close the door and lower her exhausted body onto the chair at the desk. Heavy eyelids drifted downwards. Two fingers kneaded tight muscles in the back of her neck. Teaching twenty-five, exuberant six-year-olds is a job Jenna Reynolds loves, but the end of the day, and better still, the end of the school week as it was now, was always welcome.

A knock at the door followed by a squeak as it opened, shattered the short-lived peace. With a wince, she turned her head and groaned at the sight of the principal approaching.

'Jenna, you have a new student on Monday.' John Mortimer held out a form. 'In fact, we have four new students on Monday. All from different families. This one is yours.'

She took the form and opened it out to study the details. Joshua Marcus Hunter: Father – Lucas - accountant: Mother - deceased: No siblings. 'So sad, to lose a mother so young,' Jenna murmured as she stood to walk John to the door.

'A car accident. The father is a caring man. Have a great weekend.'

When Jenna resumed her seat unbidden moisture washed over her eyes at the memory of her own loss; unforgettable memories she quickly suppressed when the second interruption to her solitude erupted into the room.

Emily Johnson is a mass of irrepressible energy. It was possible she could be classed as hyperactive but Jenna never dared voice her thoughts. The two women had taken to each other and been close friends since Jenna joined the staff at the beginning of last year. They are opposites in many respects. Where Emily is tiny, dark-haired and brown-eyed, Jenna is taller. She often thought herself to be gawky while others described her as statuesque. There is only one aspect she likes about her features - long, thick, blonde hair, which she usually wore tied back in a simple ponytail.

'Are you still coming tonight?' The question echoed around the empty room as well as Jenna's aching head. 'Lily and Erin are coming. Stuart will get there as soon as he can and Ryan asked to join us.' Emily perched on the nearest child's desk.

At the mention of Ryan, Jenna shuddered. 'Yes, I'll be there, but I wish you would stop trying to match-make. I'm not interested in a relationship.' The thought of Emily's older brother sent a tremor of distaste through her. She couldn't recall the number of times she had been invited to functions to discover she'd been matched up with Ryan. To start with she hadn't minded his company when they went out as a group but she certainly had no romantic inclinations towards the man. He wasn't her type and opposite his sister in nature. It had been three or four weeks since she'd last seen him, thank goodness, for on the last occasion he had come on too strong. More than once she had to ask him to remove his arm from her waist. His surly attitude after he'd complied had scared her to the extent she'd avoided most social get-togethers since.

'He was at a loose end and asked if he could join us. We'll meet you in the lounge at six. Stuart booked a table so we shouldn't have any trouble this time.' Emily glanced at the wall clock and jolted. 'Is that the time? I have to go, catch you later.' She scooted outside without shutting the door.

With hands clenched, memories surged about the last time they had gone to the hotel for a Friday night meal. The place had been packed, forcing them to wait ages in a rowdy bar that reeked of beer, before a table became free. It hadn't been her most pleasant experience. Fighting off Ryan had made it worse.

Most days she stayed at school to prepare lessons but today she was too tired so decided to go home. Before leaving she prepared an empty desk for the new pupil, wrote down his details in her register, gathered together the bits she needed and was glad to lock the door before the two block walk home.

Halfway, a sudden darkening of the sky accompanied by a brisk wind gust, had her peer skywards. Leaden clouds scuttled and the atmosphere became dank in mere seconds. The first smatter of icy drops fell near her front gate. She quickened her pace, grabbed the mail poking out of the letterbox and ran the last few metres along the brick path. A sudden gust whipped the skirt of her jersey dress upwards as she stepped onto the small porch. One hand tugged her skirt down to prevent indecent exposure. She tucked it between clenched knees and balanced all the gear on the other arm, the papers held down with her chin so she could scrabble in her bag for the house key.

The moment she stepped inside, a different silence enveloped her; one which beset her every day she crossed the threshold of her home – soul-sapping loneliness. With the door re-locked, she wondered if it was the metaphysical atmosphere of the house that gave her this depressive sensation or if it was because she hadn't yet laid her ghosts to rest. But how long does it take to get over these traumas? Surely twenty plus months is long enough.

She glanced along the passage of the tiny house she'd bought when she began her new position at the school after her husband decided he couldn't handle the responsibility or commitment to marriage and parenthood. Euphoric after confirmation of her pregnancy, she'd waited until Rob came home to make the grand announcement. Euphoria turned to devastation when he walked out the same night and sought an immediate divorce after only a year of marriage. There had been no real explanation, which left her confused with emotional shock. Grief overwhelmed her five months later when she lost her precious little girl who had died in her womb. It was the darkest day of her life. The anguish of her husband's betrayal had paled into insignificance the day she gave birth to her stillborn daughter.

Rob had never bothered to contact her after he packed his bags and as far as she knew he had no idea whether he was the father to a son or daughter. All communication had been via a lawyer. She didn't know where he lived, nor did she care. With no time to grieve she had mere weeks to find a teaching position to support herself. All she had gained from their divorce was enough money to purchase this tiny home.

Her shoulders dropped on a hiss of breath. It was possible she wasn't over it but how does one forget and begin to live again? As she passed each door along the short passage, she peeked in each room. The bare necessities were there and the rooms that mattered held a homely atmosphere. She hadn't been able to afford to replace the items of furniture Rob took but had made gradual purchases of odd bits and pieces and now possessed enough she could invite a small group of friends home without embarrassment. Most items came from second-hand shops: few matched but she was debt free.

The almost empty spare bedroom held a few boxes of teaching equipment and items she rarely used. In the study at the end of the passage, she dropped the schoolwork on a small wooden desk. A scan of the room brought a smile. This room was cosy with its filing cabinet, basic computer equipment and a tall bookcase along one wall. A comfortable rocking chair sat next to a small side table, which held a compact sound system. Her smile was warm while she eyed her sanctuary: the one place she could work in comfort or lay back to relax.

She sifted through the few mail items on the way to the kitchen where she set the kettle on to boil. A caffeine hit might give her an energy boost for the evening. The three bills were set aside in preference for the short missive from her brother, Mark, who lived overseas. It wasn't often he wrote since they kept in contact via email, but a card to wish her a happy birthday was included. A smile broke out at the cryptic message but she had to swallow down the yearning to be able to catch up with him and his family more often, especially her two young nieces since they were the only family she had left.

While sipping black coffee, she searched the wardrobe for an outfit to wear to the pub. With a spring storm now on a rampage, warm clothes were needed. She pulled out a pair of tailored black slacks, teamed it with a pretty, long-sleeved blouse plus a leather jacket for protection. It was only a casual fun night but, as always, she wanted to look her best, especially tonight since it was her birthday.

As a gift to herself, she wallowed in a bath to ease unusual tension. The liberal dose of bath oil sent up a sweet, spicy aroma; scents that would cling to her skin for the night. The shampoo had the same scent and negated the need for an additional spray of *eau-de-parfum*. Not one for much make-up, she figured the occasion deserved a touch of mascara and a blush of peach lipstick, although she'd told no one of the significance of the day, so what would they care? She dried and brushed her thick hair, tied it back but changed her mind and let it flow loose with a small sparkly clip each side to keep it out of her eyes. A final inspection in the mirror created a smile of satisfaction. Not too bad. 'Happy birthday, Jenna,' she said to her image.

Water still bucketed when she drove into the hotel car park on the other side of town. It took a couple of rounds before she found a spot close to the hotel entry when a car left, but she had to wait for a break in the downpour before she dared make a dash.

It appeared everyone else had the same idea for a large group converged at the same time. In the scurry Jenna was knocked off balance. With a muffled cry, she tottered backwards and was torpedoed into a hard body.

'Humph,' she heard when arms swept around her waist to steady her.

'Oh, sorry, Jenna,' said Emily as she struggled to find her balance after she'd careened into Jenna. It had to be Emily.

'Who's your friend?' Emily stared over Jenna's shoulder.

With the arms still held tight, she twisted her head around to be startled by the dark eyes of a tall, powerfully built man who smiled down at her.

'I'm sorry, err, thank you.' She struggled free to hide the inferno racing up her neck.

'You're welcome,' the stranger said as he released his hold.

Emily's boyfriend, Stuart, arrived and gave Emily a hug and brief kiss. Keeping his arm draped around her shoulder, he leant over and planted a friendly peck on Jenna's cheek. 'You've already met Luke.' He reached past her to shake the stranger's hand.

'Err, no.' Embarrassed, she moved through the doorway, desperate for a few moments to gather her wits but the entire crowd moved into the hotel lounge in one surge, carrying her inside.

'Over here.' Stuart nudged Jenna's arm and guided her towards the only empty table in the room. Because the end was so close to the next table, he re-arranged the chairs to squish four down each side. Luke eased onto a seat. Emily wriggled between him and Stuart. Erin and Lily sat together on the opposite side. Jenna was about to sit next to them when Ryan nudged her out of the way and sat, leaving her the end seat with no one opposite. Eyes shut she wished she dared to move to the other side but it would be too obvious.

Only after the drink orders were taken did Stuart stand to introduce the tall stranger. 'Luke here, has recently moved into the house next door to me and since he knows no one in town, I asked him to join us tonight. Luke, this is my girl, Emily, and her brother, Ryan, is opposite you. Across the table are the terrible two, Lily and Erin. They teach with Emily. Next to Ryan is Jenna.' Each of the group acknowledged the newcomer with nods and smiles as their names were mentioned.

With no option but to spend the evening next to Ryan, Jenna figured the night wasn't going to be as pleasant as she would have liked. Happy birthday, Jenna, her sarcastic brain yelled.

First course of shared garlic bread arrived. She took a piece, sniffed and bit off a corner. Yum. A hand landed on her thigh. Eyes closed, she drew in a breath, nudged Ryan's arm away and inched her chair closer to the end.

Ryan leant towards her — too close. 'How was work?' Garlic breath brushed her cheek.

'Good.' She leant away, used her backside and feet to move the chair a few more centimetres.

'Playing squash this weekend?' His hand landed on her forearm.

She dislodged it by lifting her hand to scratch an imaginary itch on her face. 'I'm not sure.' She was but wasn't about to let him know.

'What are you doing tomorrow?' He scraped his chair close enough his arm brushed against hers. 'Shopping?'

'No.' She wanted to tell him it was none of his business and to get the hell away. Good manners kept her mouth shut. Another shift of her chair closer to the corner and she lifted the knife to cut the bread into bite-size pieces, deliberately elbowing him hard enough he grunted. To keep him away, she used the arm to put piece after piece of bread into her mouth until her plate was empty. It might have appeared she was starving but who cared?

'Got a date Saturday night?' Ryan asked when he finished his own bread.

'I might, I might not?'

'What type of an answer is that?'

'The only one you will get.' It was a relief when her grilled fish, salad and chips landed in front of her. To keep Ryan at bay, she hoed in although there was barely room for her right hand to cut the food when he leant closer again. She wasn't sure if the newcomer noticed for all of a sudden he asked Ryan a heap of personal questions, which she was more than thankful for. It gave her a chance to eat without constant interruption. A fantastic birthday dinner, she thought when she placed her knife and fork together and pushed the plate towards the centre.

Conversation ceased while the server moved behind each person to serve sweets and/or coffee and remove the used dishes. The rich aroma of the fresh brew she'd ordered, tantalized her nostrils when it settled in front of her. With the teaspoon, she swirled the creamy froth, picked up her cup, sniffed the pungent aroma and took a sip. Perfect. While sipping she pretended an intimate study of the room and almost dropped the cup when she spied the back of a man across the room. It can't be. The cup rattled back on its saucer. When the man turned, she gasped and dropped her head to hide. Desperate to not be noticed, she unhooked her shoulder bag from the back of the chair, took enough cash from her purse to cover her meal and handed it to Ryan.

'What's this?' he asked.

'I'm not so crash hot. I need to go home. Can you pay for me?' When she stood on jellified legs and twisted so her back was to the man, she swayed for a second, grabbed her jacket and bag, and left with head down.

'Are you okay?' she heard Ryan ask.

Unable to answer, she was thankful he didn't follow. Unshed tears blurred her vision while blundering a way through the lounge area, mumbling apologies when she bumped into other patrons. The rain was still a steady stream when she stumbled outside but she took no heed and ran until she reached the safety of her car. Inside, she thrust the keys in the ignition, planted her foot on the accelerator and ignored the spin of the wheels in the sheet of surface water before they gripped the bitumen. She shot out of the parking space so fast, she had to jam on the brakes and only missed the car behind by a small gap before coming to a sudden standstill when the engine stalled. She swore, blew out her cheeks to steady shot nerves, restarted the engine and took a damn sight more care to ease out of the car park where she paused at the edge of the road to wait for oncoming traffic.

It took a minute to catch her breath before easing her foot on the accelerator. 'Happy birthday, Jenna,' she yelled with a fist slam on the steering wheel. Why had her ex-husband been at the hotel? The last person she ever wanted to meet again, well apart from creepy Ryan. To twist the knife, Rob sat next to a woman she had thought of as a close friend; close enough to be a bridesmaid at her wedding. A traitor who sat with her arms draped over Rob while they both laughed.

How long had they been together? Nancy had never mentioned Rob on the few occasions Jenna had rung her over the past year and a half. The same Nancy who was married to another man and had two young kids. Another slam on the steering wheel when she realised Nancy had never rung since the divorce. It had been Jenna who made the calls. Now she knew there had been a reason for the lack of contact.

Too afraid to let go of the principal's hand, Joshua trudged beside him. Nanna always told him it was butterflies in his tummy when he was scared but he had a huge kangaroo jumping up and down in his tummy. They stopped in front of a dark blue closed door. The loud knock made him jump and the kangaroo did a somersault.

'Come in,' said a lady's loud voice.

The principal dropped Joshua's hand and yanked on the door handle but it didn't budge. He knocked again, louder. When the noise echoed in Joshua's ears he shut his eyes and held his breath.

'I'm coming,' the teacher called. Her voice was too loud. He didn't like shouty teachers.

A click. The door moved, opened wider and wider. With his head down, Joshua spied black shoes. Not those high clickety heels but flat like his school shoes. Ever so slow, he lifted his head. The skirt was blue, his favourite colour. The top was white with a frill down the middle and long sleeves. His eyes widened at the face. She was pretty, with white hair tied back in a ponytail. Now he remembered Mummy had a ponytail – until she cut her hair short. But Mummy had brown hair.

Before the teacher squatted in front of him he noticed there were no other children in the room. The kangaroo did a tumble-turn and jumped when the teacher put one hand on his shoulder.

'Hello, Joshua, I'm Mrs Reynolds. I'm so pleased you have joined my class. Come with me to your desk to put your books in before we have a look around outside. We might be able to find a few boys from our room to play with you.'

She stood, grasped his hand. Her fingers were warm and soft. When she tugged, the kangaroo did an almighty backflip inside him but he stepped forward. At a desk, she helped him unpack his bag of the workbooks from his old school. It worried him when she flicked through the pages. There was no smile. What if he wasn't good enough?

'I like how neat your letters are,' she said, this time with a teeny smile. 'And you are a good speller. Do you like learning new words?'

Too terrified to answer, he nodded and put his pencil case inside the tray, next to the ruler.

'We'll sort your workbooks later,' she said and slid the tray back under the desk. 'Let's go outside so I can show you your play area, the toilets and other places you might need to go. This is a big school so it's easy to get muddled at first.'

Since she held his hand, he followed. The toilets were the last doors at the end of the veranda, not too far to go but he bet they were stinky. They were at his old school. At the end of the veranda was a big patch of grass with three giant trees.

'This is where all the junior classes eat their lunch,' she said. 'You can't play until a bell goes.' They walked back towards the veranda. 'Oh, look, here are two boys from our class. Brendan, Scott, this is Joshua. How about you two play with him and take care of him for his first day?'

'Okay, Miss. Come on, Joshua.' The boys moved to either side of him, both much smaller than him but the kids at the other school were smaller as well. They led him back to the grassed area. They had only reached the other side where there was a low wooden fence, when the siren went. Behind the fence was an oval, he guessed it was where they did sport. Sport was good.

'Come on,' said Scott, 'let's run so we can be first in line.' When the other two ran Joshua walked so he could be last but Scott ran back, grabbed him and shoved him between the other two at the line.

He hated it when Mrs Reynolds made him stand in front of the room so all the other kids could look at him. The kangaroo did so many jumps he felt sick. They all said 'Hello, Joshua.' He nodded and hurried to his seat so he could sit and hide, ever so glad he was in the back row.

A few kids told news. He shook his head when asked if he wanted to introduce himself. Next they did number work. Easy adding up. He liked maths. He already knew his two times table and the five and ten. Daddy showed him how easy it was to count by twos, fives and tens. He could count up to a hundred. He could count that far when he was four. He smiled when he remembered how Poppy once told him how to count to a hundred. Poppy said, 'One, two, miss a few, ninety-nine, a hundred.' It was a good joke. He liked jokes, especially knock, knock jokes.

They learned words with the same sound. He already knew those words. The other kids read aloud, a book he read ages ago, but it was way too scary to stand up and read. The kangaroo must have gone to sleep when the siren went and he could escape to eat his apple by himself after he went to the toilet to pee. The smell wasn't so bad.

At lunch time Scott and Brendan sat either side of him on a wooden seat under one of the huge trees. They opened out their lunchboxes.

'Watcha got in yours?' Scott nudged him.

Joshua lifted the corner of the triangle to show his favourite, cheese and Vegemite.

'Wanna swap one? I've got mooshed up egg.'

Joshua nodded and handed over one of his triangles. The egg was so yummy he might ask Daddy to make him egg sandwiches.

'You like tuna and lettuce?' Brendan asked.

Joshua screwed up his face and shook his head.

'Okay, how about sultanas. I've got two boxes.' Brendan held one out.

Not sure what to do, Joshua opened the box, tipped out a few in his hand and gave the box back.

'Nah,' said Brendan. 'Have 'em all, I don't like them much but Mum says we have to have a healthy lunch. I usually chuck 'em in the bin.'

'Okay, thank you,' whispered Joshua. Daddy said it was good manners to say thank you whenever a person did something nice for you.

Surprised Joshua's father hadn't come to meet her, Jenna made her way to the principal in the staffroom before she sat for lunch and a much-needed caffeine hit.

'John? Did Mr Hunter bring Joshua to school and if so, why didn't you bring him to meet me?'

'It was a young babysitter who brought him in and she will pick him up after school each day. I met Mr Hunter when he enrolled Joshua. He's a pleasant man, concerned about his son. He mentioned he goes to work early and drops Joshua off at his babysitter on the way. Is there a problem?'

'No, Joshua is a lovely young boy and quite bright. He hasn't said a word to anyone in class yet but I guess he could be overawed and frightened. I like to meet and chat with all the parents. It helps me understand their children better.'

'Would you like me to make an appointment for Mr Hunter to come in?'

'No, if he's so busy we'll wait until we need to make contact. There may not be any problems.' With a smile to indicate the conversation was over she joined the short queue at the urn, made her coffee and sat next to Emily.

Jenna liked to have her pupils do a form of physical exercise each day and since the weekend storm had disappeared to show off the warmth of a true spring day, she took her class outside for the last session of the day, playing *follow the leader* on an obstacle course around the grounds. The children laughed the entire time they followed her as she skipped, ran, jumped, hopped and walked over, under and around obstacles. The laughter increased when she raced them back to the classroom at the final siren. The mad scramble to sort out raincoats and bags when the parents came to collect their youngsters, finally ended, leaving only Joshua on the veranda. He looked bewildered so she squatted in front of him.

'Is your babysitter picking you up?'

A single nod with his eyes averted.

'Do you know where you are to wait for her?'

Another shy nod.

'She might be there; you go and check.' Jenna watched the boy wander towards the gate. He was tall for his age, the tallest in her class. And smart. The drawing he did about the story she read, showed a maturity beyond his age. The fine details he'd added were intricate and he'd picked out minor items mentioned in the story. Details no other child included.

'Bye, Joshua,' she called after him.

It twisted her heart when he turned towards her and gave a tiny wave accompanied by the barest of smiles. Back inside, she spent half an hour tidying the room, preparing gear for the next day and happy everything was ready, picked up the items she was taking home. Near the gate, it was a shock to find Joshua still outside the front fence. Tears rolled down his sad face.

With her heart on a mission to melt, she gathered him into her arms and gave him a cuddle. 'Sweetie, you must return to the classroom if your babysitter doesn't arrive. I'll look after you while you wait.'

Deep concern twisted her innards since most of the staff and all the students had gone. She could take him home, but it would cause problems if the babysitter arrived and couldn't find him. A search both ways along the street yielded no sign of any human let alone a babysitter.

'What can we do while we wait?' she asked. Receiving no answer, she led him back to the classroom where she collected a soccer ball. The pair kicked the ball around the empty car park, using Joshua's bag and jumper set on the bitumen to indicate the goalposts. The sound of his giggles and laughter each time he scored, warmed her heart but not a word did he say.

It was close to five when a young girl of about sixteen strolled up and grabbed Joshua's hand.

'Excuse me, what time are you supposed to collect Joshua?' Jenna stepped in front of the girl to prevent her walking away.

'After school. I take him home and Mum looks after him,' the girl replied with a hint of cheek and a sharp jerk on Joshua's hand.

Since the children from the high school at the end of the road were dismissed ten minutes before the primary school, Jenna reached out and grasped a hold of the girl's shoulder when she turned away. 'What took you so long? School finished over an hour ago.'

'I was talking to my friends, Miss.' Without another word, the girl dodged to one side and strode past Jenna with a tug on Joshua's arm. He had to run to keep up with her.

With a shake of her head, Jenna picked up the ball, returned it to her room and strode home with anger simmering.

'After five,' Jenna muttered at the glance on her watch, Wednesday afternoon. 'This has gone on long enough.' When she released Joshua's hand he ran towards the teenager who approached the gate. Frustrated at having to keep an eye on the boy every day, she spun around to collect her handbag. It wasn't the staying back that upset her because it gave her the opportunity to complete all her lesson preparation which left the night free to catch up on household chores, and Joshua's company was much better than the loneliness at home. She was more concerned about Joshua not being cared for properly. If she didn't take the time to keep him company he would be left standing in the street alone. Anything could happen to him. Most of the things she thought of were not of the pleasant variety.

When the same thing happened Thursday afternoon, Jenna vowed to rectify the situation. She set Joshua to sorting out a box of building blocks while she wrote a note to his father. The fear on Joshua's face when she handed him the short missive, sent a shiver across her shoulders. Surely the man wouldn't chastise his son for bringing home a note from the teacher.

With a smile to ease his fear, she grasped his hand. 'You aren't in any trouble. You are a delightful young man and I'm glad you are in my class. I'm worried about your babysitter not picking you up straight after school. You shouldn't have to wait so long each day. I'd like to speak with your dad to figure out if we can fix the problem. This note is to ask if he can ring me here at school. I've given him the phone number and the times he can phone.' To ensure Joshua understood, she opened out the note and read the words aloud.

It was a relief when he visibly relaxed and gave a tiny smile. He slipped the refolded note into his bag, zipped it shut and ambled over to the gate.

A lump settled in her throat at the sight of the boy drag his feet with his head down. He looked so lonely and forlorn. She stood at the window to keep watch until he was out of sight.

'I look forward to your call Mr Hunter,' she said to the gate when she passed through on her way home.

'There's a message for you, Jenna. Can you ring Mr Hunter back as soon as possible? Here's the number.' John Mortimer handed her a piece of paper when she walked past the office on her way from making coffee before the day began. Placing her mug on the bench by the phone, she dialled the number scrawled across the small scrap of paper and asked to be put through to Mr Hunter after she gave her name.

'Mrs Reynolds, you have a problem with my son?'

Surprised at the terse comment without so much as a hello, Jenna stiffened. 'No, Mr Hunter, Joshua gives me no trouble at all. He's a wonderful student. I wish they were all like him.'

'Thank you, but your note indicated you needed to speak to me about Josh.'

Taken aback by the tone of his voice, Jenna wondered whether Mr Hunter had a bad night or whether he was always so grumpy and terse.

'My concern is about his afterschool care, Mr Hunter.'

'With respect, Mrs Reynolds, I don't believe it is any of your business what happens to your students either before or after school. So unless you have a problem with my son's behaviour or work at school, I'd appreciate it if you would leave the rest of his upbringing to me.'

Speechless, Jenna stared at the phone while a spurt of anger shot through her. How dare he speak to her like that?

'Well, Mrs Reynolds, does my son misbehave in school?'

'No, but...'

'Is he coping with the work?'

'Yes, certainly but…'

'Then I don't understand why we are having this conversation.

I'm busy and have a client waiting. Have a good day, Mrs Reynolds.' There was a definite snick.

Stunned, Jenna stared at the silent receiver. Coming to her senses, she glanced at her watch and realised she needed to hurry. With the first siren imminent she didn't have time to call the rude man back. But she certainly would at lunchtime. She picked up the tepid coffee along with the scrap of paper with Mr Grumpy Hunter's phone number.

Mr Hunter was out with a client at lunchtime but Jenna was assured her message would be passed on.

After she'd checked her empty cubbyhole after school for any messages to say he had rung back, she dialled his number again. Again, he was with a client.

'Did Mr Hunter receive my earlier message?' she asked the receptionist.

'Certainly, I passed it on myself.'

'Can you be sure Mr Hunter receives this message as well. It is important, or you could give me his mobile number. Or the direct line to his office.'

'When our accountants are with clients, the calls are fielded through me and you are not on the list for Mr Hunter's personal phone. I'll make sure he receives the message, I promise.'

'Thank you, I appreciate your help.'

Jenna played soccer with Joshua next to the office so she would hear the phone but it remained silent. She should have given her mobile number but why should she when she wasn't on his list to be given his private number? After having to wait back until five again while she kept Joshua amused and safe, Jenna had had enough.

It was eight before she had a chance to phone Mr Hunter again. Although she only had his office number, she figured he would get the message first thing Monday morning. Determined to put an end to things, she decided she would play his game and be as terse and direct as he had been. She didn't care if she appeared rude. The man deserved her rudeness.

'Mr Hunter, you may not think your child's safety and welfare is any of my business, but I cannot stand by while a six-year-old child waits, unsupervised, on the side of a busy road, until five every afternoon. From now on I will keep him with me in my classroom and he can be picked up from there.' She paused for a second. 'At least my conscience will be clear in knowing your son is safe and not the target of a perverted predator. I, at least, will be able to sleep at night. Will you?'

'W'hy are we here, Daddy?' Joshua unclipped his harness, opened the car door but waited for an answer before he got out.

'A barbecue lunch.'

'Why?'

'The staff at work want to welcome us to town.'

'Why?'

Daddy laughed and turned around. 'It's what people do to make newcomers welcome so we can get to know each other better. All of my new workmates are bringing their partners and kids so there will be other kids for you to play with. You might find a new friend.'

'I like my old friends.' Joshua wriggled to the ground and slammed the door.

'Door, Josh.'

'Sorry.' He wasn't. He didn't want to be here. It was scary when you didn't know anyone. And he'd been scared all week at school although Brendan and Scott had been cool fun at playtime. And he liked the egg sandwich he swapped for one of his. And the sultanas. Which reminded him.

'Daddy, can you make mooshed up egg sandwiches for school sometimes?'

'Huh? You don't like egg sandwiches. You always want cheese and Vegemite.'

'I like mooshed up egg.'

'Since when?' Daddy held Joshua's hand as they walked side-by-side along the path made of bricks. They weren't all even and there were lots and lots of tiny weeds between them.

'Since Scott gave me one of his.' Josh hopped over a bumpy bit so he didn't trip.

'Who is Scott?'

'My new friend at school.' Up two steps and a jump onto the veranda.

At the door, Daddy knocked, glanced down and smiled. 'Told you it wouldn't take long to make new friends. Are there any other friends?'

'Brendan. Only Brendan and Scott. Nobody else likes me.'

'I'm sure that's not true. You've only been there five days. How about the teacher? Do you like her?'

'Yes.'

The door opened. There was a lot of grown-up talk while they went inside, through a ginormous house with a hundred rooms and out onto a bigger veranda with a roof way up high. A long, long row of tables was at one end. He hid behind Daddy's legs when so many strangers stared at him. The kangaroo woke up in his tummy and bounced up and down.

'For those of you who haven't already met him, this is our new partner, Lucas Hunter and his son,' yelled the man so loud Joshua jumped as high as the kangaroo.

'Joshua,' Daddy said.

Too scared to look, Joshua put the fingers of one hand over his eyes and kept a hold of Daddy with the other. There were lots of 'Hi' and 'Hello' before everyone started to talk at the same time. They walked to the table. Daddy tugged out a chair.

'Why don't you go and meet the kids?' Joshua was turned around to face the backyard. There were big trees way down the back, behind a humungous lawn which spread from one side fence to nearly the other. A bunch of bushes hid the bottom of the other fence. A group of younger kids played in a sandpit near the veranda. One, a boy, he thought, was throwing sand at the others. A teeny, tiny girl bashed a plastic spade on a pile of sand. No way was he going to join a bunch of babies.

Much older kids were running all over the place. It looked like they were playing chasey and most were twice his size. The only kids around his age were two girls sitting on a bench behind the sandpit. No way. He didn't want to get girl germs.

'Go on,' said Daddy with a gentle shove in Joshua's back. 'Go and meet the other kids.'

'Why?'

'So I can meet the adults. Off you go.'

He really, really, really didn't want to go but also didn't want to make Daddy cross so he walked away with his head down.

'Watch out!' yelled a lady's voice.

With a jump, Josh peeked up. Three ladies had come out of the house, carrying big bowls of food. 'Oops, sorry.' He hopped sideways to let them pass, dawdled to the edge of the veranda, jumped off and veered across the grass to the furthest corner. To pretend he was exploring, he looked at every tree, every bush, every rock and spotted a couple of garden gnomes. They were cute but dumb. Close to the fence, he scuffed towards the house, past the end of the veranda and along the skinny path to the front where there was a tall white gate with a padlock. He had to go back. He turned, leant his back against the gate and watched one foot make a pattern in the dirt on the path to waste time.

'Who's the new dopey kid?' said a loud voice.

'Looks like a sooky la-la,' said another.

Joshua dared a tiny peek and the kangaroo did high jumps. They were big kids. Had to be teenagers and he didn't like the looks on their scary faces.

'Who's the sooky la-la, who's the sooky la-la?' they both sang as they headed towards him side-by-side which made it impossible to get past. The kangaroo got stuck in his throat. Head down, he ran full pelt. Barged through them. They laughed – a laugh which wasn't funny. Still he ran, around the corner and almost tripped over one of the teeny kids. He jerked sideways, slowed and now he was close to the adults he wasn't quite so scared so shoved his shoulders back to pretend everything was okay. When he noticed Daddy, he stopped.

Daddy was laughing. Next to the lady who had growled at Josh. She had her hand on Daddy's knee. Has Daddy already found him a new mummy – a growly mummy?

The two big boys came from around the corner, laughed funny

and punched him on the shoulder. He headed for his father.

'Daddy?' he whispered.

'You have a kid?' said the lady.

'A son, yes.'

'Oh, you didn't say you were married.' Her hand lifted as she leant back.

'I'm not.'

The hand went back onto Daddy's leg.

'What's the problem, Josh?' His tummy squirmed when Daddy didn't hold out his hand or move around to face him. It squirmed more when the lady's hand rubbed up and down Daddy's leg.

Joshua crept closer and put his mouth near Daddy's ear. 'You told me to walk away when people weren't nice to me. I walked,' he said in his softest voice.

'Who wasn't nice?'

'Two big kids.'

'Nothing will happen to you here with so many adults. Stay with the younger kids.'

No way was he going anywhere. 'I need a drink.' He didn't but he could stay while Daddy found a drink.

'There are soft drink cans in the big blue Esky near the barbecue,' said the lady who lifted her hand from Daddy's knee and pointed to the other end of the veranda. Her face screwed into an ugly toad. 'How often do you have him stay with you?' she asked when she put her hand back on Daddy's knee.

'24/7,' said Daddy.

Joshua didn't know what it meant.

'You were granted full custody?' The lady leant closer to Daddy with her eyes on Joshua. She flicked her fingers towards the Esky. 'Go get yourself a drink.'

Daddy turned his head and nodded. Since he didn't want to get in trouble with so many people around, Joshua figured he'd better do as he was told. He dawdled towards the Esky. Two men were at the barbecue with long tongs in one hand and a can of drink in the other. Smelt like yucky beer. A long row of sausages sizzled on the barbecue with smoke twirling up in the air. They smelt yummy.

A huge pile of already cooked onions sat on a plate at one end and a row of handlebar chops were along the front. Gooey blood oozed on the top of the chops. He liked the chops with a handlebar. Much better than the curly tails. At the Esky, he lifted the lid and grinned. His favourite although he wasn't allowed to drink it often – red creaming soda. And cola. He lifted a few cans to check what else was there. Lemonade, lemon, orange. His hand hovered over the cola and red creaming soda. A quick peek. Daddy wasn't watching. He grabbed the red soda, turned his back to hide it from Daddy and popped the can open. Red froth fizzed and bubbled through the round hole. He lifted it to his mouth, sucked and slurped. It was cold and tickled his nose but tasted the bestest ever.

'Move away from the barbie, Son,' said one of the men.

Joshua nodded and jumped off the veranda. So Daddy didn't know what he was drinking, he held the can in front of his tummy while walking towards the back fence. The game of chasey had to be over for the older kids now stood together in different groups. He sure kept an eye out for the two nasty kids and was more than happy when they weren't anywhere in front of him.

A hand punched his back. Joshua yelped and spun around.

'Who's the sooky la-la?' sang the biggest boy at the same time he shoved on Joshua's shoulder so hard a big splotch of drink slopped over the top and onto the ground.

'You want to say that to me?' asked a voice Joshua was ever so glad to hear.

The two boys spun around, said a naughty word and stepped backwards. 'Huh, no,' one said.

'Why not?' Boy was he glad Daddy had come.

'We were only having fun,' said the other boy who swished one foot in a half-circle on the grass.

'Fun for whom?' asked Daddy. 'Certainly not for the six-year-old. Do you think it's fun to abuse younger kids?

'We didn't hurt him.' The biggest boy edged away. Daddy stepped in front of him and he was way bigger than the boys.

'You hit him and said nasty words to him. It's called abuse.'

'What's going on here? Matty?' The lady who had been next to Daddy came up and put her arm through his elbow.

'Your son?' asked Daddy.

'Yes, why?'

'You might want to teach him better manners.' Daddy tugged his elbow away.

'Excuse me?'

'Teenage boys who think it's fun to bully much younger kids, grow up to think it's fun to abuse their partners. I don't appreciate my son being the subject of abuse by a couple of hooligans. Come on Josh, let's eat.' Daddy lifted Joshua up and held him against his chest.

'Sorry, Daddy,' Joshua whispered.

'You don't need to say sorry. You did nothing wrong. I'm proud of you for the way you walked away and said nothing to them.' Daddy pointed to the can and grinned. 'Red creaming soda, hey? I guess it's okay for a special occasion. But only one. No more. Okay?'

'Okay. You like that lady?'

'Not if she can't teach her son how to be nice to people. It's never okay to be a bully.'

'I love you, Daddy.'

Daddy turned his face, smiled and pressed a kiss on Joshua's head. 'And I love you. Let's eat.' He dropped Joshua to the ground, picked two plates off the table near the barbie and asked for a chop and two sausages on both plates.

'You sure that's enough. There's steak as well,' said one of the men.

'More than enough for Josh, and I need to keep room to sample all of those salads the ladies have put together. I appreciate you putting this on for us.'

'You're welcome. I noticed Rebecca has got her hooks into you,' said the man with his tongs pointed towards the nasty boy's mother. 'Might warn you, she's on the prowl for husband number three. Took the first two to the cleaners.'

'Well, it certainly won't be me,' said Daddy with a laugh. 'I'm happy with just Josh and me.' He grinned at Josh and handed him one of the plates. 'Make sure you eat a rainbow of salad.'

Joshua rolled his eyes. Always a rainbow although Daddy still hadn't found him a blue vegetable and blue was in the rainbow. The closest he'd come was the skin of a pumpkin but it was bright orange inside. And blueberries had purple skin and were pale green inside. They should be called purple berries. He was glad he was allowed to sit next to Daddy until they went home. He wasn't so happy about the *just Josh and me* bit.

'**D**ADDY!'

Luke shot from the chair at the panicked scream, leapt across the room, ignored the pain when his shoulder *whacked* against the door frame. The short passage to the back door was too long. One hand hit the back flyscreen at the same time it opened. Joshua was almost flattened when Luke stumbled. In an instant he dropped to his knees, grasped Joshua's shoulders and ran his eyes up and down in search of a dastardly injury.

'What is it? Are you hurt? What happened?'

'The lady scared me.' Tears appeared, dropped and poured.

'What lady? Where?' Luke swept the tears away with one hand, lifted his eyes and gasped. With Joshua held against his chest, Luke rose. 'What the hell are you doing in my backyard?' he yelled at the approaching woman. Josh whimpered and pressed his fingers into Luke's neck. 'Sorry, Josh. Didn't mean to scare you.' He placed one hand against the back of the head which had fallen onto his shoulder and snuggled in. Tears soaked through his shirt while sobs echoed against his eardrum.

'I want to talk.' Rebecca had the good sense to pause five metres away.

'Talk?' Luke held up his hand in the stop position when she took a step forward.

'Yes.' She took another step, smiled.

Luke backed up and stood in the doorway. 'Front door.' He pointed to the fence she'd climbed over.

'Excuse me?'

'When you call unannounced at a person's home, you knock on the front door. It's not appropriate to climb the fence and trespass into their backyard.'

'But…'

'Go.' Barely able to suppress his anger, he again pointed to the fence at the side of the garage.

'Aren't you going to invite me in?' The voice was as sugary false as the smile.

'No. Go. Knock on the front door, which has a perfectly adequate bell.'

'I did.' She came closer.

His eyebrows rose. 'You lie as well as trespass? You didn't knock. I would have heard it and the bell is loud.' To make sure she left, he backed inside, shut both the flyscreen and the solid door.

'Luke?' yelled a male voice accompanied by several thumps on the front door.

He spun around, strode along the passage, opened the front door to find Stuart standing there with his fist high, ready to thump again.

'I was having a kip, heard Joshua scream, came to see if he's okay.'

'He's fine now after a scare.'

'What happened?' Stuart ruffled Josh's hair.

'Had a trespasser in the backyard. Scared Josh.' Luke pointed to Rebecca who was straightening the top of what appeared to be an expensive slack suit. Gold chains around her neck, dangly earrings and an arm of bracelets glinted in the sun. The long, dark smear down the front of the pale blue pants was appropriate karma.

'She's trouble,' murmured Stuart.

'You know her?'

'Know of her. Got a reputation as an easy…' He cut of his words when Joshua lifted his head and eyed him. 'You know what I mean.'

'I was warned at a work function yesterday.'

'You want me to stay?'

'No. How about you keep within hearing. If she doesn't leave quick-smart, come back, ask if we are ready? And thanks for coming to investigate, I appreciate it.'

Stuart turned and strode away with one hand waving in the air.

'Who's that?' Rebecca asked as she approached.

'My neighbour came when Joshua screamed so loud. He *knocked* on the front door. I heard it from the back. Now, I'd appreciate it if you left.'

'I want to talk.' The tone had changed from simpering sweet to more of a whine.

'About what?'

Rebecca pointed to Joshua who wore a serious frown on his red, tear-streaked face. 'In private.'

'Josh stays with me. Say what you came to say.'

Rebecca reached out; fingers gripped his forearm. 'I want to apologise for my son's behaviour yesterday. He didn't mean any harm. He's sorry.'

Luke shook her hand off. 'If he's sorry, why isn't he here apologising to my son. Too much of a coward to be here in person.'

'That's not true.'

'Yes it is.'

'Matty didn't mean any harm. I'm sorry.'

'You son and his equally callous mate, deliberately hunted down a newcomer who is half their size and a third of their age, tormented Josh with cruel words and punched him.' Luke turned to Josh. 'How many times did the two boys come up to you?'

'Three,' Joshua whispered.

'How many times did Matthew punch you?'

'Two.'

Luke turned to the woman. 'That is not an accident. It's deliberate. And you making excuses for your son will never teach him right from wrong.' He dropped Joshua to the ground. 'Go inside, wash your face and get a drink.' With hands on hips he straightened in front of the vile woman. 'Before you go, how did you know where I live?'

Her face paled before a blush rose from the neck up. 'Err, I asked someone from work.'

'Who?'

'Err, Natalie.'

The receptionist wouldn't have his private details. They were in a password protected file available to only him and his partner. 'Liar. Try again.'

'I'm not lying.' The body language said different.

'Yes, you are. There is only one person who knows any private details about me and it certainly isn't the receptionist. Which means you hacked into the personnel files.'

The blush heightened. 'You can't know that.'

'Let me tell you about myself. I'm regarded as a computer geek: know how to trace files, including deleted ones. Before you get home I will have found the IP address of the person who hacked into the private personnel files of our company. If it is you, you'd better start looking for a new job.'

'You can't fire me.' Her face was fierce but panic flared in her eyes.

'You want to bet? I own half of this company so I can damn well do what I want.' He paused for effect. 'As per protocol, I will discuss what I find with all the senior accountants. Now, Josh and I have places to go.'

Her eyes ran up and down his daggy shorts and top. 'Neither of you are dressed for going out.'

With an insidious grin, Luke leant forwards. 'That depends on where we are going, which is none of your business.' He pointed to the only visible car, parked far enough away it was obvious she'd been sneaky. 'Now go.'

'I'll call the police. Tell them how you abused me.'

A laugh gurgled up and out. 'Go ahead. I look forward to their visit.' He turned, went inside and slammed the door. It was pleasant to hear the squeal of tyres as he returned to the room he'd set up as an office to search the data base of the office computer he had already been logged onto to complete a client's monthly B.A.S statement.

'Daddy.'

He turned towards the quivering voice. 'Yes?'

'I need a cuddle.'

'I need one as well. So, how about you come over here and give me the biggest hug ever.' He held out his arms and gripped Joshua tight when the shaking body scrambled into his lap. 'Are you okay?'

'Yes – but – is that lady going to be my new Mummy?'

Stunned, Luke held Joshua at arm's length. 'What on earth gave you such an idea?'

'She had her hands on you at the barbie and you were laughing with her. I thought…'

'Josh, Josh, Josh. One day I might meet a woman who I can love enough to marry. But you have to love her as well and she has to love you for we are a team. As for Rebecca – I don't much like her.'

'But she likes you. She was touching you the way Mummy used to.'

'You remember that?'

'Yes.'

'And do you remember tha way I used to touch Mummy and kiss and cuddle her because I loved her?'

'Yes.'

'Did you see me touch Rebecca? She might have touched me but I didn't like it. I didn't want to be rude in front of all the people at the barbie so I didn't say anything. In the end, I got up and moved away the same way you did with the two big boys.' He pressed a kiss against Josh's brow. 'I would never date a woman you didn't like. How about a session on your computer? I need a cover page for a report I'm writing. Do you remember how to set up a cover page? I could sure do with your help.'

'Sure.' Josh wriggled free and scrambled to the computer Luke had built for him, set up on a smaller desk.

*K*nock, knock.

When Luke lifted his eyes, shock hit. Two police officers stood at the office door.

'Mr Lucas Hunter?' asked one.

'Yes, can I help you?' The reason they were here, shot through his brain. He stood, crossed to the door.

The man held out his badge. 'Senior Sergeant Jim McIlroy. This is Constable Peters.'

'What's this about?'

'We need to ask you a few questions.'

'About what?'

'We had a complaint this morning.'

He had to bite back a smile at Rebecca's audacity. 'I need more information. Please sit.' He pulled out the client's seat and dragged another from against the wall. To give himself a few seconds, he ambled back to his chair, rolled it backwards and sat with his long legs stretched out in front of him and fingers steepled together in his lap.

'A woman came in early this morning. Says you raped her last night.'

'When and where did this salacious act take place?'

'Last night. In the back of your car.'

When laughter bubbled up it was a struggle to straighten his face. 'What time was this supposed to have happened? And you don't need to tell me who made the accusation.'

'So you know the woman?'

'Yes, she was sacked last night and I didn't rape her. I didn't even touch her. Excuse me a moment.' He lifted the receiver for the internal phone, pressed one. 'Sam, I need you in my office pronto.'

'Who is Sam?' asked the constable.

'My business partner. You didn't give me the time.'

'Between eight and ten.'

'What's so urgent? Oh, err, wow. What's going on?' Sam appeared, stepped in, raised his hands in shock and took a step back.

'You need to tell these guys where I was at eight o'clock last night.'

'Here, why?'

'Anyone with me?'

'Of course, me and young Joshua. Why? What's going on?'

'And after I took Josh home and put him to bed, what did we do?'

'Had a video conference with the senior accountants. Why?'

'How long did the conference last?'

'About ninety minutes? Why?'

'It appears I was in two places at once. I've been accused of raping our friend Rebecca, between eight and ten last night – stretched out in the back of my car.'

'In your car?' Sam sniggered. 'God, man, you're six feet four. You wouldn't fit, especially with young Josh's booster seat.' Sam turned to the officers. 'I can guarantee Lucas was here and thirty minutes later, on a video conference – discussing this woman to figure out what to do with her because she hacked into and downloaded a number of our customer's private accounts, as well as the files of our employees. We fired her last night. Rang after ten and told her not to present herself at work today.'

'And…' Luke interrupted, 'I can show you the tapes of my home security system for the past twenty-four hours. It will show when I was home, when I left to come here, when I returned and who was with me. It will also show how this ghastly woman trespassed into my backyard, scared my son. In fact, I can log onto the tape from here. You might want to study it so you have proof of my innocence. You are free to examine my car, which is a sedan by the way. I can guarantee you won't find a skerrick of her DNA in it. I can set up the feed on my laptop. I'm sure we can find a free spot for you to study it for right now, I've got a client waiting.'

'How can you see the tape from here?'

Sam grinned. 'Lucas is a computer whizz. He knows computers inside-out, back-to-front and upside-down. He's our new forensic auditor who tracks down secret accounts and hidden paper trails for you guys as well as the legal fraternity. I'll leave you to it. If you have any more questions, ask our receptionist to hunt me down. We're rather busy today, cleaning up the mess this woman left us. There's a good chance we'll be laying charges against her when Lucas gets a chance to track down all the files she downloaded.' Sam saluted as he left.

'So, guys, how do you want to do this?' Luke opened his laptop, punched in keys, opened a file. It took him a minute to log onto the home security system. 'Here we are, 8a.m. yesterday. You can sit in the reception area. If you're not satisfied, I can copy the tape after I've dealt with my client.' After handing the laptop to the sergeant, he ushered both men into the reception area and greeted his client.

It was lunchtime before the officers left, satisfied, and Lucas had a chance to listen to his messages for the day. He jotted down the names and numbers of the first few messages. His pen stopped, mid-air, at the angry tirade from Josh's teacher. Unable to believe what he heard he pressed the replay button. While he listened to the harsh words a third time he made a frantic search of the top of his desk for the note he had received, when was it? Friday? No Thursday. He'd rung on Friday. He was still searching when his next client was ushered in.

The poor client didn't get the attention she deserved when the teacher's message replayed over and over in his brain. When he couldn't stand the tension any longer, he apologised to his client, paged the receptionist to find the phone number of Josh's school and asked her to make coffee for his client.

Number and mobile in hand, he left his client with her refreshment while he moved outside to ring the school. Since she was in class with her students, all he could do was ask if Mrs Reynolds could ring him back the moment she was free. Only then was he able to give his full attention to his client's needs.

He waited on tenterhooks for the return call.

It never came.

By school closing time panic had set in. He still had another client waiting so left another message for Mrs Reynolds. When worry overtook his ability to concentrate he cut the interview short with the promise he would visit his client at his place of work, making another appointment for him before he ushered the hapless man out.

The instant the man departed, Luke flew to his car and sped away until he noticed how much over the limit he was and a vision of his wife's wrecked car centred in his brain. He forced his foot off the accelerator. The devastation left behind was a stark reminder.

To add to shot nerves, the car park was empty when he reached the school. He unfolded from the seat so fast his head connected with the top of the doorway. He swore. It was only when he strode towards the nearest building, he realised he had no idea which classroom was his son's and the place was deserted. Even Mrs Reynold's car wasn't there. At the eerie silence bile surged when his stomach clenched in fear. Where was Josh? He broke into a run, tore across the bitumen, along the nearest veranda, jumping up to glance in the narrow row of overhead windows as he passed each room.

Empty. Nothing. At every door he grasped the handle, twisted at the same time he shoved against the thick wood. All were locked.

He raced across the quadrangle and repeated his search along the facing veranda. Still nothing. He spun around the corner to search the next wing, raced down the concrete veranda. 'Josh,' he yelled, praying he was still there.

'Daddy!' he heard a split second before a door further along squeaked open and Joshua ran full pelt along the veranda.

Lucas scooped his son up into his arms and hugged him tight. The relief was so overwhelming a rush of moisture swept across his eyes. 'Am I glad I found you. Where's your teacher? Which is your room?' When he set Joshua down, he couldn't bring himself to release the firm hold he had on the small hand.

'This way, Mrs Reynolds is in here.' Joshua tugged his father along the veranda - into a doorway.

'You're Joshua's father?'

Lucas glanced up at the shocked voice. The woman who stood before him with arms akimbo had a stunned face. It took a moment to recognise her with her long hair tied back away from her face. It suddenly dawned on him who she was. 'Jenna? Are you Mrs Reynolds?'

Her chin rose, jutted out a fraction and eyes turned glacial. 'Yes, I'm Mrs Reynolds and yes, I'm Joshua's teacher and yes, I'm angry at the way you spoke to me over the phone.'

'You have a right to be angry. I didn't give you the opportunity to explain why you were concerned. I sincerely apologise for my manner. Which is why I'm here. Your phone message had me extremely worried and I'm mystified as to its content and why my son is still at school at this late hour.'

A knock at the door had all three turn around. The young babysitter strolled in. Her shocked 'oops' when she noticed him had her back out again, spin on her heel and take off full pelt along the veranda.

'Wait a minute, young lady!' Lucas bellowed as he followed the young girl. 'Would you mind explaining why you are only now coming to pick Joshua up from school?'

With no answer, the girl vanished around the corner. The echoing footsteps weren't walking. When he returned to the classroom, Jenna was on her knees in front of Joshua.

'Your father is angry at your babysitter, not you.'

'Josh,' he called softly and knelt next to him. 'I'm certainly not angry with you. Come here?' He enveloped Josh in his arms and lifted him to his chest as he stood and planted a kiss on his head. After searching for a place to sit, he lowered his massive body onto one of the small desks, settling Josh on his knee.

'Now, perhaps one of you can tell me exactly what is going on here?' He honed his eyes on Jenna.

'As my phone message indicated, I'm concerned about Joshua having to wait so long after school. It has been close to five each day, sometimes later.'

'I take it you have stayed behind to supervise him.' The light blush on her cheeks told him he was correct. 'I appreciate your concern and thank you most sincerely. I had no idea. I was under the impression Josh was being picked up straight after school as per the arrangement. That young lady was supposed to be waiting at the gate when Joshua was released for the day.' He turned to his son. 'You should have told me.' Joshua squirmed and dropped his eyes.

Luke thought for a moment. 'It's obvious the babysitter isn't suitable, which leaves me with a dilemma until I can find another one. Jenna, do you know of anyone else, perhaps other children in your class have after school care while their parents work?' He shook his head. 'I had a devil of a job finding that one. I had no idea it would be so difficult to find good babysitters when I made the decision to move here.'

'I could make inquiries. It might take a few days.' She paused; her brow furrowed in thought. 'In the meantime I could look after Joshua until you can find a new sitter. Although, I'd prefer to take him home. I don't live far away. You could pick him up from my house.'

'I couldn't impose on you like that.'

'I wouldn't mind, truly. Joshua is no trouble. He's a lovely young boy.' With a smile, Jenna ruffled Joshua's hair.

'What would Mr Reynolds think of the idea?' Luke tried to hide his surprise when he noticed the brief grimace of pain in her eyes. 'I assume he's no longer on the scene. Is that why you left with such haste the other night?' A look of alarm passed over her face. He had to be right. Logic hit. 'He was there, wasn't he? That's why you raced away so distraught.'

Jenna spun around, hurried to her desk where she pulled pen and paper from the drawer and wrote on it. Shoulders rose as though taking a deep breath before she turned back. It didn't take genius status to figure she was close to tears.

'This is my home phone number. Ring tonight if you would like me to look after Joshua tomorrow afternoon. Now I must go.' After handing Luke the piece of paper, she picked up her bag and stood at the door with eyes averted.

He took the hint. He'd been too personal and it wouldn't be wise to delve any further. Jenna Reynolds was still in a lot of pain. He knew how it felt. It had taken two years for his own pain to ease after his wife died and he still missed Lisa a great deal.

'Come on, Josh, let's get you home.' He took Josh's hand, paused at the door. 'Thank you for the care you have taken of my son. I appreciate it a great deal and apologise for my rudeness. Either way, I'll ring tonight.'

As they walked along the veranda he thought about the night

he'd met Jenna. He'd liked the tiny bundle of energy that was Stuart's girlfriend who chattered non-stop with an unceasing grin spread across her face. He would never be able to live with a partner who was so irrepressible and boisterous despite Emily being a sweet young woman. The brother, Ryan, appeared to be more introspective and obviously keen on Jenna. It was equally obvious Jenna wasn't so keen on the advances he'd made by the way she kept edging her chair away from him. At the time he'd been amused and intrigued.

When they reached his car, Luke buckled Josh into the booster seat he was too big for. Law required a child to be seven before they didn't need a booster seat. The law didn't account for kids who were taller than other kids their age; kids who inherited oversize genes from their dad. A safety seat had saved Josh's life in the accident so Luke was happy to cram Josh into a booster seat for as long as he could.

'Why didn't you tell me about the baby-sitter?' he asked. 'You said school was good.'

'School is good. I like Mrs Reynolds. Brendan and Scott have asked me to be their friend.'

Luke raised an eyebrow. 'It's great you have new friends but you know what I mean. You didn't tell me you had to wait so long for the babysitter. Why?'

Josh shrugged. 'I don't want you to be sad anymore.'

'Sad? I'm not sad. And I wouldn't be mad at you either. It's important you tell me anything you feel isn't right. When you are uncomfortable about situations in here.' He tapped Josh's gut. 'We talked about this with Katerina.' A year and a half with a child psych had done wonders for Josh after the ordeal he'd been through.

'I know. Sorry. I like Mrs Reynolds.'

Luke laughed. 'Enough to keep her at school to spend time with you. It's not fair on your teacher. She works hard to prepare lessons and has to put up with a class full of scamps like you all day.' He tousled Josh's hair. 'Teachers need time to relax the same way I do after I've had a tough day at work. So how about we give her a break?'

'You mean I can't stay with her after school?'

'I'll find us another babysitter. A much better one than Mrs Rogers and her daughter.'

After a week of neglect because she stayed at school with Joshua, it sent a tingle down her spine to stand in the one place serenity surrounded her. It was hard to believe a simple vegetable garden could have so many different scents. The intensity of dark organically enriched soil, the sweetness of peapods, the sharpness of onions and pungency of various herbs. The hum of bees brought a smile while she tugged on protective gloves. They enjoyed these beds as much as she did. This was her happy place which always brought a smile while she dug, weeded, planted and harvested. The high beds were jam-packed with a wide variety of vegetables, too many for her but her friends and neighbours never complained about the surplus.

As she moved among the beds to harvest for a stir-fry, she pulled the few weeds that had dared to poke their heads up this past week. Darkness surrounded her by the time she carried the dish of fresh goodies inside. Working outdoors usually re-invigorated her, but Lucas Hunter had stirred up unpleasant memories she now found difficult to send to the deep recesses of her mind where they belonged.

With her mind on a roundabout, she rinsed, chopped and tossed the ingredients in the wok with herbs and spices. A shrill ring of the landline brought her out of a painful reverie. Startled her meal was ready, she turned off the gas flame before lifting the receiver.

'Jenna Reynolds speaking.'

'Hi, it's Luke Hunter. I'm afraid I have to take you up on your offer to look after Josh for a couple of days. That is, if your offer is still open. I haven't been able to find anyone else at such short notice.'

'That's fine, Mr Hunter, I'll bring Joshua home with me after school.'

'I appreciate your help. Of course I'll pay you the same rate, and please call me Luke.'

At the plea in his voice, Jenna paused. 'I won't accept any money. Did you meet with the babysitter? Oh, sorry, it's none of my business.'

'I figure because you were the one who suffered the consequences, you have a right to know. It wasn't pleasant. After I expressed my disappointment, Mrs Rogers became defensive and served me a bitter tirade how working parents shouldn't have children to start with. Given the circumstances of my single parent status I'm afraid I reacted badly and used a few words and phrases I would wash out of Josh's mouth if he ever used them. I apologised on the spot but after I'd cooled down I realised I'm relieved Joshua will no longer be in the woman's care.'

'It's obvious he wasn't her number one priority so I don't blame you.'

'Trouble is, I've made innumerable phone calls and can't find anyone else – yet. I'll keep trying. And I need to apologise for I was abominably rude to you and think I may have stirred up bad memories with my questions. Please forgive me.'

'Nothing to forgive. I'll bring Joshua home tomorrow. He is a pleasure to have. Good night. Oh, I'd better give you my address.'

'Give me a sec to find a pen. Okay, go ahead.'

Jenna gave the details.

'Thank you and have a great evening.'

When she replaced the receiver, her thoughts centred on Joshua's father. Twice now, he had touched her. Both times she had blushed like an idiot and pulled away like a naïve teenager, afraid of the sensations that had welled up. She no longer had any faith in men to the extent she kept up a barrier whenever she was alone with one. It was obvious by the men's reactions she gave the impression she was cold and aloof. The wall wasn't so rigid with Stuart because he and Emily were so close and there was no fear he would make a pass at her. She was aware Ryan tried hard to melt her icy exterior but she had no intention of dating him. She'd made a few friends since moving to town but had steered away from any romantic liaison and rarely went out on a social basis, although a one-on-one date with a guy sure would ease the loneliness. It didn't help that she wasn't game to take the chance. A weekly game of squash to keep her skills honed was her only real commitment outside work.

Luke had been kind and polite at the hotel function. From what she had seen, he appeared to treat his son with utmost tenderness and care. She'd jumped when he yelled at the teenager, but his voice turned gentle with his son. She had been on the receiving end of his terse tongue but she paid him back to ensure she got his attention. A grin broke out at the memory as she spooned her meal onto a plate. The grin turned to a frown when the phone rang again.

'Hello, Jenna speaking.'

'Hi, I want to know if you will be at squash on Saturday.'

'Hi, Emily. Probably, why?'

'Ryan needs a partner.'

The last person she wanted to play with but if everyone else was partnered up, she had no choice unless she didn't go. Eyes closed; she sighed. She loved the game and needed the exercise. Deep down she figured this was another attempt to get them together but if Ryan came on too strong, she'd give him no mercy with the squash ball. She'd played him many times but always pulled her punches because he wasn't a good player. She usually played poor shots so he could win because he was a surly loser.

'Okay, what time?'

'Two.'

Jenna gave Joshua a few chores to help tidy the room before they walked home hand-in-hand. He still wouldn't talk even when asked direct questions so instead she chatted about her young nieces. Once home, she gave him milk and a snack while she sipped black tea.

'Would you like to help me pick the vegetables for my dinner?' she asked when the last of the milk went down.

His face lit up at the sight of the vegie patch hidden behind a band of mature shrubs and trees. The house might be small but the large block made up for it. Eyes, wide, he turned around slowly, paused at the peas, reached up but couldn't touch the top. 'How come they are so big?'

She laughed to hide her delight that he finally spoke. 'The same way you can get different apples, there are different types of peas. This variety grows extra tall and I give them lots of fertilizer to make sure they grow well. Stand next to them.' She nudged him closer and smiled. 'You could hide behind these and nobody would spot you. Here, taste them. I think they are delicious.' Picking a couple of pods from the mass of extra tall plants, she opened them up and smiled while he scooped them out and popped them into his mouth.

'How about you fill the bowl. Pick the nice fat ones, like this one.' She showed him one and how to pick it off. While he searched, she washed the dirt off a young carrot and handed it to him to eat. The pleasure in his eyes caused a permanent grin on her face while they worked their way through the various vegetables.

Once inside, she set Joshua the task of shelling the peas, smiling each time one escaped onto the table or floor. The burst of laughter when he chased after it, delighted her. A breakthrough in their communication as far as she was concerned. The sad, remote look disappeared when he laughed. Half of the produce went into a plastic bag for him to take home.

'Is Daddy a good cook?' she dared ask.

Joshua nodded at the same time there was a knock on the door. She sent Joshua to open the door, delighted with his excited voice while he related about the peas. A warm fuzzy swept through her innards to hear his voice after the week-long silence. She marvelled at how Luke squatted down to his son's level to give his full attention for a few minutes. When Luke stood he acknowledged her.

She handed Joshua his bag of goodies. 'I hope you can use these. Joshua helped me pick them and there are far more than I can use.'

'Thank you and thank you for taking care of him. I'll sort out my dilemma as soon as I can.' He grasped his son's hand and led him outside.

'Bye Joshua, I'll see you in the morning.' Jenna smiled when he turned and gave her the biggest grin, followed by a wave. After he'd gone, loneliness surrounded her like a dark, oppressive mantle.

Each night after Joshua left, the loneliness bit with sharp fangs. To ease the emptiness on Friday evening, she ate her meal in front of the television. Soon bored of the inane programme she switched it off and opened a book. The oppressive silence soon had her close the book and search around for something – anything, to do. While wiping down kitchen benches a thought came. A brisk walk might ease the depression. One block later, the quiet amble turned into a slow jog to work off frustration. A sudden return of stormy weather put paid to the exercise when she was caught in a downpour. By the time she reached home she was soaked through. Under the warm shower she was glad she had agreed to play squash tomorrow. There would at least be people to talk to.

Emily and Stuart had begun their game when Jenna hurried into the squash courts - late. The tardiness had been deliberate in the hope all the regular gang, including Ryan, had partnered off.

'Where have you been?' At the same time mouthwash breath brushed against her cheek, an arm went around her waist and gripped tight. 'We're on court three.'

Miffed at the curt question and unwanted liberties she jerked around to dislodge the arm. She was more miffed when Ryan aimed a kiss towards her mouth, which missed its target when she turned her head away at the last second and scarpered towards the stairs. She wanted and needed company but not from the over-zealous Ryan. When he grasped her elbow as though she was too decrepit to descend by herself, the unease increased. It boiled when his fingers lingered too long as he placed the ball in her hand. Instead of lifting his hand away fingertips brushed along her skin. Creepy.

Already, she'd had enough. No more Mrs Nice to pander to his ego. 'Ready?'

'Yes, you serve.'

She smashed the ball against the wall near the corner. He missed. Game on. It was hard to suppress a grin each time he was forced to run from side-to-side, forwards and backwards in pursuit of the balls she placed with practised precision exactly where she wanted, hardly ever moving herself. Bubbles of delight jiggled inside her the entire game and burst to a showy rainbow when he attempted to return her final serve, missed, skidded and lost his balance. He lay sprawled on the floor, seemingly too exhausted to get up.

At the applause from the viewing gallery above she turned,

peered up and was startled at the sight of Joshua clapping madly. Her eyes swung towards Luke who stared down. He saluted with two fingers and a grin.

Ryan picked himself up and stormed from the court without a word. Blowing out her cheeks, she watched his retreating back with a silent prayer he would think twice about inveigling his way into partnering her again. She hoped he wouldn't want to.

'Jenna!' Luke called. 'I've finished my match. I'll challenge you to a game since your partner has deserted you.'

She nodded but wondered if she would regret her decision. Luke was a huge, powerful man and he'd probably wipe the floor with her as she had done with Ryan. Luke had the advantage of having seen how she played while she had no idea what type of a player he was.

It didn't take long to discover how adept and agile he was. He was an equal match, which caused her to work hard to keep the scores close. She finally came out the victor with a couple of well-placed shots and a few strokes of good luck.

'You play well, congratulations,' Luke gasped as they left the court.

'So do you - I was lucky on the last serve. Thank you for the game.' She stopped to catch her breath.

Joshua came running down the steps. 'Did you win, Dad?'

'Not this time but I will try to next time. That is, if Mrs Reynolds will allow me the opportunity for a rematch.' Luke lifted his eyes to Jenna and smiled. 'How about it? Same time next week, but let's make it the best of three.'

'I'm game.' She turned to Joshua. 'Do you think I can beat your dad again?'

He grinned, shook his head.

Luke lifted his son up into his arms. 'I'd better let you get back to your boyfriend.'

'He's not my …'

'But it's obvious he'd like to be,' Luke countered with a nod towards the top of the staircase.

When she raised her eyes the anger on Ryan's face was a shock.

She didn't know if it was because she hadn't let him win again or if it was because she'd played a game against Luke. Probably the former because he'd been the one to walk off in a huff. His pride may have been dented a tad.

'I think I'd better go.' She fled along the narrow corridor towards the change-rooms.

The decision to not bother with a shower was easy. Instead, she slipped a tracksuit over her skirt and top and gathered her belongings. Unease was strong as thoughts tumbled. Why did she allow Ryan to get away with so much? Was she too nice – not ever wanting to hurt people? But he didn't give a hoot about her. Head down, she returned along the passage in deep contemplation, paused, blew out her cheeks, pulled her shoulders back and lifted her head high before jogging up the stairs to say farewell instead of joining them for drinks as per normal.

'I'm off, guys,' she called in a forced bright voice.

'You're not joining us for drinks?' Emily called above the chatter.

'Not today, I have a lot of work to do,' she lied. 'Thanks for the game, Ryan. Catch you all soon.' It was so darn good to escape.

The weekend finished with a phone call from Luke. 'I hate to ask you this but can you care for Joshua for a while longer? I've had no luck finding another suitable carer.' The tone of his voice indicated he hated asking but she was delighted at the prospect of the continued break from loneliness.

Knelt next to Joshua, every cell in her body had sparkled to life. It was sheer joy to have his company after school. Jenna leant forwards. 'Make the hole deep enough for the roots to hang down straight.' She made a hollow with the trowel. 'Hold the baby plant where the stem begins and dangle it over the hole.' She guided his small fingers. 'With the other hand, scoop the soil around the roots and tamp it down.'

'What does tamp mean?' He dug his fingers in the pile of soil and scratched it into the hole.

'When the hole is full, press the soil in so there are no air bubbles but not so hard you damage the plant.' She showed him.

'Oh, okay. Like this?' He used two fingers to pat the soil.

'Perfect. How about you do the next one by yourself?'

'Okay.' He took the trowel, made a hole and lifted the next spinach seedling from the ground where she had already laid them out after easing them from the punnet.

She sat back on her heels to watch. The entire week had been a joy. Each afternoon they collected vegetables while she taught Joshua about a different variety each day, allowing him to taste while she explained what they could be used in and how they should be cooked. They baked biscuits the first afternoon, half of which were packed into a container for Joshua to take home. She noted the genuine look of appreciation Luke gave when he collected Joshua. Homemade treats might not be a regular menu item.

A game of soccer in the nearby park on the second day had them running late. Luke was leant up against the fence when they ran down the street.

Another day the pair played hide-and-seek and tag inside the house, making so much noise with squeals and laughter, they didn't hear Luke knock. He rang her number from his mobile to ask to be let in.

Today she was showing Josh how to plant new seedlings. The last plant went in. 'Great job, Josh. We need to water them now so the soil settles around the roots and to give them a drink.' They stood at the same time, brushed dirt from their hands and legs - Joshua mimicking every action she made. When she turned to fetch the hose she jerked. Luke was leant against the wall with his arms casually folded.

'How long have you been there?'

'Long enough.'

'Daddy,' Joshua yelled. 'We planted lots of baby plants.'

'So I noticed. Now you better water them so they will grow.' Luke handed Jenna the end of the hose and turned on the tap.

She showed Joshua how to spray the plants gently. Happy with the light spray, she left him to complete the task and moved over to Luke. 'We've had fun today.'

'So I heard - it's fantastic to hear Josh laugh again. I haven't heard him laugh so much for over two years. You've done wonders for him and you have a smut right there.' When he reached out and brushed his finger down her cheek she froze, thankful it was getting dark to hide the blush she knew was there for an inferno burnt her cheeks.

'What are you so afraid of? I would never hurt you.' He finished brushing the dirt off and withdrew his hand while her eyes searched for and found a small spot on the ground to stare at. 'Is it me or men in general you're afraid of?'

'I'm not afraid of men. It's…'

'You don't enjoy Ryan's company.'

'No. He's too pushy and I'm not interested in a relationship, especially with him but he doesn't take the hint.'

Luke straightened. 'Are we still on for my revenge tomorrow? I've booked the court for two.'

'Most definitely.' Glad of the diversion she turned off the tap to prevent the plants from being drowned. 'Come on, Joshua, it's time for you to go.' To not give Luke the chance to pursue the matter she grasped the small grimy hand and led Joshua inside to clean up and collect his bag. She went outside to wave them off and was heartened when Joshua suddenly turned around, ran back and flung his arms around her waist to give her a hug goodbye. She knelt, wrapped her arms around him, delighted when a soft kiss landed on her cheek as he held her tight.

'Goodbye, Sweetie, I'll see you tomorrow,' she whispered in his ear, released him and stood, gently pushing him towards his father. Her heart exploded with love and warmth for the young boy. After they had driven off she couldn't bear the thought of returning to her empty house to face the lonely solitude. Instead, she went for a power walk until the physical pain overpowered her emotional ache.

'When will she be here?' Joshua asked for the umpteenth time. He wrapped his lips around the straw and slurped the last of the juice.

'When she gets here. It's still early.' Luke was amused at his son's impatience but delighted with the eagerness after two years of struggle to get him over the trauma of the accident. This move had begun to show benefits, more so for Josh than for him. 'Those noises aren't polite so how about you toss the carton in the recycle bin.'

Josh sent him a cheeky grin. 'Okay.' But he had to have a final slurp followed by a giggle.

Luke fought to keep his grin at bay when Josh skipped to the bin. Thoughts of Jenna didn't want to give him any peace. Since arriving today, he'd tried to make head or tail of the incidents from last week. He and Joshua had been partaking of refreshment at the kiosk when Jenna arrived. He'd already finished his game with a work colleague and noticed the way Ryan greeted Jenna with a missed kiss when she turned away. Ryan must have said or done something to upset her for her to have played so dramatically, for she whipped his butt and the man hadn't been happy about it.

And there was yesterday when he got the impression it wasn't only Ryan she held back from. There had to be another reason. A more sinister thought came to mind. Had she been abused in her marriage? Is that why she is so afraid of men? Pictures of her continual actions of withdrawal from Ryan's ministrations flooded through his brain. Logic took hold and things fell into place. The woman intrigued him and he wanted to get to know her better but he realised he would have to take things slow and easy.

'She's here, Daddy, she's here!' Josh ran, arms wide, grabbed Jenna around her waist and gripped as though his life depended on it. A vice clenched Luke's heart when Jenna ran her fingers through Josh's hair and he smiled broader than Luke had seen for years. This woman had brought life back into his son. When he stood to greet her he couldn't help but smile at the way Josh grabbed her hand and tugged her along the walkway.

She smiled at Joshua. 'Your dad's waiting to be beaten again is he?'

Joshua shook his head, a grin splitting his face.

'Afternoon Luke, young Joshua is barracking for you. I hope I can disappoint him again.' Her smile was wicked.

'Not a chance, I'm out for revenge.'

'Give me a minute to dump my gear in the changeroom. I'll meet you on court. Which one?'

'Four.' While she jogged down the stairs, he settled Josh in a seat at the front of the viewing glass. 'Don't move from there. Stay where I can see you.'

'I'll keep an eye on him.' Emily plonked onto the seat next to Josh.

'Thanks, I appreciate it.' Luke turned away and hurried down the steps.

'Hi, Joshua. Do you mind if I sit with you?'

Joshua shrugged. 'Okay. Do you know my daddy?'

'Yes. We had dinner together at the hotel last week.'

Dinner. Together. Daddy has a girlfriend already? 'I thought he went with Stewart from next door.'

'Yes, Stewart was there as well. And your teacher along with a few other people.'

'Oh.' He needed to think about this. 'You teach the year twos at my school.'

'That's right.'

'Do you like my daddy?'

'Yes, although I've only met him a couple of times.' She nudged him. 'He must be a nice man if he's got such a super boy like you.'

Joshua smiled. He liked Miss Johnson and she liked Daddy. 'You're not married, are you?'

'What makes you say that?'

'Your name is Miss Johnson. Miss means you're not married.'

'How do you know?'

'My nanna said ladies are called Mrs when they get married.'

'Your nanna is right. Knock, knock.'

Joshua stared at Miss Johnson and grinned when she nodded her head. 'Who's there?'

'Joshua.'

'Uh, me?'

She nodded again. 'Come on ask me.'

'Joshua who?'

'Joshua smart.'

'Uh, I don't get it.'

Miss Johnson laughed. 'Josh – you – are - smart.'

He stared at her. 'Wow. You made up a good joke about me.

I've got a joke. Do you want to hear it?'

'Sure.'

'What has five toes that isn't your foot?'

'Five toes, eh? I can't think of anything else with five toes, so I think you'll have to tell me the answer.'

'My foot.'

Miss Johnson clapped and laughed. 'Wow, that's such a clever joke. Do you have any more?'

'Sure. How do you make a tissue dance?'

'A tissue as in a paper handkerchief?'

Joshua nodded.

'I don't know. How do you make a tissue dance?'

'You put a little boogie in it.'

'Oh, that's so gross.' She laughed. 'But it's also funny. I like your jokes.'

'What are you doing with that brat?'

Joshua jumped at the growly voice and shrank next to Miss Johnson when a man came close and leant over. The man who played squash with his teacher last week. The angry face came too close. It was so scary the kangaroo woke up in his tummy and did a mighty backflip.

'Ryan,' said Miss Johnson. 'Don't scare him and he's not a brat. Why would you call him one?'

'He's the kid of the new bloke. Comes into town and thinks he can stick his nose into other people's business.'

When Miss Johnson stood, Joshua hid behind her. The kangaroo bounced up into his throat.

'What are you talking about?' asked Miss Johnson.

'Take a look.' The nasty man pointed over the rail at Daddy and Mrs Reynolds.

'Jenna's my partner. She's supposed to be playing with me.' The growl was much louder.

'Did you make a time and date with her?' Miss Johnson asked.

'We've played together every weekend.'

'I didn't notice your name on the court schedule. Did you book a court? Did Jenna know about it? Luke had booked a court for this time.'

'She should know. She's my partner.'

'Jenna can partner anyone she wants. She comes here every Saturday and plays against anyone – not just you. If you didn't make an arrangement, tough. Go find another partner and next time make an arrangement beforehand and book your own court like everyone else does. Now if you don't mind, Josh was telling me some super jokes.' She shoved Ryan out of the way, sat and leant towards Joshua.

Joshua fisted his eyes to stop any tears. He didn't like this Ryan. He was scary like the bogey man who scared him in his bad dreams at night.

Miss Johnson put her arm around Joshua and gave him a hug. 'Come on, sit back down next to me.'

'What's a brat?' he asked as he sat and wriggled close to Miss Johnson.

'You're not a brat. A brat is a naughty person who gets into mischief and doesn't much care if they hurt other people.' She nudged Joshua and smiled. 'More like Ryan a minute ago. He was naughty and didn't care if he hurt you. So he's the brat. Let's watch your dad play squash. Who do you think will win?'

'Daddy, of course.'

'Okay, you barrack for your dad and I'll barrack for Jenna, oops, sorry, Mrs Reynolds to you. We can't have you calling your teacher by her first name.'

The first game was hard fought with both on equal footing until Jenna dropped an unplayable ball low in the corner and won. Luke applauded the shot and laughed when she gave Joshua a salute with one finger pointed back at herself. Emily smiled and clapped while Joshua shook his head and pointed at Luke.

To earn his son's approval he fought hard in the second game and was lucky to win the final point. When he checked on Joshua this time, he was surprised at the number of spectators watching but Joshua stood in the front and yelled, 'Yay, Daddy.'

The crowd above grew larger while they slogged it out for the third game. It was point for point until Jenna conceded defeat after she missed a particularly hard serve which must have hit the corner exactly right for it dropped to the floor as though made of lead. He wished he knew what he'd done so he could play the same shot again in the future.

'Well done,' Jenna huffed. 'Joshua will be happy.'

Loud applause erupted from the gallery. They both glanced up. When Jenna gasped, Luke eyed her to see her pale in an instant. He searched the crowd and noted two men who stared down but neither cheered nor applauded. Both appeared tense and angry. One was Ryan but Luke was sure it wasn't him who had caused the pallor. The other man was about the same height as Jenna, slightly built and wore an angry scowl.

Luke scrambled after Jenna when she made a hasty retreat through the rear doorway. He had to increase his speed to catch up. 'Jenna, are you all right?' He reached out, grasped her elbow and turned her around. It was obvious she was fighting back tears. 'Go and have your shower while I collect Josh. We'll wait for you here.'

Gut instinct told him to accompany her to the change rooms where he left her to collect Josh. By the time he reached the viewing gallery, most of the crowd had dispersed with no sign of either man. He picked up his son, gave him a hug, carried him back downstairs where he had a quick shower, changed into jeans and sweatshirt and was waiting when Jenna exited the female change-room.

He reached out to take her bag. 'Can we go for a drink? Preferably away from here because I need to talk to you about Josh.'

'Okay, I'll put my bag in my car.'

When they exited the main entry she retrieved her bag and headed towards her car but stopped in her tracks with a groan. Without warning she spun around and cannoned into his chest. 'Sorry, I've changed my mind. Please, get me out of here?'

When Luke noted the pained expression, he eyed her car. The man he had seen in the gallery straightened and sauntered towards them. With her frantic actions and words, it was obvious Jenna had no desire to speak to the man so Luke slung his free arm around her shoulders, called Joshua to walk faster and steered them across the bitumen to his car. He pressed the remote so they could get in straight away and drove off before they had their seat belts on. Once they reached the entrance onto the main road, he checked Josh was buckled up before he sped away.

'My place is closest but if you're uncomfortable about coming home, please tell me and we can go somewhere else.'

'Your place will be fine.' Jenna's voice was so strained she sounded as though another planet would be preferable. What had this man done to hurt her so badly? They had driven only a few blocks when Luke turned into his drive.

'Oh, no,' Jenna mumbled.

Luke trained his eyes in the direction she stared. Ryan was easing out of his car in Stuart's driveway. Both Stuart and Emily stood next to the car.

'I'm sure they didn't notice you. No one was looking this way,' Luke murmured so Joshua wouldn't hear. He switched off the engine with his eyes on Jenna, who leant on the dashboard with her head in her hands.

'Here, Josh, you go and open the door.' He handed the keys to Josh who ran off with a smile.

'Are you okay?'

She gulped in a deep breath, straightened and turned towards him. 'Yes, I'm fine. I'm sorry, I've spoilt a good day. It's been a long time since I've had such a good game.' Her forced smile was weak.

He opened his door. 'Come inside. I promised you a drink.'

Hopping from foot-to-foot, Joshua stood waiting for them and led the way into the kitchen.

Amused at his son's action, Luke smiled and turned his attention to Jenna. 'What would you like, tea, coffee, wine, water? By the look of your face, you might prefer something stronger.'

'I'd love a glass of water and wine if you have it. I'm not a lover of strong liquor.'

She perched on the high barstool Luke pulled out for her. He poured fruit juice for Joshua and water for both Jenna and himself to re-hydrate. With the need for privacy, he suggested to his son it might be a good idea if he went to play while he spoke *grown-up talk* with Jenna. He took two crystal wine glasses from an overhead cupboard before opening a bottle of chilled white wine. After pouring both glasses he perched on a stool opposite her.

'First, I want to thank you for caring for Josh and to let you know I've found a new sitter, starting Monday.'

'Oh. I'll miss him. I enjoyed every minute of it.'

'I've imposed on you too long. Now, what was all that about today? I gather the man at your car was your ex-husband and you want nothing to do with him.' No matter how much she tried to hide it, the hurt in her eyes was obvious.

'You assume right, but I don't want to talk about it.'

'And Ryan, where does he stand with you?'

'Emily has urged me to go out with him for ages, although he's never actually asked me for a date. Somehow, we keep ending up together.'

'Does this fear only relate to Ryan and your ex-husband, or are all men off the agenda? Which would be a pity because I planned to invite you out for a meal to thank you for all you've done for Josh.'

She glanced at him, surprise lighting up her features.

'No strings attached - I promise,' he added when he noticed her hesitation.

She smiled. 'I would love to go, but only if you'll allow me the opportunity to challenge you to a rematch. Today was one of the best games of squash I've played in a long time.' Jenna's smile widened as Luke held out his hand to shake on the deal.

'Done.'

While they sipped the wine, Luke did his best to lighten the atmosphere by talking about general subjects. When she intimated it was time she left, he called Joshua and they drove back to the squash courts to Jenna's car.

Jenna suppressed the scream, swallowed the noise and opened her eyes. Woken from a restless sleep, she wasn't sure whether a noise from outside had disturbed her or if it was one of those too regular nights when sleep was intermittent. When she was able to drag groggy senses to full alert, she lay still, too scared to breathe with her ears honed for more unusual sounds – if was a real sound.

A shadow passed the window.

Every atom in her body jiggled with alarm. The silhouette paused at the draped window. Shadowy hands reached up, jostled the frame. The shadow moved away. Heart jammed in her throat, she eased from the bed and crept to the next room where she made out the same shadows in the gloom while the frame emitted tiny grates and rattles. The person was trying to find a way in.

Unsure what to do, she followed the shadow from room-to-room while it made its way all around the house. She prayed the person would simply disappear once they discovered all the doors and windows were secure, thankful she had a regular routine of drawing the curtains across all windows each night but now she realised the drapes weren't heavy enough to conceal all the light from the street lamps which outlined the shadows. Although it could be a good thing, her inner conscience added while her innards did wild, crazy things, clenching tight before somersaulting at random.

Panic surged when the shadow returned to the backyard. Now certain the person wasn't going away she crept to her phone and rang the only person she could think off – Luke. He lived closer than the police station and would arrive sooner.

'Luke, please help me?' she whispered at the hello.

'Jenna, where are you?'

'Home. There's someone trying to break in.'

'I'm on my way.' The phone clicked.

The house wasn't large, with one room devoid of furniture, which meant she had few places to hide. At the smash of glass, she fled to the lounge room – at least there she had furniture to hide behind with enough room to escape a prowler's clutches. With a silent prayer heavenwards asking she could remain hidden long enough for Luke to arrive, she attuned her ears for the slightest sound and crouched behind the sofa with backside against the wall.

A door opened at the far end of the short passage. The study, she was certain. Too fast – too close.

The silence was heavy until another door opened. It must be the spare room for the pause was short before the third door opened and closed. Bathroom. A quiet squeak was familiar - her room. A lengthy silence. The prowler must have entered the room for a muffled curse came. Whoever must have discovered the empty, rumpled, still warm bed. The hushed voice was definitely male.

Soft, slow footsteps crossed the hallway - entered the lounge. With held breath, her racing pulse drummed in her ears. Every muscle tensed. Every nerve readied itself to fracture. It wasn't so easy to follow the footsteps now they were muffled on carpet.

A sudden movement behind. The sofa yanked away from the wall. She squealed, stood and fled in the opposite direction. Hands grabbed the fine fabric of her nightdress at the hem - pulled her backwards. A frantic tug, the fabric ripped but she was free. She ran.

'Damn!' A whispered curse. Footsteps followed her through the dining area, around the table. She turned down the passage, headed back to the lounge, the man in hot pursuit.

There was nowhere else to go except round and round the same route. All the other doors led to a room from where she wouldn't be able to get out. The front and back doors were deadlocked. By the time she stopped to open them, she would be caught – he was so close, the heavy breaths audible. Why oh, why didn't she open the darn door to escape as soon as she noticed an intruder? Stupid, stupid woman.

Twice more she pelted along the same circuit.

Twice more he followed.

The footsteps ceased.

She paused, mid-flight. Which way to go? Had he turned back? Was he waiting around the corner? Which corner? Where the hell was he?

Hot breath on her back the same moment fingers clenched tight below her elbow. She screamed, lashed out with one hand, yanked hard to free her trapped arm. Searing pain ran down her arm when rough fingernails gouged but the grip released.

She spun on her heel and fled in the opposite direction: turned the corner into the passage.

The shadow loomed in front of her.

She spun back the way she had come. Her breath rasped in gasps. She reached the doorway that passed from the lounge room into the passage and paused to listen. The only sounds were her own laboured breaths. Too loud to make out soft footsteps.

She had no idea where he was.

Thwack! Her head ricocheted when a closed fist whacked across her cheek the moment she poked her head around the corner. Pain surged. Arms tightened around her chest, dragged her across the passage, into the bedroom and flung her across the bed. A second thump with a closed fist onto the same side of her head silenced her.

Dizziness, darkness, nausea. It was as though she stumbled along a dark, airless tunnel, desperate to find a way out.

A moan escaped, the blackness lifted, consciousness returned to the hiss of a belt as it was yanked out of its keepers. She screamed, flung herself over the other side of the bed in an attempt to flee but couldn't control the fall to the hard floor.

The man swore under his breath, lunged over the bed. The springs crunched. A body landed on her and pinned her to the floor.

She screamed and was hit for her troubles.

The man stood and pressed one heavy booted foot on her heaving chest. The slither of fabric at the same time she wrapped both hands around his calf. Trouser fabric fell to her hands. The man dropped on top of her, straddled across her hips. A thrust of his swollen erection pressed against her hip. She screamed, writhed from side-to-side in an attempt to dislodge him. Again and again, she screamed. A hand clamped over her mouth. The other hand grabbed a firm hold at the top of her nightdress and yanked. The fabric ripped apart.

'Shut up.' Harsh words followed: filthy words - describing in explicit detail exactly what was going to happen to her. He lifted his hips in an attempt to penetrate. With an almighty effort she swung her hips to one side.

'Damn you to hell, bitch,' he cursed under his breath. 'Bloody whore!'

She knew the voice.

Luke reached Jenna's house, pulled into a driveway two houses away, glanced into the back seat to check Josh was still asleep, locked the car and pelted barefooted along the pathway to find the metal side gate open. His heart hammered while he crept along the side of the house, searching for either the assailant or a forced entry point.

A piercing scream.

He forget about being quiet, quickened his pace, found the rear window that had been smashed and flung one leg over the sill. A piece of jagged glass pressed into the denim of his jeans. Not sure what to do, he tore off his sweater, flicked it out in front of him and gave it only a couple of seconds to settle on the floor inside before he clambered inside, felt the crunch of glass but no sharp edges cut through the soles, not that he had time to care.

The frantic cries were easy to follow but with little light to guide him, he stumbled against a side cupboard in the hallway. By the time he straightened it and himself, Jenna had gone quiet. Not certain which was her bedroom or if she was in her own room, he paused to listen.

A muffled cry came from behind. He turned, felt for the door and found it ajar. His fingers ran up the inside wall until he found the light switch and flicked the tiny lever. Light flooded the room. When his eyes adjusted to the sudden light, he spied a man's bare buttocks rise from the floor. Heart in his mouth, Luke craned over the bed. The sight of Jenna under the man's body, his trousers around his ankles caused a surge of bile. A hand pressed hard against Jenna's mouth but her terrified eyes stared at him. A surge of adrenalin pumped through his veins. His heart thundered in his chest while a vice-like grip squeezed his diaphragm tight as a fierce anger rose from the pit of his stomach. He was too late.

In the brief instant the man lifted his head in surprise at the light, Luke noticed Jenna's nightgown had been torn apart to expose her naked body. A deep animalistic growl started low in his chest, gurgled up his throat and whooshed out like the roar of an angry wildcat as he leapt around the bed, bent over and grabbed the man's shirt at the collar.

Luke hauled with all his might, jerked the man away from Jenna and pounded him against the wall. Flakes of dislodged paint fluttered to the ground.

'Run, Jenna. Get out. Open the front door for the police.'

In a flash, she tugged the torn shreds of her nightdress together, scrambled up, stumbled and fled, tears pouring down her face.

The man struggled but couldn't free himself. He tried to turn. Swung his fists in a wild frenzy, but Luke's longer arms held the attacker far enough away the punches flailed in mid-air. Luke grabbed a threshing wrist and jerked it up behind the man's back as hard and high as he could, not caring how much he hurt the bastard who stilled and yelped in pain.

Feet pounded along the hallway. The man tensed.

The same footsteps prevented Luke from doing a severe physical injury to the man.

When two police officers spun into the room, Luke dragged the man up to his feet and shoved him towards them, pleased when the bastard tripped over his dropped trousers and thumped to the ground. Luke stepped over the prostrate man to search for Jenna.

He found her slumped by the open front door. Her head rested on her knees with her hair fanned out as though a shroud. She was too quiet, too still. Instinct told him she would be in shock. He sank to his haunches, went to gather her into his arms.

'Don't touch me.' She shivered and hunkered backwards.

With arms raised in submission, Luke shuffled backwards. 'Okay. I won't harm you. I promise. How about you let me help you up?' He held out one hand, palm up.

Jenna shivered again and her hand shook as she lifted it slowly, reached out, grasped his fingers. When he hauled her upright she stumbled but managed to lean against the wall. It appeared she wasn't breathing until she hauled in a long breath as though finding courage. He didn't dare assist her until she took a step and her knees buckled.

'Easy, hold my hand.'

She gripped tight, stumbled to the lounge, flopped onto the sofa and curled into a ball. Luke grabbed a throw rug off the single chair and held it out.

'Wrap this around you. Your nightie is torn.'

She glanced down, groaned, grabbed the rug and wrapped it tight around her torso with the ends gripped tight under her chin. The warmth didn't stop her shivers.

One police officer came to the door to ask questions. Answers Luke also wanted to know but he doubted she was capable of answering.

'His name is Reynolds - Jenna's ex-husband. I don't know his first name. I found him on top of Jenna, on the floor with his hand clamped over her mouth. That's all I can tell you,' Luke offered. Jenna tensed. Surely she must have known who he was.

The police officer sat on the edge of a chair opposite. 'Ma'am, I need to know exactly what happened. I know there's no easy way to ask this, but I have to know whether or not he raped you.' The words were gentle but there was no real way to lessen the harshness and brutality of the question.

Luke's breath stalled when Jenna went rigid. She was so still. Grasping the edges of the rug tighter she straightened, turned her head towards the officer.

'He tried to. M…m…more than once. Almost succeeded. Luke arrived in time. I couldn't have fought him off much longer.'

Tears fell in large plops then streamed while Luke expelled his held breath. Why had the man wanted to hurt her? Had he done this before? Is this why Jenna was so afraid of men?

'Can you tell me all that happened ma'am?' asked the officer.

Jenna paused, gasped, sucked in a breath. She stumbled through her version of events, words interspersed by wracking sobs.

'He said… I should have… talked to him earlier today. He kept calling me horrible, sick names.' Jenna stopped, stared at Luke; the hollow, vacant eyes scared him.

'Why did he do that, Luke? Why did he hit me? Why rape me? I've never done anything to hurt him.'

With no answer he leant forwards, settled one hand on her knee and ignored the wince. 'I don't know. It's up to the police to find out. Are you up to finishing your story or do you want to stop now?'

She continued; her voice muffled against the fabric of the blanket which she had edged up as though desperate to hide away. 'I screamed as loud as I could, hoping the neighbours would hear. That's when he put his hand over my mouth and he was trying to...' Wracking sobs finished the sentence.

The officer stood. 'I'll leave it for now but we'll need a formal statement tomorrow. Mr Reynolds is in custody and won't bother you for a few days. He'll be cooling his heels in a cell until the initial hearing. I'll have an officer call in tomorrow. Will you be all right? Do you need a policewoman here to help you? We have specially trained people for situations like this. If you like, I could call in to get someone here.'

At the barely perceptible shake of Jenna's head, Luke assured the officer he would take care of her. After the police left, he didn't move until he sensed she had calmed. 'I've got Josh in the car. I have to go and check on him. Will you be all right for a few minutes?'

At the weak nod, Luke ran outside and brought his car into Jenna's drive. He hated the idea of leaving Josh in the car a moment longer so he lifted him out and carried him inside. Jenna had disappeared, but the rush of a shower came through the wall. He laid the still sleeping boy on the lounge, placed a cushion under his head and switched the light off on his way to the kitchen where he filled the kettle and set it on to boil. Too restless to sit still, he retrieved his sweater, manoeuvred the heavy bookcase to cover the broken window and searched the cupboards for all he needed to make a hot drink.

I n the shower, Jenna scrubbed and scrubbed to get rid of the filth of the touch of Rob. No matter how hard or how often she soaped her skin, she still didn't feel clean. Her tears had stopped, her mind gone numb but finally she reached for the tap and shut off the water. After towelling herself dry, she dressed in jeans and jumper to hide her ravaged, filthy body from Luke's scrutiny. Still in a daze, she combed the tangles from wet hair, gathered up the desecrated nightie and without acknowledging Luke who stood leant up against the sink, walked through the kitchen to the backyard and hurled the garment into the garbage bin where it belonged.

The sensation of Luke's eyes pressed into her. He stood motionless at the back door. She paused in front of him, head down but couldn't control the waves of tremors until he placed his hands each side of her shoulders. She melted into the secure warmth of his arms where she stayed until the tremors ceased and logic took hold. She wriggled free and set about completing the job Luke had begun. Coffee made, she flopped into a chair at the table, ignored the screech of legs on the floor and wrapped still shaking fingers around the mug for warmth. For the first time, she was game to catch Luke's eye.

'Thank you. I hate to think what would have happened if you hadn't come when you did.'

'I'm glad you had the good sense to ring me. Do you want to talk about it? I don't mind - I'm a good listener but it's okay if you don't want to - whatever is right for you.' He reached over, grasped one of her hands in his. His thumb ran up and down the back of her fingers.

'I'd rather not right now, it's too… too raw. Too painful. Can I ask another favour from you?'

'Of course.' The gentle movements with his thumb around the inside of her palm continued.

'I don't want to be alone tonight. I don't think I can handle it - especially with a broken window. I know he's in gaol, but I'm so… I guess the right word would be petrified.' The word shame, centred in her mind but she couldn't say it. Luke had seen her at her worst: half-naked with a man, no, an animal on top of her. He had seen her at her most vulnerable and for that she was ashamed. Ashamed for not being stronger, ashamed for letting him into her past.

'Could I make a suggestion? Come back to my place where you will be safe. I can put Josh in his own bed and there's a bed made up in the guest room you can use. I'll make sure your window is fixed tomorrow. Go and gather a few clothes and toiletries while I clean up in here.'

He eased her from the chair, led her along the passage. She hesitated at the bedroom doorway, too afraid to step over the threshold. It took a monumental effort to suck in a deep breath and sidle to the wardrobe while keeping eyes away from the bed. The sensation of filth eased when she entered the bathroom to collect basic toiletries but returned when she skittered along the wall of the bedroom to find a bag and underwear. A breath of relief whooshed out the moment she slammed the bedroom door.

'I moved the bookcase over the broken window.'

She jumped at the voice, spun around with a squeal. Joshua was draped over Luke's shoulder.

'Sorry. Let's get you out of here.' Luke followed her to his car.

The drive was silent. She couldn't find words and was thankful Luke didn't ask questions she figured would be rolling around in his mind. Questions she didn't want to answer - if she could find one.

After he'd tucked Joshua into bed, Luke showed her to the guest room and bathroom. 'My room is right next door so don't be afraid to call if you need me, even if you only want to talk or fear takes hold. Try to sleep and you don't have to get up early.' After checking she had all she needed he left her at the bedroom door. The second he left the fear returned. She doubted she would be able to sleep.

Each time she closed her eyes, the claustrophobia of a hand clamped over her mouth returned as did the sensation of Rob's body pressing her to the floor. Her skin crawled every time she recalled his hands on her.

Sometime during the night she must have slept but was wide-awake when Joshua stirred. Still in her clothes, she rose from the bed and went to him so he wouldn't disturb his father. When Joshua's eyes widened and mouth opened she put her fingers to her lips to hush him.

'Hi. Don't wake your father yet. He's tired. A man broke a window in my house last night and your dad thought I'd be safer if I stayed with you until it is fixed. You don't mind do you?'

Joshua shook his head. 'Was it a bad man?'

'Yes, but your dad called the police and they caught him. Now he's in gaol.' Not wanting to alarm the young boy, she changed the topic. 'How about you get dressed, sneak past Daddy's room so we can get breakfast. You can help me find everything.'

Since she was in someone else's house, it wasn't right to intrude beyond cereal, toast and fruit juice. It was a worry when Joshua gobbled his food as though he hadn't eaten in a week. Too bad. He could eat more with Luke.

'What can we do while we wait for your dad?' She asked after she'd rinsed dishes and put back the breakfast items.

'Dunno.'

'What do you like doing?'

'Lego.'

'Sounds like fun.'

'You like to build with Lego?'

'Sure,' she lied. 'Have you got much?'

'A bucketful.'

'Well, go get it.'

'Okay.' Joshua ran full pelt. He was back within seconds. The bucket was three times the size she thought it would be.

'Wow, you have so much.' She knelt on the lounge room carpet.

'What do you want to build? My brother used to build space stations on the moon.'

'You have brother?' The bucket was upturned. Blocks of every colour, size and description ended up on the floor in front of them.

'Yes but he doesn't live here. I told you about his two girls – my nieces.'

Joshua knelt next to her and brushed through the pile, picked up four flat bases and placed them next to each other. 'My baby sister was still in Mummy's tummy when she died. This can be the property for the station.'

Without a clue about what to say she picked out a few long grey blocks and clipped them in a line around the edge. 'Okay. We need a fence in case there are moon monsters who want to invade the station.'

Joshua hunkered forward. 'I'll make a big strong building for the astronauts to live in. Big enough the monsters can't get into it. Is Miss Johnson your friend?'

'Yes, my best friend since I moved here.'

'I like Miss Johnson. We just moved here too.'

'Yes, I know but I've been here for over a year and a half.'

'I've got a secret.'

Flummoxed, Jenna didn't know what to do. Kids had a habit of keeping unpleasant things secrets because they'd been told by less than scrupulous people that what went on was their special secret. 'A good secret?' she asked.

'The best.'

'Do you want to tell me what it is?'

Joshua laughed. 'Nah. If I did it wouldn't be a secret.'

'Earth calling Mars.'

Both Jenna and Joshua jerked at the loud voice.

'It's not a good idea to scare me like that right now, Lucas Hunter and it's the moon.' Jenna fought to calm the frantic beats of her heart.

'Daddy,' Joshua yelled at the same time. 'We're building a space station on the moon.'

'So I can see. Sorry, Jenna, I didn't think.' Luke knelt on the floor opposite them. He reached out and ran a gentle finger down her face. 'That looks painful. Why didn't you tell me last night? And why did you let me sleep so late? Have you two had breakfast?'

'One, because I had other things to worry about last night. Two, because you'd been up half the night and were tired and three, yes,' Jenna replied to all three questions.

'And how much sleep did you get?' Luke stared into her eyes. 'Not much if I read the blush right. How about you join me for a coffee after which, you can go back to bed while Josh and I go to repair your window until we can organise a new sheet of glass.'

'No thanks to the coffee but bed sounds amazing.' Embarrassment hit when she realised the connotation after Luke raised his eyebrows and grinned.

'Come on Josh, we've got men's work to do.' Standing, he hauled Joshua up, gave him a hug and kiss and offered his hand to pull her up.

'You don't have to do this. I can get a tradie.' She stumbled upright.

'No need. Go get some sleep. No-one knows you're here so you'll be safe.'

'Okay.' Still embarrassed by her *faux pas* she turned and fled to the bathroom where she drowned heated cheeks under a cold tap until the heat dissipated. After taking care to pat it dry, she studied her face in the mirror. The red marks from the punches had already turned indigo. It hurt like blazes when she waggled her jaw from side-to-side but she didn't think there were any fractures. Time would heal it and concealer would hide the worst until it healed. There was a long rough gouge down the inside of her lower arm where Rob scratched her. She had already scrubbed it clean but she shivered in distaste at the sense of filth she couldn't get rid of.

Still in her clothes, she climbed under the bedcovers, pulled them around her shoulders, but doubted she would be able to sleep.

'W'hy are we here?' Joshua asked when the car turned into the humungous car park. 'This isn't Mrs Reynolds' house.'

'We need a sheet of wood big enough to cover the broken window.'

'Oh, okay.' Joshua clicked open the buckles on his harness as soon as the car engine stopped. He opened the door, slid out and slammed it.

'Careful with the door. You'll wear it out if you slam it all the time.' Daddy grabbed his hand.

'Sorry, I forgot.' Joshua had to walk real fast to keep up.

'You forget every time. What would happen if I forgot to cook you dinner tonight?'

'Mrs Reynolds can cook it for us. She makes yummy food.'

'You don't like my food? And we don't ask visitors to do our chores – remember? They are guests. We take care of our guests.'

'Okay, but I like her food. Those biscuits were scrummy. Did you like them?'

Daddy laughed. 'The one I could get before you snaffled them all up, was delicious.'

They turned into the big shop. The doors were always open. Joshua liked it when they came to the hardware store although he thought it was a funny name for a shop. To him it was an everything except food shop. Although you could get drinks and snacks at the food bar right down the other end. And there was a sausage sizzle at the front on the weekends. He liked the sausages but not the onions. They are yucky. And no mustard, but lots of barbecue sauce.

'Come on, we need to go to the back wall where the wood is.' Daddy tugged Joshua's arm, they turned down a long aisle and he had to run to keep up.

Daddy took out lots of pieces of wood, ran his hand over them, shoved them back in the slots. 'This one,' he said at last: 'It's nice and thick. Now we need to get it cut to size. Here, you can help carry it.'

Joshua put both hands on the end of the wood while Daddy wrapped his long arm over it and gripped his fingers around the edge. This time Daddy walked slow as they went into the big workshop at the back. A man with a growly face came up to them and asked what they wanted.

'Children aren't allowed in the workshop.'

'Sorry,' said Daddy. 'I'll take him back inside in a second. There's only Josh and me so where I go, he comes with me. I need this cut 1.25 by 1.6. I'll be in there.' Daddy pointed to the big doorway. 'Come on, Josh. We have to wait in the store.'

'Why?'

'Safety. In case a piece of wood flies off.'

'The wood could hurt a big person too.'

'I know but places like this have insurance policies which tell them to not take any chances. They think kids might be in more danger.'

'I can run fast.'

Daddy laughed. 'True but there are rules and we have to obey rules the same way you do at school.'

'Like when you drive a car.'

'Exactly.'

'Rules are dumb.' They were now in the shop, but he could still see the growly man slide the big sheet of wood along a bench where a whizzy saw cut off a slice and spewed sawdust behind it. It looked like fun. He cut a smaller piece off the end, lifted it from the bench and nodded at Daddy.

'Wait here,' said Daddy. The man gave Daddy the wood and a piece of paper. 'Okay, let's go and fix a window.' With the wood under his arm Daddy grasped Joshua's hand. This time Daddy walked slow enough Joshua didn't have to run until they got to the check-out where Daddy handed over the piece of paper and used his card to pay.

In the car, Joshua squished into the dumb booster seat.

'Buckle up,' said Daddy the same time he tugged the straps together and clicked them into place.

'Too uncomfortable,' said Joshua.

'I know but you aren't seven yet. It's safer for you even though you are big enough to not have a booster seat. And you pass the five rules.'

'What rules?'

'There are five rules a child needs to pass before they can sit on the seat without a booster seat. Because you're so big, you pass them all except for one. You have to be seven.'

'More dumb rules.'

Daddy laughed. 'Yes, a road rule I have to obey. All children under seven have to use a booster seat. Wriggle to get more comfortable.

'Dumb rule.' Joshua wriggled while Daddy opened the boot and put the wood in back. The door shut with a shake of the car.

They passed the new school on the way. It was still a scary place although Mrs Reynolds was nice and Miss Johnson was fun.

'Daddy, do you like Miss Johnson?' They drove into the drive, parked in front of the shut garage door and Daddy turned off the engine.

'Yes, why?'

'She's funny.' Joshua unclipped the seatbelt and rubbed at his chest to ease the scratchy bit.

'How do you know?' Daddy opened the front door.

Joshua opened the back door and slid to the ground. 'She talked to me at the squash court. She knows cool *knock, knock* jokes. She made up one about me. She talks to me in the playground at school, too.' He slammed the door and winced. 'Oops, sorry, I forgot again.'

'Looks like I'll have to forget to cook two nights in a row.' Daddy opened the boot and took out the wood, and a hammer, and a pile of big nails.

'You should get a new mummy.'

'Excuse me?'

'A new mummy can cook dinner for you.'

Daddy squatted next to Joshua. 'Nanna is my mother and Poppy is my father. I don't think Nanna will be happy if I tell her I don't want her to be my mother anymore.'

'But I don't have a mummy. You can get me a new mummy.'

Stunned, the only thing Luke could do was hug his son tight. Words defied him. Where had this idea come from? He dropped the tools, lifted Josh from the ground and gripped him in one arm. On eye level he noted Josh's face. There were no tears, no sadness in the depths. 'I'm not good enough?' he asked when he couldn't think of anything else to say. 'I love you to bits. We've done all right so far with only the two of us.'

Joshua wriggled, dropped his eyes but said nothing.

'Where did this idea come from?'

Joshua shrugged. 'All the other kids at school have a mummy.'

'All the ones you know about. Lots of kids have only one parent. Some don't have a daddy. Some have stepparents as well. Some live in two different houses so they can spend time with both their mum and their dad when the parents split up and divorce. I loved your mummy a great deal. So did you. And she loved you to pieces. She died in an accident. You know all of this.'

'I know.' Tears welled, tumbled over. Thin arms wrapped around Luke's neck and a head landed on his shoulder.

Luke's heart exploded as he hugged his son tight and ran one hand up and down his back. When tears soaked into his shirt, he searched for a place to sit. On the front step, he continued to hold Josh against his chest until the boy wept out his pain. It had been months since he'd been in such a dark space. He prayed this move hadn't unsettled him too much.

'Daddy?' Josh pulled his head away.

'Yes?' Luke studied the tear-wracked face, swept his hand over to wipe away most of the moisture.

'I'm sorry.'

'Ah, Josh, you have nothing to be sorry about. I know you miss having a mummy. So do I. One day I might meet a woman I can love enough to get married again. But not yet. We need time to settle into our life here. To make new friends. You already have two class mates who want to be friends with you. Maybe we can invite them over to play one weekend.' He lifted the bottom of Joshua's T-shirt to wipe his face clean and smiled. 'And you have a nice new teacher who needs our help right now. So how about we nail this piece of wood to the window so she can be safe, eh?'

'Okay.' Josh wriggled from Luke's lap and picked up the hammer. 'Where is Mr Reynolds?'

'Huh, what are you on about?' Luke picked up the wood.

'Nanna said a lady is called Mrs when she gets married. Nanna is Mrs Hunter because she married Poppy. Mummy was Mrs Hunter because she married you. So Mrs Reynolds must be married to Mr Reynolds.' Joshua walked next to him with one hand on the wood, to the fancy metal gate, which was open, along the side path until they ended up at the back of the house.

'Mr Reynolds didn't want to be married anymore so he divorced Mrs Reynolds. It's like getting unmarried. Lean on this.' Luke held the wood up to cover the window.

'So she's not married anymore?' Joshua put his back to the wood and leant on it.

'No.' Luke banged in a nail and swore when it bent.

'You said a naughty word.'

'Sorry.' The nail tinkled on the path. Luke took more care with the next one and the ones after until he was happy the wood was secure.

Back home, he checked on Jenna. Noting she was still asleep, he closed the door and put his finger to his mouth to keep Josh quiet. In the kitchen he gave Josh a drink and snack. 'We need to do a load of laundry.'

'Why?'

'You need a clean uniform for school tomorrow.'

'Why?'

'So you don't stink.' Luke ruffled Josh's hair. 'You don't want your new friends to think you don't have clean clothes. What would Mrs Reynolds say if you went to school all stinky?'

'Okay.'

'Come and give me a hand. You can toss the clothes and soap powder in the machine.'

It was early afternoon while he folded clean clothes from the drier, Luke heard Jenna rouse. She went into the bathroom for a few minutes, came out. Footsteps came along the passage. Luke poked his head from the laundry.

'Hi, I'm in here. Do you feel better?' The dark red and blue marks where Rob belted her, stood out. Luke fought to hide a wince.

'Do you have any painkillers? My face aches.'

'Of course, it looks pretty painful. He must have given you quite a hefty whack. Come into the kitchen.'

Jenna followed and sat on the stool he pulled out for her. He searched a high shelf in a cupboard for the required medication. After emptying two tablets from the foil into her hand he gave her a glass of water.

'You must be hungry; would you like something to eat?' Luke filled the kettle and set it on to boil. 'I'm about to make coffee for myself.'

'Yes to the coffee, please. I had breakfast with Joshua and until these take effect, eating will be painful. Where's Joshua?'

'Building towers with three packs of cards. We nailed a substantial board to the outside of your window. I thought about phoning a glass repair place but it's Sunday and wasn't sure about your insurance arrangements. I figured it was better to not interfere.'

'Thank you. I'll phone my insurance company tomorrow. I forgot the police were going to visit to ask questions.'

'I rang them to say you were here and not in the space for questions. They did ask for you to contact them today if possible.' Luke spooned coffee powder into two cups, added hot water and stirred.

Jenna closed her eyes, breathed deep three times, opened them again. 'Okay. I'll phone them after I go home.'

'Are you sure you're up to it? You're welcome to stay as long as you need.' He pushed a mug towards her. 'You have it black, don't you?'

'Either. Thank you.' She lifted the mug, sniffed at the coil of steam. 'Smells so good.'

'Can I ask a personal question? But you don't have to answer.'

'Ask away.'

'Was your husband abusive before you parted company?'

With closed eyes, Jenna took her time to place the mug on the bench. Her shoulders rose and fell. 'No. Never. It wasn't the reason he walked out on me. And I don't want to talk about it right now.' She lifted her eyes: bleak eyes.

'Sorry for intruding. It's… I can't abide men who think it's okay to abuse a woman. I wanted to punch his lights out last night but to do so would make me no better. It was fortunate the police came when they did.' Luke reached out and placed one hand on Jenna's wrist. 'Sorry, it's none of my business.'

'I rang you for help. You were much closer than the police. I'm glad I did for I couldn't have held him off any longer and the result would have been much worse.' She dropped her head into her hands and went silent.

'Ring me any time you feel threatened.' He slammed his mouth shut when Joshua joined them.

Amusement tickled his lips at the way Joshua crept to Jenna, leant against her with his head on her lap. Jenna's hand found its way onto his head where she gently ran her fingers through his hair. When she lifted her head and smiled his heart managed a tumble turn. After this morning's meltdown, this was probably exactly what Josh needed. Jenna as well.

'Can you take me home?' The sudden question surprised him.

'Sure. If it's what you want.'

'I'm sure. I've got lessons to plan for this young scallywag.'

Joshua lifted his head and grinned. 'And I'll have clean clothes so I won't be stinky.'

Jenna raised her eyebrows in question.

Luke laughed. 'I needed to explain why it was important to do a load of laundry. Josh helped. Needed an extra rinse to get rid of the overdose of powder. Come on mate, we need to get the lady back to her home.'

It wasn't until after he walked her to her front door he noticed the trepidation on her face. 'Are you sure you want to stay here?'

'Yes, I'll be fine. I've got chores to do, lessons to plan, laundry.'

'Okay, but ring me if you change your mind. I'll phone tonight.' He was sure she wasn't being totally honest for he both felt and heard the anxiety in her voice.

The second the door closed a shiver beset her before taking the first step. Creeped out, she slithered down the door and sat on the floor with arms gripped around bent knees. Vivid images galloped through her mind. 'He's in gaol,' she yelled. 'He can't hurt me now.' The words echoed along the passage. The same passage with a creepy vibe.

She humped along the floor to the lounge opening, peered in, shivered. The sofa was skewed away from the wall where Rob left it. Determined to get rid of his presence, she stood, ran, jerked the sofa into place and skedaddled to the kitchen where it was a relief to find nothing out of place. But he'd been in here.

She took out disinfectant, wiped it over every surface, including the floor. To gain courage she gulped down half a glass of water before she was game enough to go into her study. It was so dark she switched on the light to find the window boarded up behind the bookcase Luke had dragged across the floor.

Rob had been in here as well and violated her haven.

Broken glass was scattered over the floor, the seat of the rocking chair and reached under the desk. Furious, she swept up the glass shards, scooped them into the rubbish bin and dumped them in the outside bin. A mop spread disinfectant over the polished floorboards. A cloth rubbed off any of Rob's skin cells from every surface on the furniture, wall and window sill.

Her skin crawled the entire time she sat at the desk, scribbled out scanty lesson plans for the next day, packed up the gear she would need and shoved them into the basket she used to get gear to and from school. When the phone rang, she ignored it. If she didn't answer, the police couldn't ask her to relive the horror with their questions.

For dinner, she opened the fridge door, took out odds and ends and dropped them onto a plate. Tonight was not the time to care about healthy options. A glass of red washed down cheese and crackers, a sliced apple, a wedged tomato and half a block of white chocolate. Another glass of red went with her to the bathroom where she washed, scrubbed, rinsed and scrubbed again until her skin tingled and stung. Dollops of shampoo washed the filth from her hair three times. Wrapped in a towel with another around her hair, she stood outside the bedroom door, too scared to enter.

Tired and a tad tipsy, she grabbed two carving knives from the knife block, turned on all the lights in the house and went into the lounge where she sat huddled in a corner to wait for sleep to take her from this horror. At one stage she crept to the bedroom, stood at the door but couldn't move across the threshold. With a sensation of cockroaches crawling over her skin, she turned away, took her old sleeping bag, a spare pillow and heavy rug from the linen cupboard and crept to the door leading to the garage. Ears alert for the slightest of sounds, she dropped the rear passenger seat of her SUV down, spread the sleeping bag out and wrapped the blanket around her for warmth. No-one would think to look for her in the car. Doors locked, she slid the two knives between seat and door and curled up. A nightmare, accompanied by screams, woke her more times than she cared to count, until she abandoned sleep and sat in the front with the radio to accompany her until slithers of sunlight crept under the door.

Before leaving for school, she did her best to cover the injuries on her face. The harsh red mark on her cheek had deepened to an indigo swollen and painful bruise. She hid the red scratches on her arm under a long sleeved blouse, thankful the weather was cool enough to wear such a garment.

Emily was the first to notice her injury when she bounced into Jenna's classroom for their usual early morning catch-up. Too ashamed to disclose details, she made up a story about slipping on the bathmat and catching her face on the corner of the vanity top. Such a lame excuse most battered women used but she didn't care and since she didn't have a partner, it was kind of valid.

By lunch, exhaustion had taken hold. It was a struggle to maintain enthusiasm for the students and their artistic achievements when she gave them a free *draw anything you like,* session to round up the day instead of physical activity outside.

Home again, she decided to move her bed into the spare room since she would never be able to sleep in the main bedroom again. She had only dragged the mattress into the room when a loud knock on the front door sent her nerves on a frantic race to tighten.

'Who is it?' she called from behind the door.

'Police.'

Damn, the last thing she needed but she plastered on a smile and opened the door. 'Sorry I haven't got back to you. It's been… I've just arrived home.'

'Can we come in?' asked one with her I.D. card held out.

She nodded at the two female officers and led them to the room of least fear – the kitchen. 'Please sit. Can I get you a drink? Tea, coffee?'

'No thanks, we're fine. Are you up to giving us a more detailed statement?'

Jenna shrugged. 'Not really but let's do it.' She sat opposite, took in a large breath and eased it out. The questions were easy, the answers tough. One officer wrote in a pad even though they recorded it as well. The beauty of mobile phones. When there were no more questions one officer handed her a form.

'We suggest you apply for a restraining order to keep Mr Reynolds away from you. He was given bail after the first court appearance earlier today.'

'Given bail!' She shot from the chair and leant over the sink, desperate to find enough air to breathe.

'He did promise to not come near you but an order will carry more weight.'

'More weight for what?' Jenna turned on limp spaghetti legs. Needing to sit, she stumbled to a chair and plonked into it.

'It's a legal order to keep away from you. You will need to appear before a magistrate. In cases like this, the wait time is minimal.'

'But what if he comes back tonight or before I can get this order in place?'

'If you have your own legal representative they can lodge it on-line for you.'

'I don't. I'll need to get time off from school tomorrow and I will. But what difference is a piece of paper going to make? He deliberately sought me out, broke into my house, hunted me down and knew exactly what he was doing. Made ugly threats. Look what he did to me.' One hand swept across her face. 'He was caught in the act. How come a physical abuser can be released while the victim has to live in fear he'll come back and try again?'

'Sorry. We can only make the arrest and press charges. The judge makes the decision.'

'Has to be a male judge.'

'Mr Reynolds had a lawyer to advise him and make the bail application.'

'While the victim wasn't given a chance to plead their case. Terrific legal system we have.'

'Do you know why he came?'

'No. I haven't spoken to him since the night he walked out on our marriage two and a half years ago.'

'I'll arrange for a squad car to cruise around during the night. Phone us if you suspect he's around. Here.' The younger officer handed her a card with two phone numbers. 'You could stay with friends.'

'I could. I'll think about it.' As if. The only people she knew well enough to couch surf were fellow teachers, which would require explanations she was too ashamed to give. And Luke, but she'd already imposed on him too much.

The officers stood and packed up their gear. Jenna showed them out, shut the door and double-checked the deadlock was in place.

It was fortunate she had the task of moving furniture to ease sensations she couldn't describe. Hollow dread, marshmallow brain and plain exhaustion were words she came up with while she struggled to pull her bed apart, drag the pieces down the passage and set it up again, but the bed was made in time for her to use it - with clean sheets. The defiled linen went into the bin. Sleep still eluded her so to fill the lonely, empty hours she moved other pieces of furniture from room-to-room, a few pieces more than once, until physical exhaustion and a muddled jungle of furniture dragged her back to bed.

Despite being determined to fight the fear, the same pattern occurred each night. By Thursday, the house had been transformed with not a single item in the main bedroom. It hadn't prevented her from missing Joshua after school. On the walk home, she wished Luke hadn't succeeded in his search for another babysitter.

By Friday afternoon the loneliness and dread had intensified so much she couldn't face going home. With nothing else to do, she dawdled, studied every garden and house-front along the way. Spotted things she'd never noticed before. The spiderwebs woven in a wire fence, the almost dead daisies desperate for a drink, the veranda crowded with junk next to a house where the veranda was spotless and there was a small cloth on the round table between two comfortable-looking chairs. Each house owner had different priorities. Hers was to move out and figure out why an intense sensation of dread had grown over the week. At the corner, she paused to let two cars pass before crossing the road. Thoughts rambled, sorted themselves out. Luke hadn't called all week, not that there was a reason for him to call after the first evening when he checked she was okay. She lied - said she was fine. After all she was nothing more than his son's teacher, they had enjoyed a couple of games of squash against each other and he had helped her in a time of crisis. Now it was obvious it was all he wanted, so she determined she would keep it that way and stepped onto the road, jogged across and hurried home. No more maudlin depression.

Not sure whether he would turn up for the rematch on Saturday, she made sure she was early, not only so she had a chance to warm up but also so she didn't have to remain in her house a moment longer. At the courts there were people: people she could talk to, a crowd to hide in.

The moment she entered the courts a shiver beset her when a memory surged. Rob had been here last time. Un-nerved, she took care to survey the entire inside and study the features of every person to ensure there weren't going to be any unwelcome spectators. After a check to find which court was booked she deposited her bag in the change-room, moved onto the empty court to hit the ball around as warm-up. If Luke didn't come, she would leave.

At an excited shout from above she turned, waved, held up one finger in the air and pointed to herself. Unexpectedly, Joshua nodded in agreement.

'You've turned my son against me. He's barracking for you today.' Luke's husky admonish came from the open doorway.

'I can't let him be disappointed can I?' Jenna quipped with what she hoped was a wicked smile as she spun around and hit the ball against the wall. The sudden sight of Luke had set her pulse hammering so she took out the sense of unease against the small rubber ball, whacking it hard.

'How have you been?' Luke stepped in front of her and caught the ball in his palm when it rebounded from the front wall.

'I'm fine.'

Luke scoffed. 'I doubt it. Bruises have faded but still there. Scratch down your arm is still vivid and believe me, I know how long it takes to get over a trauma.' He hit the ball. 'Warm-up time.'

The warm-up was brief before the game began in earnest. She pulled out all stops to gain the upper hand, played hard from the outset in the hope he would tire early while she took her anger and frustration out on the tiny, black, round rubber ball, belting it as hard as she could. Luke's height, long reach and physical strength gave him an advantage but she was lighter on her feet, more agile and a tad fitter. She won the first game and acknowledged Joshua's cheers by turning to give him a wave. Again they had amassed quite an audience, although she couldn't figure out why? This time she studied the crowd to make sure a certain face wasn't among them. She didn't realise how the thought tensed her nerves tight until they eased off when he wasn't there.

Luke won the second game by playing two virtually unreturnable serves. She applauded his skill by tapping one hand against the taut strings of her racquet when she conceded defeat, but she was ready for him to try the same tactic again. She had figured out his weakness and kept playing to his backhand, which enabled her to win the third game by the biggest margin yet. She gave the victory sign in response to Joshua's yell of approval.

'Well done. You outplayed me this time,' Luke gasped with a pat on the back of her shoulder. Sweat poured from his brow and his chest heaved. They both glanced up at the sound of loud applause, astounded at the packed gallery. Both acknowledged the applause with a wave before moving from the court to the change rooms for a shower. When Jenna emerged, Joshua flew at her. She knelt to give him a hug, her heart contracting at the feel and smell of him. How she missed him.

'Josh, you and I need to have to have a serious talk. Where's my hug?' Luke queried from behind.

'Jenna was the winner so she gets first hug,' Joshua chirped but immediately turned around and reached his arms around Luke's waist to hug him as well.

With a bite of guilt for Joshua's defection, Jenna stood and turned away to leave. A small hand tucked itself into her fingers. Warmth flooded her heart. No way could she let him go until they climbed the steps to the upper level where they were stopped by one of the spectators who introduced himself as the captain of the club's pennant team.

'The club could use players of your calibre on the pennant team. How about joining us?'

'Not for me, I don't have the time at the moment,' said Luke.

'Sorry, but no,' was all Jenna said after a long pause. She would love to but not at the moment. She wasn't in the space.

Luke took Joshua's other hand and they walked side-by-side. Like a family. One she should have had but now probably would never have. The pain of loneliness returned with a vengeance while they continued on their way to the car park, their small steps accommodating Joshua's shorter stride. To make the ache worse,

Luke was so silent. In fact he'd been unusually quiet the entire afternoon. He'd hardly said a word after the initial greeting, his silence reinforcing her thoughts how he wasn't interested in anything more than a passing friendship. So when they neared her car she dropped Joshua's hand and turned towards her car.

'My car is over here. Thank you for the game, Luke. You stretched me to my limit and I enjoyed it a great deal.'

At Joshua's forlorn face, she knelt next to him and enveloped him in her arms. 'I'll see you Monday morning.' On the pretext of giving him an extra-long cuddle she held him longer, breathing in the sweetness she had become used to. 'Bye Josh,' she whispered in his ear, overwhelmed by her fragile emotions. Releasing him, she turned and hurried towards her car, fighting back unbidden tears. It was ridiculous how easy tears threatened lately. After stowing her bag, she drove off, allowing the tears a free rein.

She couldn't face going home to the loneliness of an empty house: the house she was now too scared to enter. The house which was no longer her haven and could no longer be called a home. Her private sanctuary had been invaded, violated and she now hated crossing the thresh-hold of the front door. Desperate for fresh air and a different environment she drove to a nearby park from where she walked around and around the edge in an attempt to rid herself of a sensation she couldn't put a name to.

'You didn't ask her, Dad,' Josh admonished while Luke stood staring after Jenna.

'Jenna was in a hurry to get away.'

'Because she's sad.' Josh peered up with serious eyes.

'How do you know she was sad? Jenna thrashed me at squash, she should be happy.'

'She was crying.'

Luke stared down at his son. 'Are you sure?'

Josh nodded, his hands on his hips as though to let his father know he should notice these things. And he should have.

The moment they arrived home, Joshua raced to his room and slammed the door.

'Door, Josh,' Luke called after him.

'Don't care,' Josh yelled back.

It was all he needed, a recalcitrant son and an upset Jenna. To make sure she was all right and get an answer, Luke dialled her number but her answering machine was off and the phone rang out. He had no idea what her mobile number was or if she had one. He had planned on asking her to join them for dinner that night and couldn't for the life of him figure out where things had gone so badly askew. She'd pushed him to exhaustion in the game. She was one of the best players he'd ever encountered; smart too for she'd figured out and played to his weakness in the last game and he'd have to practise a lot if he wanted to beat her again. And he sure needed to rebuild his fitness levels.

He rang again, several times, each call unanswered. After the fifth call he thought she might not answer on purpose. Or she could be too upset to speak. Unable to settle, he figured a visit might give him the answer and also cheer up Josh.

At least Joshua was happy as they drove to Jenna's house. He chatted and wriggled non-stop. The grumpy face returned when Jenna's car wasn't there and there was no sign of her.

'We have to wait for her,' Joshua demanded when he refused to get back in the car.

'We could be waiting a long time. It's possible she could be visiting friends or might have a dinner date.'

'She should be having dinner with us.'

'Next time we'll invite her a week ahead so we know for sure she can come.'

Back home, Joshua tore to his room, slammed the door. With raised eyebrows, Luke ignored it. Instead he set about peeling vegetables and set them in the roasting pan with the small hunk of lamb. Joshua's favourite meal and the one he'd insisted they cook for Jenna.

It was a shock when Joshua refused to eat. 'Don't want it. Jenna isn't here. You made her so sad she doesn't want to visit us any more,' yelled Josh from behind the bedroom door.

Luke knocked, waited, opened the door. Josh lay on his bed with his shoes on. The bleak face twisted Luke's innards. Joshua had been like this before, in the early days of grieving for his mother. What had amazed Luke was how quick Joshua had taken to Jenna, because he'd been socially withdrawn and reluctant to show any affection for anyone other than Luke and his parents since the accident.

'If you want to blame me, it's okay but neither of us did anything to make Jenna sad. I think she may still be upset about the man who broke into her house. She was scared and could still be scared. How about you eat half of your dinner so you have lots of energy?'

'Don't want any.' Josh turned his back and curled into a ball on his side.

'Okay, take your shoes off and hop into bed. You might be better after a nap.' To make sure, he slipped the shoes and socks from Josh's feet and tucked him under the covers.

It didn't take long after Josh fell asleep before the first scream. Luke ran, swept the frightened boy up in his arms. It had been a while since the last distressing nightmare.

'Shush, Son, it's all right. It's only a bad dream,' Luke whispered.

'Jenna! I want Jenna!' he sobbed.

'I'm here, it's okay.'

'No, want Jenna.'

Luke whispered, caressed, cajoled while holding his distraught son close. Nothing worked. When Joshua became hysterical, Luke carried him to the phone, dialled Jenna, huffed out a breath of relief when she answered.

'Hi, it's Luke. I need to ask a favour. Joshua has had a nightmare and keeps calling for you. Nothing I say calms him. Can I bring him over?'

'Of course, put him on.'

'Here, Jenna wants to talk to you.' He put the phone to Joshua's ear but doubted he would hear with all the hiccoughs and sobs. At last he quietened – listened. A teary smile broke out.

'Come on, let's go, Jenna wants to see me.' He wriggled, slipped to the floor and pelted towards the garage door.

Stunned at the dramatic change, Luke grabbed a jacket for them both. He drove as fast as he legally could, but no-where near fast enough for Joshua who kept urging him to hurry. When they reached Jenna's house, Joshua was out of his seatbelt, out of the car and knocking on the door before Luke could turn the engine off. When he arrived at the door, it was to find Joshua enveloped in Jenna's arms. She knelt on the floor with his tousled head on her shoulder, talking to him in a subdued, gentle voice, one hand holding his head to her and the other rubbing gently up and down his back. 'I miss you too, Joshua, as much as I miss my own little girl.'

When Luke gasped, she paused. Her shoulders rose but she said nothing. Instead she rubbed Joshua's back again and kept him wrapped in her arms until the crying ceased and he wriggled free.

'Come into the lounge room, both of you.' Jenna led Joshua to the sofa and laid him down with his head on her lap. She stroked his hair, talking to him until the exhausted boy was asleep.

Luke sat in the armchair opposite, his long legs stretched out in front of him, crossed over at the ankles, watching and waiting. Once he knew for sure Joshua was asleep, it was time. 'We need to talk. Do you mind?'

'Put him in my bed to let him sleep in peace.'

Luke stood, moved across to the sofa and lifted his son into his arms. He walked to her bedroom but she swiftly moved in front of him and guided him to the room next door.

'In here.' She pushed the door open.

It was the same bed and furniture from her bedroom. Puzzled, he said nothing. Settling his son under the covers, he gave him a soft kiss, moved into the passage, noted the new security lock on the inside of the door. His mind began to work in overdrive and without saying a word he went to the room where Jenna had slept before. Upon opening the door he found nothing - absolutely nothing. The room was empty but had a strong odour of bleach. It was obvious Jenna had scrubbed the room clean in an attempt to rid it of any trace of Rob. Closing the door behind him, he returned to the lounge where he sat opposite Jenna. Her head rested in the palms of her hands, elbows on her knees.

'I'm sorry about tonight, but Josh was distraught. We had planned on asking you to have dinner with us tonight but you fled after our game and I didn't get the chance to offer the invitation. Josh was pretty forceful in letting me know I hadn't asked you. He wouldn't eat his dinner, went to bed upset with me and woke from a nightmare not long after he fell asleep. From then on things went from bad to worse. He kept blaming me you didn't want him anymore. Why were you upset this afternoon? Josh said you were crying when you left.' When she wouldn't look at him, he stared at her for the slightest indication of what was going on.

'I wasn't in a good space. I haven't slept much this week.'

Gut instinct told him she was being evasive. 'Hmm! Let's start with last week. I recall asking you to ring if you needed me. It's pretty obvious you've had a hard time of it - hence shifting all your furniture. Why didn't you ask me to help?'

'I managed.'

'I can see you managed but it's not the answer to my question.'

He moved across the room and knelt on the floor in front of her. 'Why didn't you ring me?' He hooked his fingers under her chin so they were eye-to-eye.

'Because it was my problem and you had done more than enough to help me,' she whispered.

'I'll accept your answer but I'm not sure I'm happy with your reason. Now, why were you upset this afternoon? You whipped me to the point of exhaustion, my son deserted me, his allegiance with you; we walked to the car hand-in-hand. I thought everything was hunky-dory until you just up and left. I couldn't, and still can't figure out what went wrong. Can't you at least give me a hint? Joshua, of course, blames me for making you sad.'

At this, Jenna gave a weak smile. Luke seized on this tiny indication of wavering. 'Come on, help me out here? I hate us being at odds, especially when I don't have a clue as to why.'

'I couldn't figure out why you hardly said a word to me. I hadn't heard from you all week and I thought it was possible you didn't want to associate with me after...' She pulled away.

'I hardly said a word because I had no breath left. With little free time to play any sport over the past two years, I've become fairly unfit and you worked my butt off. And if you think for one nano-second that because a scumbag hurt you it would make any difference on how I feel about you, you don't know me very well.' He smiled. 'There's something I always want to do when I'm with you.' Reaching behind her he slipped the elastic from her ponytail, ran the fingers of both hands through her hair and pulled a thick strand forwards over her shoulders. 'You have beautiful hair and I keep wanting it the way it was the first time I met you. Now where were we?' He perched next to Jenna, twisted his fingers together in his lap. 'I guess I should have rung you during the week to check if you were coping but I've worked long hours after Josh goes to sleep, to get on top of everything at work. An entire new bunch of clients to get a handle on as well as staff. Are you coping all right now? I noticed the lock on your door.'

'Rob is out on bail. I took out a restraining order and he's not allowed within a hundred metres of me, but it's only a piece of paper. I pray he won't attack me again but I keep getting this uncomfortable sensation as though I'm being watched. It's probably just nerves and an over-active imagination. I couldn't sleep in such a defiled room again and have even considered selling my house to find a new place to live. This place has an unpleasant aura about it now and I don't feel safe. I feel dirty, violated.'

'You know you can ring me any time, even if all you want is to talk.' Luke reached out and lifted Jenna's hand in his. He'd read about the feelings of worthlessness and disgust rape victims have. An issue he didn't know how to handle. 'I haven't been interested in a relationship since Lisa died, but you have made an impact on me, and on Josh. I get the impression you have been badly hurt and have built up a few barriers against the male half of the population.'

She gasped.

'The hurt lives in your eyes but I would like for us to get to know each other better. Let's take it one step at a time to see how things work out. Can we start by me asking you to come over tomorrow night to let Josh and me cook you dinner? Josh might actually speak to me again if you agree. Please?'

Jenna smiled. 'I'd like that, thank you.'

'Wonderful. Now I must get Josh home and let you get a decent night's sleep. I've taken up too much of your time. I appreciate your help.' Luke stood and drew Jenna up from the lounge. Desperate to give her a thank you hug, he instead stepped away and went to the bedroom. The last thing she needed after such an ordeal was to be touched in any form on intimacy by a man.

When Luke picked Joshua from the bed, he stirred, called out Jenna's name.

'Jenna has agreed to come to dinner tomorrow night. We have to go home so we can cook it and I need your help,' Luke whispered.

Still half asleep, Joshua smiled, snuggled against Luke's chest and closed his eyes.

With an almighty flying leap Joshua landed on Daddy.

'Oomph.' Daddy groaned and tried to turn over.

Josh tickled him. 'Come on, you have to get up now.'

'Why?' Daddy pulled the pillow over his head.

Josh tugged it away. 'We have to get ready for Jenna.'

'Mrs Reynolds to you. You know the rules.'

'What rules? Rules are dumb.' Joshua tugged at the Doona.

Daddy tugged it back. 'You never call an adult by their first name unless they ask you to. It's called having good manners. And it's still dark. What time is it?' He lifted his head, glanced at the bedside clock and groaned. 'It's not six yet. Go away.'

'We have to get ready. Come on.' Josh grabbed the pillow, tossed it across the floor. He went to the bottom of the bed, tickled Daddy's feet and when Daddy went to grab him, he yanked the Doona away and ran with it dragging behind.

'I will pay you back young man,' Daddy called but Josh heard him go to the bathroom so he was up.

He dumped the Doona in the doorway, ran to his room, tore off his PJs, dragged on a pair of clean undies, yesterday's shorts and a Star Wars T-shirt. He was about to leave when he remembered Jenna was coming so he straightened the Doona on his bed, belted the pillow into shape, rolled up his PJs and hid them under the pillow. Another belt to lower the lump. He grabbed all the clothes on the floor, bundled them together and shot to the laundry where he tossed the lot in the basket. Daddy won't have to hassle him today. Back in his room he knelt on the floor and shoved everything under the bed. Leaning back he used his feet to make sure everything was right at the back where it couldn't be seen.

Jenna was a teacher so she would want his school things on the desk in neat piles. He stacked and restacked when they pile wobbled and fell. Two stacks made it better. He shoved them at the back so the wall would hold them up. All the pencils got swept into the open drawer. Happy, he placed the chair right in the middle of the desk so it was neat, the same way he had to at school. It was hard to get the wardrobe door shut. He shoved but something was stuck. Door open, he dropped to the floor, wrestled a shoe free and tossed it inside. At last, the door shut.

'Good grief, what happened in here?' Daddy stood in the doorway. He rubbed his eyes, stuck his head in and moved it around.

'I tidied it so Jen… oops, Mrs Reynolds can come in and play with me.'

'Oh, can she now? We have invited her to share dinner with us, not play games. And remember, we take care of our guests. How about we decide what food we're going to have while we eat breakfast? Not that the shops will be open yet for us to go buy what we need.'

'Okay.' Joshua ran, opened the pantry and took out the cereal. He had to wait for Daddy to get the bowls because they were too high. Instead, he got the spoons and knives and clattered them onto the table. When he took the milk from the fridge door his fingers slipped on the cold carton and he had to catch it before it fell.'

'Slow down or you'll have an accident.'

'Sorry.'

Daddy poured Corn Flakes in both bowls and added the milk. 'What do you think we should have for dinner tonight? We need to make a shopping list.'

'Pizza.'

'Not for an important guest.'

'Hamburgers.'

Daddy laughed and shook his head. 'Uh, uh.'

'Spag Bog.'

'No, we need an elegant dish, nice food a lady would like to eat when she dines out.'

'Do you know what Je… Mrs Reynolds likes to eat? You had dinner with her at the pub. What did she eat there?'

'How do you know she was at the pub?'

'Miss Johnson told me. Do you like Miss Johnson?'

'Yes, why?'

'She likes you. And she's not married.'

'What difference does it make whether she's married or not?'

'You can't marry a lady who is already married.'

'Josh! I have no plans to get married again. And Miss Johnson has a boyfriend. Stewart, next door is her boyfriend. He won't be pleased if he hears you want her to marry a different man. And quit trying to find me a new wife.'

'Okay.' Not Miss Johnson, although she's lots of fun.

'Jenna had fish with salad and chips so we know she likes fish. We could do baked potatoes and vegetables to go with the fish. What about dessert?'

'Ice-cream.'

'Not elegant. How about a chocolate cheesecake?'

'The one Nanna makes?'

'Yes, I've got the recipe. You can help make it. And we need a first course – entrée they call it. How about soup?'

'Yuck.'

'I know, bruschetta, you like it and so do I.'

Joshua shrugged. 'Okay, but not too much yucky onion.' He licked the spoon, lifted the empty bowl and tipped the rest of the milk into his mouth.

'And don't you dare lick your bowl tonight. It's bad manners.' Daddy collected the dirty dishes and put them in the sink. 'You go and wash up and make sure you scrub your teeth well while I write out a list for shopping.'

It was a relief to get home after the shopping experience from hell. Josh had driven him nuts with constant questions whether Jenna would like different foods. There had been no stop button. The only time he shut up was when he stuffed sausage roll in his mouth and slurped his way through a chocolate milkshake. Bags on the bench, Luke sorted the ingredients, put cold stuff in the fridge and added a couple of bottles of wine, one, a sparkly Rose and the other, a Semillon Blanc.

To make the cheesecake first, he had Joshua open packages, crush biscuits for the base, tip in ingredients, stir and generally get in the way until Luke sent him to set the table. There was no budging from his insistence Jenna had to sit next to him. They had to pick a bunch of flowers to make the table look pretty, which had Luke search through an unopened carton for a vase he knew he had kept. The search filled in an hour. The resultant bunch of torn off stems jammed into a too large vase looked ragged to Luke but Josh wouldn't allow his father to re-arrange them.

Under normal circumstances it took a lot of prompting for Joshua to have a shower and dress, but not this time; he came out clad in his best outfit. Luke couldn't help but smile when his son sat in a chair near the door, waiting for Jenna to arrive. He certainly didn't wait with patience - he was up and down like a yoyo, going to the window, looking out, returning to the chair, swinging his feet to-and-fro. While Luke dressed in a more casual outfit of slacks and a light crewneck knitted top he kept poking his head around the corner and grinning at his impatient son.

The moment a crunch of tyres came from outside, Joshua shot like a torpedo from the chair and had the door open before she had a chance to knock. 'Jenna!' he yelled and flung his body into her arms when she crouched down to greet him.

'It's polite to ask your guest inside first, Josh.' Bemused, Luke watched, the sight of them together causing his chest muscles to tighten. When Josh released his arms from Jenna's neck he grabbed her hand and dragged her inside. As she flew past him Luke whispered in her ear. 'I think he might be wooing you.'

'Oh,' was all Jenna could get out as she flew past and was led to the dining room where she was shown where each was to sit and the flowers they had picked especially for her. Next, she was dragged to Joshua's room to check how neat and tidy it was. He took her no further, but suggested she might like to sit on the floor and play with him.

Luke trailed after them. 'It might be a good idea to allow Jenna to sit in a comfortable lounge chair and offer her a drink.'

Joshua grasped her hand again and led the way. A soft snort came from Jenna when Luke caught her eye. It appeared she was doing her best to suppress a giggle. He lifted his shoulders in an act of hopelessness and smiled. Jenna was forced to sit on the lounge with Joshua settled next to her.

'Oh no, you ask the lady if she would like a glass of wine. You need to ask if she would prefer red, white or sparkly Rose. Next job is to go and pour it for her.'

Joshua was the perfect gentleman in his solicitous request. 'Would you prefer white wine or red wine or sparkly… umm…?'

'Rose,' she finished for him. 'White, thank you, Joshua.'

Luke was glad he could disappear in the kitchen so he could hide a permanent grin but had to force his face into a mask when Joshua joined him to help open the bottle. Joshua returned to Jenna, ever so slow, the tip of his tongue held firmly between his teeth while he concentrated on not spilling a drop from the delicate, crystal glass.

'Thank you, Joshua.' Jenna tasted the wine, made a show of swilling it around in her mouth before she swallowed. 'This is perfect. Now come and sit by me.'

He needed no second invitation. He sat so close she had to wriggle over but it didn't stop him from snuggling into her side. Luke sat opposite, fighting to suppress his mirth. Jenna led the conversation by asking Joshua pertinent questions. He snuggled in closer and closer until Jenna slid her arm around his shoulder.

Unable to control his laughter any longer, Luke stood and left the room, his body shaking with suppressed laughter as he swallowed any sound, choking in the process. It took him a few minutes to regain control and return. 'Music, Son, you forgot the music.'

'I forgot.' Joshua leapt across the room, picked up a remote control from the coffee table, pressed a button to start a preset CD. 'Daddy said we needed nice quiet music so we could still talk.'

'Your dad chose lovely music. I like this a great deal.' Jenna's response sounded tortured as if she also found it difficult to hold back her mirth while Joshua snuggled into her again.

Luke returned to the kitchen, took out the already prepared buttered ciabatta slices for the bruschetta. He set the bread under the grill, waited for the garlic butter to melt into the lightly toasted surface and spooned the diced tomato, onion and feta onto each piece. No onion in Josh's. In the doorway, he nodded to Josh as per their pre-arranged signal.

Joshua stood and gave a tiny bow. 'Will you please come with me? Dinner is ready.' Studiously, he placed one hand behind Jenna's elbow, held her fingers with his other hand, exactly as Luke had shown him earlier.

It was obvious Jenna fought to suppress her giggle so Luke snuck up behind her to whisper in her ear. 'I'm finding it hard to keep a straight face.' Pulling Jenna's chair out for her, Luke sent Joshua to the kitchen to help bring out the first course. Joshua was judicious in serving Jenna and then sat in his own seat to wait for Luke to bring in the other two plates.

'This looks and smells wonderful, Joshua. Did you cook this by yourself or did your dad help?' Jenna scooped up a forkful of diced tomato and placed it in her mouth, making a big show of tasting the food.

'Daddy did most of it and I just helped him.' His pride and honesty was almost Luke's undoing. He had to grab his glass to take a sip of wine in an effort to wash down the half chewed morsel he was choking on.

While they ate, Joshua narrated in minute detail, what part he had played in the preparation of each dish. The meal continued in much the same vein, with Luke managing to keep his amusement under control as he guided his son on how to entertain a lady. By the time they had finished sweets, Joshua had let loose with several long yawns. Luke wasn't surprised as the day had been extra-long with Joshua on a high most of the time.

'How about you go and get into your PJs? Luke suggested.

Joshua frowned. 'I'm not...' Another yawn finished the sentence.

Jenna placed her hand on Joshua's arm. 'If you hop into bed, I'll come and say goodnight.'

'Promise?'

'I promise but only if you hurry.'

'Okay.' He shot from the chair and ran.

To give Joshua privacy while he readied for bed, Jenna carried an armload of plates into the kitchen. Luke removed the plates and put them on the bench. He placed a hand each side of her face, lowered his head slowly and brushed his lips against hers.

Shocked, she gasped but didn't pull away as instinct told her to. It was the first time a man had kissed her since Rob had walked out of her life.

As quick as he'd kissed her, he dropped his hands, jerked his head up and stepped back. 'I'm sorry, that shouldn't have happened. Please forgive me.'

'Oh, uh… sure.' The stab of pain at his rejection was unexpected. Miffed and unable to think of anything to say, she turned away, hurried to the door. 'I'd better go and say goodnight to Joshua.' When she was out of sight she paused, eyes shut, brain in a whirl. Why did he jerk away? Was she such a bad kisser? Is that the real reason Rob left her? Why did it hurt so much? Good one, Jenna Louise, you finally let your guard down, a man you like kisses you and he rejects you. Well, darn it. Shoulders back, spine stiff, she crossed the lounge, crept into Joshua's room but he was curled on his side with his back to the door and appeared to already be asleep. He was so cute, so adorable. Well, if Lucas Hunter didn't like her, she would give her heart to his son. With a soft smile, she ran her fingers through tousled hair, bent and kissed Josh on his brow and returned to the kitchen where she picked up the tea towel to dry the dishes.

'Tell me about Lisa. There's a picture next to Joshua's bed. She was a lovely woman.' At least this was a safe topic.

'Yes she was lovely. A few inches shorter than you but darker in complexion and hair. She died in a car crash two years ago. She was five months pregnant with our daughter at the time. Josh was in the car with her and unfortunately, watched his mother die. It was pretty traumatic for him, hence the nightmares. But I think he is over the worst of it now. Which is why I had to bring him around last night. The picture had always been in my room but Josh asked if he could have it when we moved here.'

'I'm sorry. It must have been hard for you as well.'

'It knocked me for six at first. I loved Lisa a great deal, but no amount of grieving will bring them back. I'm thankful I had Josh. Having to dedicate my time to him helped me work through my grief. You had a child. What happened?'

Jenna stilled on a hissed in breath. This topic wasn't safe. 'You weren't supposed to hear.'

'I didn't mean to eavesdrop. It was impossible to miss.'

'She was stillborn at seven months. One day she was alive, healthy and kicking me from the inside, the next day there was no movement. So I went straight to my doctor. They did a scan but could detect no heartbeat. She'd died. They had to induce labour. It wasn't the best day of my life. She was so perfect and they have no idea why she died.'

Luke dried his hands on the towel Jenna frantically twisted around her fingers, removed it and grasped her hands in his. 'I couldn't begin to imagine how heartbreaking that would be. Is that why you and your husband split?'

A snort of derision escaped. 'He doesn't know. He walked out the day I found out I was pregnant. Couldn't face up to the responsibility and commitment of parenthood and he's never bothered to contact me to find out whether he had a son or daughter. Last week was the first contact he's made.'

'You know he's not worth your anguish.'

'It still doesn't make it easy to forget.'

'Or to trust again,' Luke murmured. 'Which is why you don't want anything to do with Ryan.'

'Not the entire reason. I don't much like him. He comes on so strong it's creepy.' She took back the tea towel and wiped the last plate.

'We're almost finished. Would you like coffee?' Luke placed a handful of cutlery on the sink.

'Sounds good.'

They worked in silence; each wrapped in their own thoughts, until the last dish was put away. Luke put the kettle on and spooned coffee into two mugs. While he waited for the water to boil, he reached over to Jenna, loosened off her ponytail, smiled and brought forward a strand of hair.

'It reminds me of the first day we met. I found my face buried in the sweetest smelling blonde waves and my arms around your waist. I thought it was rather nice of you to throw yourself at me with such enthusiasm.' He laughed at the indignant look she sent him then turned away to finish making the coffee. After handing her a mug he took possession of her free hand.

Confused by the action after he'd pulled away from the kiss, she lifted her hand to brush hair from her face to avoid his touch. It was disconcerting when she sat on the lounge and he settled next to her, the same way his son had earlier. To pull away would be obvious so she didn't move. The warmth of his body against her side unsettled her for she liked it. Liked him. Loved his son. Enjoyed the friendship. And she sure needed a few more friends. She'd been here close to two years and got on well with most of the school staff, but only Emily could be classed as a friend. The regulars at the squash courts were all friendly but not true friends and she had no other social outlets. Such a loser. And now she'd had a fun night where she'd forgotten about Rob and hadn't had the hollow sensation of loneliness, yet it was obvious Luke wasn't up for anything more than a friendship.

While they sipped, they chit-chatted about general topics for which Jenna was grateful. Coffee finished, she stood, eager to get away to think and make sense of everything. 'Thank you for a wonderful night. It's been a long time since I've enjoyed an evening so much. And thank Joshua.' She grinned. 'It was hard to not burst out laughing, he was so sweet.'

'He was determined to make the night perfect to the extent he tidied his room without six million threats. I didn't have to ask once. I might have to invite you to dinner more often if it means Josh keeps his room neat.' He stood next to her, both hands on her shoulders. 'I never thought I would have to compete with my own son for a lady's attention. Do you know, I was jealous of him when he was cuddled into your side?'

Stunned, Jenna took a step back. 'Joshua has been a perfect gentleman. You should be proud of him.' Desperate to avoid another touch, she picked up her handbag and keys and went to the front door.

Luke opened it, stood aside. 'Good night.'

She reached up, pecked his cheek. 'Good night and thank you.' Within seconds she was in the car, afraid if she stayed a moment longer she would turn the peck into a kiss, even though it was obvious Luke wasn't interested. Each waved as she reversed out of the drive and turned onto the road.

The euphoria of the best night she'd had in years was mixed with the confusion about Luke's actions, until she neared her house.

A weird sensation passed through her when she noted the property. Gut instinct sent her a scary message. Down to first gear, she drifted past, studied the windows, the front door, the garden.

It hit her. The light she'd left on in the hall was no longer on. Had there been a blackout? But the street lights were on. Maybe a blown light bulb?

Foot down a tad, she drove on, around the block, slowed to a crawl to pass the house again. A glow came from a different window – one towards the rear. She swore at the same time a violent shiver raced across her shoulders. Surely Rob wouldn't be stupid enough to return. The car swerved. She swung the steering wheel to get back on track and pressed harder on the accelerator. Around the first corner she pulled over. Had she brought her mobile with her? It wasn't often she used it for she had few people to keep in contact with. A scrabble around in her bag. It was there, in the bottom. She took it out, pressed the button, brought it to life and noticed how low the battery strength was. Not game to use Luke again to get her out of a pickle, she dialled the emergency number.

Panicked message given and with an assurance the police were on their way, Jenna turned off the engine and made sure all the doors and windows were locked, checking twice. It took five interminable minutes before red and blue strobe lights lit up the road. They neared, passed her car and turned into her drive. She'd been told to wait. Instead she drove home, parked on the verge and searched the area for scary shadows before game to alight.

The front door stood open. How? They didn't have a key. Eyes screwed tight she paused, wondering what to do. Her house - she was going in.

One step inside, she recoiled at the sight. The house had been trashed. Drawers were pulled out and upended, cupboard doors stood open with the contents scattered over the floor, furniture had been turned upside down. It appeared nothing had been left untouched.

'Hello,' she called to let her presence be known.

Two men emerged from the kitchen. She recognised both as the same two who had come last time.

'We seem to be making a habit of this,' commented one man with his hand stretched out in greeting.

'Unfortunately, yes.' She shook each hand in turn. 'Do you have any idea who did this?'

'Not yet, we'll need to brush for fingerprints in the morning. This is a crime scene. You won't be able to stay here.'

'You let him out on bail. Why?'

'Not us, the judge. Might not be the same perpetrator.'

'Who else could it be? So much for restraining orders.'

'We can't jump to hasty conclusions. We need proof to be sure. I'll send a team down as soon as they are free. This isn't the first crime scene tonight. We'll need you to let us know if anything is missing. I notice one room is empty.'

'I moved all my bedroom furniture out of the old bedroom. I…' she couldn't finish.

'I understand.'

He might, she didn't. None of this made sense. 'I'll book into an hotel but I need clothes, toiletries and school work and… God, I can't think.' She stared at the officer. 'Are you sure he's not here? He could be hiding in the yard.'

'Our colleague is out there now. There's no-one inside. How about we go through the house? You might notice if any particular object is missing.'

Without saying a word, Jenna crept through each room, her nerves strung so tight she was afraid they would ping apart and shatter. The mess was unbelievable but as far as she could figure out nothing had been taken, although it was impossible to be sure. Why? Why would anyone be so vindictive?

In her new bedroom, the officer watched while she scouted around the scattered clothes to retrieve what she thought she would need, trying not to move too much or to touch anything other than what she took. A wave of embarrassment hit at the sight of her underwear. Had the bastard touched them?

When she went into the bathroom to collect a few basic toiletries she found the word 'bitch' scrawled across the mirror with pink lipstick. A shudder of horror wracked her body. She flicked the ruined stick into the bin. Instantly a thought came that she shouldn't have. Too late.

She wanted to rub the offensive word off but knew she couldn't. Intense anger surged around her gut. Nausea swirled and rose. She swallowed it down while stuffing items into an overnight bag. School – she needed stuff for school. When she met the officer at the door, he took her elbow and guided her to the front door.

'I need items for school tomorrow.'

'You might have to take the day off. We want you here first thing with the forensics team so you can tell them if anything is missing.' While he spoke, he studied her face as though she knew what the hell was going on.

'Why is Rob doing this to me?' she asked. Another wave of anger surged. Anger at his intrusion into her new life, at his abusive treatment – behaviour he had never shown before.

'We don't know for sure it was him.'

'I know. I felt it when I drove past. What does he want from me? After all this time, why now?'

'I wish I could give you the answers, but I can't. He will be questioned tomorrow. We may get the answers you want. But right now, we have work to do. Can you give us a key so we can lock up and hand it to the investigators? Let us know which hotel you are booked into. Do you have a mobile number?'

'I gave it to you last time. It will be with my report. Which reminds me, my phone needs to be charged.' She returned to the kitchen, unplugged the charger and shoved it in a pocket. After handing over the spare key, she stalked to her car, shoved the bag onto the rear seat and slammed the driver's door after she got in.

Her anger hadn't eased when she registered at the hotel nearest school, nor when she closed the door of her room. A long hot shower didn't have the ability to take the edge off.

After a barely touched breakfast, Jenna rang her boss to organise the day off, which was a relief for after so little sleep she would be a tetchy teacher. At her house the police were already present, dressed in forensic suits, taking photographs, searching for clues. She'd already seen her personal belongings strewn over the floor. Daylight made the vision worse. As far as she could ascertain, nothing had been broken or taken. It was as though the intruder merely searched for a specific item or wanted to inflict fear. Well, they sure succeeded but now it was more anger than fear. The only graffiti, the scrawl on the bathroom mirror and the word 'whore' smeared on the back of the bedroom door had her wrap her arms around herself in disgust and disbelief while she stood and stared at each in turn. They were two of the words Rob had called her while he had her pinned to the floor. Her haven had been defiled a second time.

While she sat huddled in a chair on the back patio, the police searched for fingerprints and any other evidence but apart from the forced entry of the back door, the place yielded no prints. Whoever had been there had worn gloves, one officer said as he squatted in front of her.

'Mr Reynolds denied any knowledge of the incident. He had an alibi. We're fairly certain he isn't the culprit but can't count him out completely. We need an account of your whereabouts last night.'

'You think I trashed my own home?'

'No. We have to follow due process.'

A long sigh escaped. 'Okay.'

The officer sat on the top step, turned on his mobile phone and recorded her statement, after which she rested her head on cupped hands, eyes closed to wait until the police left. She was still there half an hour later when a magpie trilled close by, bringing her out of a vacuum. She stood, swore, blew out a long breath and began the arduous, soul-destroying task of cleaning up.

While working, she forced a steely determination to not let Rob win. She would not be a victim but more of a victor. It was a struggle to get her furniture back in place, although it didn't make an iota of difference for she could never live here again. It took ages to sort through her belongings and put them back in their allotted places. All her valuables were still there, not that she had many. It was afternoon before she opened the fridge door to find a snack to replenish her energy. She sat on a plastic chair in the backyard where she shoved food in her mouth, chewed but tasted nothing.

'Daddy, Daddy,' Joshua yelled as soon as the car turned into the babysitter's drive. He was at the driver's door when it opened.

'You know better than to run anywhere near a car before it has stopped,' said Daddy in his angry voice.

'Oops, sorry but you have to find Je… Mrs Reynolds.'

'What, why? I don't understand. Where's your bag?'

'I'll get it.' He pelted back inside, grabbed his bag, ran outside but remembered he had to say thank you. He rushed back, 'Thank you for looking after me. Daddy's here,' turned and sped back outside.

He hurled his bag on the floor and climbed into the booster seat. 'Come on, we have to find Mrs Reynolds.'

'I have no idea what you mean.' The engine started but Daddy twisted around to look at Joshua.

'She wasn't at school today. She might be sick. I'm only allowed to have a day home if I'm really, really sick. Which is n-e-v-e-r.'

'I'll ring her when we get home.'

'No. What if she's so sick she needs help?'

'She would have called if she needed help.'

'Not if she's so sick she can't get out of bed.'

'Okay, we'll drive past her place on the way home.'

Joshua kept his eyes glued to the front window until they came to the right street. 'She's there. Her car is in the drive.'

As soon as the car turned into the drive Joshua undid the seatbelt and waited, waited, waited until the engine stopped. As soon as it did he opened the door and ran full pelt across the small patch of grass, onto the path, up the two steps and banged on the door.

'Slow down, Josh.'

The door opened. He smiled. She was here and she was dressed in clothes so she was okay.

'Hi.' Mrs Reynolds squatted in front of him. 'What are you doing here?'

Oh, oh. She didn't have her smiley face.

A hand gripped his shoulder. 'Josh was concerned because you weren't at school today. Are you okay?'

Mrs Reynolds frowned, screwed her eyes, turned away for a long time and turned back. 'I was about to pick the vegetables for my dinner. How about you do it for me,' she said to Joshua.

'Okay.' But he didn't want to. She wanted to get rid of him so they could have stupid grown-up talk.

'Come inside, I'll get you a bowl.'

They followed her into the kitchen and sat at the table. The whole room was messy with dishes and plates and knives and forks and pots all over the benches. He wanted to know why because it had never been this messy before. A large silver bowl landed in front of him. He didn't want to take it so turned his eyes away.

'Pick enough for you as well. Peas and a few carrots, beans, spinach, broccoli. Add a couple of beetroot. You know what I like. I could do with your help today.'

'Okay.' Joshua dropped from the chair, picked up the bowl and dawdled, hoping Daddy would do what he did the other night. But he kept it a secret about what he saw.

All he heard was the water from the tap going into the kettle. Heard the switch go on, the rattles of mugs, spoons, and coffee. The door closed and he couldn't sneak a look but if he leant against the wood he might be able to hear what they said.

'Now he's gone, do you want to tell me what's wrong?'

He could hear Daddy okay.

'No.' It was hard to make out Mrs Reynold's words so he moved along and pressed his ear hard against the wood.

'According to Joshua, you weren't at school today. Are you ill?'

'No.'

'Did your ex come back and what's with this mess?'

What's an X? thought Joshua.

'My house was ransacked last night while I was at your place. I had the police here this morning, been cleaning up all day. I'm exhausted. I... I...'

'Why didn't you phone me?'

'My problem. You've already done so much for me. I didn't want to involve you.'

'Hey, I recall asking you to phone me for anything. And this isn't any old thing. This is a major issue. You don't need to face it alone. You should have come back to my place straight away. Have you had any sleep?'

'I went to an hotel last night. The police didn't want me to move anything.'

'But did you get any sleep?'

'Not much.'

'You know you can use my spare room until you get this sorted.'

'Thank you, but I'll find a place to rent for a while. I might have to put my furniture into storage until I can sort out my life.

'Holidays start next week. Josh will spend the two weeks with my parents. They cared for him while I was at work before I moved here and he's looking forward to staying with them. It will also give him the opportunity to catch up with Lisa's parents, who live close by, and his best friend, Ben. You are more than welcome to use my house as a base. I'm uncomfortable with you staying here by yourself. Which reminds me, I promised you a meal, how about Saturday night? We'll go somewhere special - you and me with no Josh for me to get jealous of.'

Josh straightened. Dinner? Without him? No way. He should stay here for the holidays. But how could he talk Daddy into letting him stay?

'Sounds wonderful, thank you. Are you coming to the Parent's Night on Thursday evening?'

'Of course, I wouldn't miss it. But the change of subject doesn't work. Is there anything you need me to do? I could help you get this kitchen to look like a kitchen and not a second-hand yard.'

'Right now, all I want is to get away from here.'

'Understood. How about we find a kid-friendly place to eat. I'd prefer a nice dinner for two but I doubt my persistent, nosey son will grant me my wish. Go get cleaned up while I rescue your vegetable garden. No fancy clothes. Casual and comfortable. And leave your hair loose.'

'Thank you. You're a lifesaver.'

At the sound of footsteps, Joshua turned, jumped from the veranda and pelted along the path until he reached the vegie patch. He grabbed two carrots, tugged, flung them in the bowl. Peas. He shot along the path, stepped in the middle of the humungous peas and searched for full shells but couldn't find any. Spied one, grabbed it and tugged but the entire plant came away. Uh, oh. He ripped off the pods, shoved the plant behind the others.

'Joshua!'

Uh, oh. Daddy's gonna be cross.

'Joshua!' Daddy yelled again, much closer.

'Yes, Daddy.'

'You can stop now; we're going out for dinner.'

Phew.

Fear followed Jenna from the minute she walked into her house each afternoon until the time she left next morning. Even after keyed locks had been installed on each window and a second deadlock on each outside door, she still didn't feel safe, although when Luke rang she insisted everything was fine. She was more than thankful preparations for Parent's Night kept her busy. Each day for lessons, the children prepared their best work for display and helped set up the room. Each night, she remained at school to pin up art and work samples.

Most nights it was dusk before she made a cautious way home on foot. Eyes searched behind every tree, wall, fence and along driveways. Ears were honed for the slightest out-of-place noise. Nerves tightened at each shadow. Walking up her footpath was the hardest. Every sound set frazzled nerves on edge. Once inside, she switched on all the lights to ensure every item was where she had left it and no crank hid inside. It became routine to search under her bed, in cupboards, behind doors and curtains – everywhere it was possible for a person to hide and in places where it was impossible for a human to fit. Too petrified to venture outside in the scary darkness, the vegetable garden was neglected to the extent she was too darn terrified to harvest for meals.

On the day of the parents' visits, she hurried home after school, gulped down an early dinner of whatever she could find in the fridge. There wasn't much. A wrinkled tomato, a too big slab of cheese but it would fill a hole. Three dates, also of suspect viability. Two pickled onions – still in good condition. The end of the squishy cucumber went into the bin, too far gone.

After a quick shower she dressed in a prettier outfit than she normally wore at school and was back in her classroom in plenty of time to receive the first group of parents at six. To her, these events were special. A time when she could have informal chats with most of the parents, plus a good number of grandparents. A lot of work went into the displays, but it was worth the effort and more important, the children were proud of their achievements and loved showing off their workbooks.

The first she knew of Luke's presence was Joshua's excited voice while he pointed out a story pinned on the board at the back of the room. When Jenna glanced up Luke's dark eyes were on her. Embarrassed, she turned away to continue the chat with the parents of a delightful young girl who struggled with number concepts.

Five minutes later she headed towards Luke. 'Hi, Joshua, have you taken your father to your desk yet? Why don't you show him your diary?'

'Okay, come on, Daddy, over here.' Joshua grabbed Luke's hand and tugged. Luke raised his eyebrows and grinned at his exaggerated stagger.

When a question came from her side she turned to the woman. During the conversation she kept peeking at Luke to observe his facial expressions while he perused Joshua's latest daily diary entries. She'd had to keep a straight face when she helped Joshua get his words correct while he wrote the last couple of entries. When the grin on Luke's face changed to alarm she knew what he was reading. He beckoned her over. Excusing herself she moved towards him.

'He saw me kiss you and you let him write it down for everyone to read?'

'Nobody else reads their diaries and it's important they write what is meaningful to them. I did manage to hide away the picture to accompany his story - it was quite realistic. He's a mature artist.'

Luke looked unnerved. 'You'll have to show me another time. I don't think I like my private life being revealed to all and sundry.'

'The picture isn't at school. I deliberately left it home, which caused consternation. I had to tell Joshua I was in a hurry and forgot. He's proud of his sketch and wanted me to pin it up on the board for tonight.' She chuckled at Luke's shocked face. 'Now go and compare Joshua's work with the other children. He's advanced for his age to the extent I've been giving him extension work. I need to catch up with a few other parents. Can you wait a while?'

Luke nodded and followed his son over to another display, giving Joshua his full attention.

As the last parents departed, Jenna emitted a long audible sigh. For her, the night had been busy with non-stop movement from group-to-group to ensure she gave time to each parent and answered all the questions about her pupils. It also gave her a few hours relief from the constant worry about her safety although the worry had returned with a vengeance when she realised she didn't think about the walk home in the dark. Nerves gnawed as she locked the door. She turned and jolted when two figures loomed.

The breath whistled through pursed lips when she recognised Luke and Joshua.

'I notice your car's not here. Would you like a lift home?' Luke took possession of her elbow and leant closer. 'Joshua isn't the only one you have lied to. Each time I phoned this week you said you were fine. Those dark rings around your eyes tell me the truth.'

'I'd appreciate the ride. What did you think of Joshua's work?' Jenna slipped the young boy's hand in hers and gave it a gentle squeeze.

'I'm proud of him and he has an excellent teacher.' As Luke piloted them along the veranda he leant closer. 'The change of subject won't work,' he whispered.

The moment they reached her house, she couldn't prevent the sudden tension of nerves.

Luke must have noticed for he put one hand on her arm. 'Give me your keys, I'll check it out.'

'It's okay. I'm fine. There haven't been any more incidents.' To prove she was fine, she opened the car door, got out and stood tall. Inside, her gut was a like a force five cyclone. Joshua's small hand slid into her palm. The cyclone decreased to force three status. They mounted the two front steps. She took the key from her bag but Luke whisked it from her hand, opened the door, turned on the lights and proceeded to check through the house while she stood in the front entry.

'All is as it should be. No unwelcome visitors.'

The lump of wood in her throat vanished. Relieved, she led them to the kitchen and filled the kettle as a way of being busy so she didn't have to answer questions. While taking down cups she wondered if there was any milk left and if there was, would it be sour. A visit to the shops for essentials hadn't happened for too long.

'Every time I've rung, you failed to mention how you are scared out of your wits. My offer is still open. You don't have to stay here.' Luke murmured in her ear as he lifted the jar of coffee from a cupboard and placed it on the bench.

'I'm edgy when I come home, not sure if a ghoul is waiting to pounce. I've rung three estate agents and booked to inspect a few rentals on Monday. Would you like a coffee?'

Luke paused. 'Normally I'd say yes, but it's way past Josh's bedtime. Are you positive you'll be all right? I know I keep repeating myself but please ring if you are anxious and have the need to talk. I'll pick you up six-thirty Saturday evening. We're going to a special place I heard about and I look forward to having you to myself without our six-year-old chaperone.' Luke bent his head and gave Jenna a brief kiss on her cheek.

He turned away, grasped Joshua's hand. 'Come on, you should be in bed.'

Luke waited until Jenna had locked herself inside before easing into the car. Eyes on the rear-vision mirror, he waited for Joshua to buckle himself in before starting the engine and reversing onto the street.

'You kissed Jenna again, Daddy. Does that mean you like her?'

Speechless at the innocent question, Luke hissed in a breath. 'Yes, I like Jenna and I'd appreciate it if you don't write in your diary every time I happen to kiss a woman.'

'If you married Jenna, she would be my new mummy wouldn't she?'

Stunned Luke veered off the side of the road when his hands gripped too hard on the steering wheel. Nerves shattered, he eased his foot on the brake pedal and brought the car to a standstill. On a deep breath to settle an adrenalin rush, he turned around with no idea what to say.

'Josh.' He paused to think.

'Yes Daddy.'

'Don't get any ideas in your head and don't you dare talk to anyone about Jenna like that, especially Jenna. Two people have to know each other a lot better and be in love with each other before they can think about getting married. Do you understand? We don't know if Jenna likes us.'

Josh nodded, smiled. 'I want Jenna to be my new mummy, so when you know her better you can marry her.'

The bald statement left Luke exasperated, but at the same time, delighted at his son's thoughts. He was too damn perceptive. With a shake of his head, he restarted the engine, veered onto the road, ever so thankful Jenna wasn't with them.

'Not going to happen, Josh, so get all those crazy ideas out of your head.'

Determined the last day of term would be lot of fun Jenna dismissed any thought of formal lessons. Instead, she planned a day of fun-filled activities. They played games, maths and word orientated of course. Played dodge in the afternoon, painted weird monsters as an art exercise and acted out simple plays, where the children had to read their parts. Exhausted by the end of the day, she was more than glad when the last child disappeared through the doorway. Two weeks to rejuvenate sounded great, but in reality one week was usually dedicated to planning programmes for the next term and these holidays she had personal problems to sort. There would be no true relaxation. First she needed to find a house nearby to live in. She hated having to move but knew she would never be content in her house again and the sooner she was able to move out, the better. She had already begun to empty cupboards and pack gear in cartons.

The evening was spent sorting. Although she didn't have a lot, there were still items no longer required. They ended up in a pile by the back door to be put in the bin when the darkness outside didn't hide unwelcome visitors. It was late before she fell into bed, exhausted enough for sleep to overtake her before doubt and fear took hold.

For the first time in a week she woke refreshed. Breakfast consisted of toasted stale bread with a thick slather of strawberry jam to give it a hint of moisture. With a hot cup of black coffee, since the milk had curdled, she sat at the table while thoughts tumbled. Tonight she was going on a date. The first since forever. A real date – well, sort of date for there was still the question of whether or not Luke liked her or if he wanted to give her a good time to ease her fear. Or it could be a simple thank you dinner and nothing else. What could she wear? The cup went on the table. A search of the wardrobe was needed.

After a good search, she dismissed the few garments laid out on the bed. All oldish, none suitable. Who needed decent date clothes when no-one ever asked you out? A new outfit might rejuvenate her depressed self-esteem. New man, new life, new outfit sounded the way to go. Glad to have an excuse to not linger in the house, she dressed for a morning in town to fill the fridge and larder with fresh supplies and wander from shop-to-shop until she found the perfect dress for a sort-of-date.

Three hours later she stared at her reflection in the dressing-room mirror. The deep green filmy fabric showed off her blonde hair and lean curves to perfection. Well, she thought so. Others might not. The calf-length skirt swirled around her legs and shimmered at every movement. To her, it was perfect.

By the time six-thirty arrived, she had been ready for half an hour and tense nerves had taken hold. For the umpteenth time, she checked her hair in the mirror. Was it okay? Should she tie it back? Was it too messy left loose? Unsure, she re-clipped the sides, took the sparkling clips out, took a bigger hunk from the front, pulled it back and caught the two strands together on the top of her head with both clips. At least they matched the silver sandals she hadn't had the opportunity to wear since forever. A couple of twirls around in front of the mirror to study the final effect, euphoria took hold and settled the nerves. Another inspection, doubt overtook the euphoria.

Knock, knock. Nerves tightened. Breathe, she ordered rigid lungs. She blew out her cheeks with a long hiss, scampered to the door to ensure she didn't flee out the back instead. Hand on the knob, she opened the door and stifled a gasp when she saw how handsome Luke was in black slacks, a black skivvy clinging to his well-defined muscular body. Over the top he wore a taupe linen jacket.

'You look so beautiful, Jenna. The colour suits you. Turn around slowly.'

Heart pounding, she turned. Luke reached out, fingered the

loose hair, moved closer. His hands landed on her shoulders when she completed the turn. He drew her into his arms, bent his head and kissed her. Really kissed her. Every atom in her body danced and spun. It had been so long since a man had kissed her this well. If ever. Had Rob ever kissed her this well?

Disappointment settled in her gut when he jerked his mouth away. His head rose with eyes shut and a pained expression. He swung her next to him, placing one arm around her shoulders. When he said nothing while guiding her to the car, it scared her. After she eased onto the seat Luke shut the door, rounded the bonnet and got in the other side.

'Has Joshua gone?' was the only thing she could think of to begin a conversation. At least the topic was safe.

'Yes, my parents collected him and I will pick him up in two weeks. I was shocked when he insisted he wanted to stay here. It took ages to convince him to go because I couldn't take time off work to look after him during the day. I don't think I need mention who he said he could spend the days with.'

'I wouldn't have minded.'

'I would never impose on you. You need the holiday as much as the kids. When his grandparents arrived he was glad to see them but left you a message. *Tell Jenna I will miss her.* He didn't say the same to me, mind you.' Luke sent her a quizzical glance.

She grinned. 'Where are we going?'

'Surprise. I asked around, was given the name of this restaurant from several people.'

An hour later, Luke guided her into the beachside restaurant to a table overlooking the water, the waves much calmer than her own innards. With the subdued elegancy of the décor, she understood why people drove the distance to dine there. Once settled, their orders taken and the first drinks served, she retrieved a folded piece of paper from her bag, opened it out and pressed one finger along the crease.

'I thought you might want to see how creative your son is.'

Luke took the paper from her fingers while Jenna settled back in her seat, amused at the astonishment on his face when he perused the picture of them kissing. And it had been such a brief kiss, which you sure couldn't tell from the picture.

'He doesn't leave much to the imagination does he? Can I keep this?'

'Oh, no, he has already asked for it. He wanted me to put it up on the board so I don't mind showing you, but you'd better not let on you've seen it until he shows you. You didn't by any chance turn over the page in his diary and read the entry after the kiss, did you?'

'There was more? Oh, Lord! I sincerely hope it wasn't what he mentioned before he went away.' Luke blushed. 'Hell, I shouldn't have said that. What did he write?'

'What did he say to you?' Jenna's curiosity had been aroused, more so by the flush on Luke's face.

'Nothing I'm prepared to talk about right now. What was in the entry? Although I'm not sure I want to know.'

'Let's say we had to have a sex education lesson.'

'Excuse me? He's only six! I'm highly embarrassed right now.'

'I had to explain how a kiss did not result in producing a baby. I left those details for you to explain.' She glanced at Luke's horrified face. 'I do believe you are blushing, Lucas Hunter.' She couldn't hold back the gurgle of laughter.

'Oh, heavens, I'm so sorry. He and I need to have a serious discussion. I think I might have to ring my parents to let them know I've taken you out on only one date and Joshua's fertile imagination is exactly that, and for them to not read anything into what he says.'

'Was that what Joshua said to you?'

'No, and we are dropping the subject right now. Young Josh took centre stage last time we had a meal together, I'd rather he didn't do the same tonight. I'd like tonight to be for you and me.' Reaching over he sought out her hand, caressed her fingers, but had to release it when their first course was served.

The food was excellent and Luke kept the conversation away from his son. By the end of a superb meal where they both related more humorous stories about their jobs, Jenna realised she hadn't enjoyed herself so much for a long time, even during her marriage. Rob had never been such an amusing conversationalist.

After the meal they ambled along the beach walkway hand-in-hand. The scenario was perfect with waves crashing onto the sand, the crisp tang of salt in the air and occasional peeks of night creatures on the scrounge for food. They stood over a small hermit crab for a while to watch it scurry sideways, find a morsel and disappear down a hole, dragging it's dinner with it. On the way back to the car, Luke's arm moved around her shoulder, drew her close enough her head dropped to his shoulder and her arm crept around his waist.

Before they reached the car, Luke stopped, turned Jenna around into his arms. He gave the impression he was about to kiss her again. Disappointment flared when all he did was peck her on the forehead. What was wrong?

It was impossible to figure out an answer since he held her hand all the way back to the car and while he drove home, pressed her hand against his thigh. It was only released for brief moments when he needed his hand for driving. Each time he released it, she slid her hand back to her own lap but Luke sought it out when he completed his chore, placing her hand back on his thigh with his large palm keeping it in place.

'Please leave it there? I like you touching me.'

Heat incinerated up her neck to her cheeks but she complied since she enjoyed the warmth from his muscular thigh much more than she thought she would and probably more than she should.

When Luke drove into her driveway, uncertainty hit. She didn't want the night to end but at the same time, this closeness was too much. He turned off the engine, sat with his eyes on her for way too long as though the same uncertainty lived with him. It was a shock when he turned away and opened the car door. To add to the turmoil in her head, he took her hand and held it while they walked along the path to the front door. Unnerved, Jenna kept her head down. Upon reaching the door, she turned to Luke.

'Thank you for tonight, it's been a long time since I've enjoyed myself so much.'

'Me too. Can we meet up tomorrow as well? Without Josh to cater to I'll be at a loose end and I'd like to spend the day with you. Please say yes?'

'I'd like that. Thank you,' she said to hide her uncertainty.

'Great. I'll be around early in the morning and we'll see what happens. Goodnight, Jenna.' Taking her in his arms again he made to kiss her again but jerked back as though hit with an electric current.

'I'm sorry, that shouldn't have happened.' He turned away and strode to his car as though the devil was after him.

The turmoil turned into chaos and disappointment. It was obvious to kiss her was a mistake but the reason why created too many negative thoughts, most of which churned too long into the wee hours of the morning.

Horrified, Luke pulled into Jenna's drive and turned off the engine. Wearing shabby cut-off jeans and a faded T-shirt, she stood barefooted at the front window. Anger showed in each swipe of a stiff brush over the cherry red paint daubed over every pane of glass along the front. *Bitch* and *whore* had been scrawled alternately on each windowpane. She didn't look up when he reached her but kept scrubbing. Remnants of tears smeared her drawn, pale face. With utmost care, he tugged the brush out of hand, gathered her into his arms and let a fresh bout of hot tears fall against his chest.

'Have you rung the police?' Her head moved back and forth against his chest. 'Why didn't you ring me?'

Her muffled response came from near his armpit. 'I only noticed it when I came outside this morning - it's on all the windows, back and front.'

Shoving the partially open front door with one foot, he shuffled Jenna inside, reached into the top pocket of his shirt and dialled the now familiar police number with Jenna tucked next to him. Despite her struggles to wriggle free, he didn't release her. Call completed, he drew a tea towel from its rail and dabbed the moisture from her face.

'The police will want to take photos. I'll help you clean it off when they give the okay.'

'But people will notice it.' With her words followed by an unladylike sniff, Jenna reached for a tissue from the box on top of the refrigerator.

'So what! You know it's not true and so do I. The rest of the world can get stuffed. People will understand what it is – graffiti. I hope your admirer has left a trail this time but if you clean it off the police will lose much-needed evidence. I suspect you have a stalker and wonder if we were followed last night.'

Jenna tugged free. 'Stalked? But why? Why would anyone want to follow us?'

'I don't know. They might not have, it's a guess. But they were here in the night for there was no graffiti when I dropped you off. And I don't think it's wise for you to stay here alone another night. You either come to my place or an hotel. Go pack a bag of clothes and anything else you may need - and pack plenty - not just for one night.' To ensure she did, he led her by the hand into her room. Once he was sure she was packing, he moved to the kitchen to make coffee while they waited the arrival of the police.

With Luke's description of what had occurred, the police sent the forensic team straight away. He joined them outside while they snapped photos and searched for clues. Moulds were made of the two footprints found in a garden bed under one of the windows, a sample of paint was scraped into an evidence bag but once again no fingerprints were found.

'Do you think the perpetrator is a danger to Jenna?' Luke asked the officer who jotted down notes. 'Her ex-husband has already physically harmed her.'

'Things are getting out of hand,' said the young constable. 'I'd hazard a guess it's possible Mrs Reynolds could be more seriously hurt.'

'I don't know,' added the sergeant. 'The damage appears to be confined to things easily cleaned. There is no graffiti on brickwork and nothing has been smashed or destroyed. It's possible the perpetrator is simply trying to frighten Mrs Reynolds.'

'Why?' asked Luke. 'There has to be a reason.'

'A question we can only ask the person carrying out this vendetta.' The constable packed up his camera equipment.

'So, can anyone assure me next time there's an attack it won't threaten Jenna's life?' asked Luke.

'Err, no. We can't make such an assumption.' The sergeant paused for a moment, a worried frown on his face.

'What can we do to ensure her safety? Jenna can't stay in the house alone any longer.'

'I believe she spent a night in an hotel last time. At least there, they have security cameras on each floor as well as the entry and lobby. We can have a word with them to ensure no strangers get to her room.'

'Word from you guys would hold more weight than from me.'

'We'll chat to them when we've finished here. I assume it will be the same hotel. I'll let you know the details.'

'Sounds good. I'll keep Jenna with me until I hear from you.' Luke left them to complete their work while he went in search of Jenna. He found her sitting on her bed, two packed bags near the door. He picked up the bags, stowed them in his car and returned to fetch a terrified, pale-faced woman.

'Come on, we'll leave the police to complete their investigation. They will organise a safe hotel room for you and until then, you're staying by my side where I can keep an eye on you.' He smiled. 'Can't complain about my task. It will be a pleasure to have you with me.' Gently grasping her hand, he levered her off the bed.

His original plans for the day were tossed out the window. Instead, he drove into town, scanning the rear vision mirrors for a sign of being followed. They spent what was left of the morning window shopping where they bought nothing until they called into a pleasant café for lunch. After a delicious light repast he took her to the cinema where he switched his mobile phone to vibration. When he studied Jenna's face while lounging back in his seat, he doubted she absorbed any of the romantic comedy. Most of the time she sat huddled back with her arms wrapped around her torso. The rhythmical movements of his fingers up and down her arm didn't break through her deep introspection.

The film was nearing the end when his phone vibrated. Easing up, he whispered an excuse and hurried down the aisle.

The journey to the hotel was silent with all attempts to start a conversation met with a stoic silence. After handing Jenna's bags to the porter, Luke followed the instructions he had been given to book her in. Registration done; he led her back to his car. This broke Jenna from her reverie for she glanced at him with a quizzical frown.

'I'll cook dinner tonight.' He returned her stare with a questioning look of his own.

'Only if you let me help.' She smiled. 'Thank you. Sorry I've been a bit… umm…'

'Absent?'

'Yes. My brain is numb but at the same time it's overcome with the knowledge a weirdo, for an unknown reason, is hell bent on terrorizing me. Most of the day I've searched my brain for a reason behind these sudden attacks. I can't recall meeting anyone over the past twenty odd months who I've insulted or slighted in any way. Rob is the only name I continually come up with, but for the life of me I can't think why he wanted to rape me, or why he came to town. He was the one who wanted a divorce and has made no attempt to communicate with me since the day he walked out – in fact he made it quite clear, through his solicitor, he never wanted any communication.' She paused. 'Sorry, none of this is of your concern.'

'Not at all. It's good to get unpleasant thoughts off your chest. I know. Had several sessions with a psych after Lisa's death. It helped – especially for Josh.'

'Speaking of Josh, it's quiet without him.'

'A blessed quiet but at the same time I sure miss him. This will be the longest we've been apart since the accident. A test for both of us, I think. There is a good side, I can have you to myself without Joshua taking centre stage.'

For the rest of the journey, Jenna sat back with eyes closed but a frown on her brow indicated she was deep in thought.

'What are you thinking?' he dared ask.

Her eyes shot open. 'Nothing important.'

He laughed. 'Liar.'

'Excuse me?' She half-turned towards him.

'The frown tells me the thoughts are serious.'

'Private thoughts.' She turned her head towards the window.

'Sorry. I didn't mean to intrude.' Her answer didn't ease his curiosity, but instead teased his brain cells. When the to-ing fro-ing of thoughts scrambled his brain, he switched off and concentrated on the road and traffic until they reached his home.

After the previous night's stab of guilt for kissing Jenna, he was wary of getting too close, so waited for Jenna to alight and head for the front door before he clicked the remote to lock the car. Nerves skittered when he brushed against her to open the door so he held back until she went in first. Inside, she followed him to the kitchen.

'Wine?' he asked.

'Sounds good.' Jenna perched her backside on a stool at the kitchen bench.

Luke opened a bottle of chilled white wine, poured two glasses, handed one to Jenna and watched her finger toy with the fragile stem of the glass and trace a cold droplet of condensation all the way down the glass bowl. Without any warning, she ceased her contemplation, shrugged, lifted her eyes and smiled.

He wanted to kiss her again but a sharp stab of guilt whacked him around the ear for daring to think it. He stepped away and set about preparing their meal, not surprised when Jenna made a rapid retreat to the other side of the bench. He'd sensed her response to his actions. With his own body doing a damn good imitation of a sergeant major standing at attention, he figured retreat was needed so he opened the fridge and took out a bundle of vegetables despite not having a clue what to cook. To keep things under control, he sent Jenna into the lounge room to select background music from his collection of CDs while he sorted through the ingredients, decided what to cook and put half back in the fridge. It could be because he'd been too long without a woman but since Lisa's death he'd never been interested. Hell, he and Jenna barely knew each other and he sure didn't want to stuff this up by coming on too strong, too soon. Didn't want to be another Ryan.

The soft music drifting through from the lounge didn't help him concentrate on the meal. Soft romantic music he normally would have thought appropriate for the situation but right now he needed more strident and raucous music to rid the atmosphere of the heightened sexual undertones. It appeared Jenna might think the same because all of a sudden the music ceased and was replaced by a more thumping rock type. The CD had been a gift: one he didn't particularly like but right now he was forever grateful to the donor.

While waiting for the onions to fry, he carried the bottle of wine into the lounge to re-fill Jenna's glass. She stood at the glass French doors staring at his backyard.

'You can go out and have a wander around if you like. I haven't had time to do much out there since we moved in. With your gardening skills you can give me a few ideas.' Unlatching the locks he opened the doors wide and left Jenna to wander while he returned to the kitchen to rescue the onions which had a darker tinge than he wanted.

Food ready, he set the table and went in search of his guest. Jenna stood in the middle of the garden, thoughtful but turned to him. 'If this was my garden much of it would be turned into vegetables and herbs.'

'I wish I had the time to tend a vegie patch. Dinner's ready.' Luke paused at the doorway; hands slipped in apparent casualness in his pockets. His fingers were gripped against the inside layer of cotton fabric to prevent them from taking a path towards the woman who had caused his body so much agony. Why this women and why now? And why these guilt trips when he touched her?

'Why don't you ask Joshua what he would like and plan it together? I'm certain he would like a larger play area. Think skateboard or rollerblades.'

'I'd rather not. Broken limbs come to mind.'

'True, but kids soon learn their limits. This garden is all *bitty* with not enough room for a young boy to be adventurous. If half these odd-shaped garden beds were removed and the area paved it would make a much larger play or outdoor entertaining area and less for you to maintain. Keep the mature trees along the back for shade.'

When Jenna moved towards the door Luke retreated slightly to keep away from her. 'An excellent idea, come inside – dinner is ready.' Luke locked the doors before following her. After serving the chicken stir-fry he moved around to the other side of the table to sit opposite, keeping the conversation to topics of a more controversial nature so they could give opinions while he deliberately sparred with her, which resulted in great repartee. By the end of the meal they were both laughing and the intense emotional atmosphere had dissipated. After Jenna helped with the dishes, Luke drove to the hotel where he left her at the door with nothing more than a head nod.

'Will you be in town tomorrow?' he asked.

'Probably. I have appointments to inspect a couple of rental places first thing, why?'

'I have lunch at one. Always away from the office to ensure I have a break. Come by my office and we'll go out for a bite. Here's my card with the address.' He took one from his wallet. 'Now I must go to talk with my parents before young Josh does any more damage to my reputation, or yours. You take care.'

At the *brnng, brnng,* Jenna groaned, turned to glance at the clock and jolted when the digital numbers indicated it was well after nine. Another *brnng* and she reached for the bedside phone, lifted the receiver. 'Good morning,' slurred out.

'Are you okay?'

'Luke?'

'Who else knows where you are?'

'Sorry, you woke me.'

'Hmm, is this because you spent half the night awake with worry or because you slept well?'

'The latter.'

'Same with me. I didn't have a bundle of energy diving on me the second the sun showed its face. I rang to let you know I've organised window cleaners to deal with the graffiti and to suggest it might be a good idea to not go there alone in case your tormentor is watching the premises.'

'As if I'm game to go anywhere near the place. Thank you for the cleaners and I'm glad you woke me for I've got house inspections booked and I need to hurry.'

'You'll be at the office at one?'

'Yes, if you're sure.'

'I'm sure. Happy hunting.' The phone clicked.

Jenna shot from the bed, dragged on the top outfit in her suitcase and bolted, not pausing long enough for coffee, let alone, breakfast. Since her car was still in her house garage, it was a good job the hotel was in the heart of town. Nerves on high alert, she power-walked the few blocks to the estate agency.

Over the next couple of hours, the agent showed her through three possible rental homes but each was a disappointment.

'Do you have any other options,' she asked.

'Sorry, no.'

'Darn it. I didn't think it would be so hard to find a decent rental. Thank you for your time.'

She walked a short distance to another agency. This time she asked for their list first, searched a map to find out where each house was located. Three were within reasonable distance to school. She didn't want to be stuck out in the never-never. Appointment made she went in search of Luke's office.

When she found a large, modern building right in the centre of town, she realised how large the firm of accountants was. The front reception area was airy and well set out. After asking for Luke, she was shown to a comfortable leather chair and offered a coffee, which she declined since she didn't want to spoil lunch. Being early, she was prepared to wait so was surprised when Luke came to meet her. She drew in her breath at the sight of him dressed in a dark grey business suit. His size made his presence felt wherever he went, but she had a new heightened awareness of him. He set her emotions on edge. Emotions she thought had gone forever.

'How did the house hunting go?'

'Not so crash hot. There are more than a few awful places out there. I have another three to look at this afternoon but right now I'm famished. I didn't have time for breakfast.'

'Let's go.' Luke led her to his favourite lunchtime haunt - a classy bistro filled with business people and only a short walk from his office. He ushered her inside to a table near the rear and pulled out a chair for her.

'Take your time to check out all the properties available. My offer is still open - you can use my place as a base if needed until the right rental comes up. Now let's get some sustenance into you.' They perused the menu and placed their orders, asking for coffee first.

While waiting, Jenna studied the surroundings and gasped when Ryan walked in. 'Does he often eat in here?'

Luke glanced over his shoulder. 'I've not seen him in here before. I thought he worked for a big metal factory on the outskirts of town. He doesn't look dressed for work. He could have the day off or is on holidays.'

They nodded to Ryan when he acknowledged them with a wave from across the room.

'Did you ever go out with him?'

'He's never asked me to go on a date. I found him okay when I first moved here. I went to a few functions with Emily where he was as well, but I don't particularly like him much now. I've made up numbers in a few group situations where he manages to sit next to me. If he becomes too much, I leave. The day I let loose on the squash court I'd had enough.'

Further thoughts of Ryan were dismissed when the food arrived and they tucked in. Jenna made short work of the toasted avocado, cheese and tomato sandwich and salad after which they ordered a second coffee. After they'd paid the bill, they moved to the front door.

'Could I ask another favour?' Jenna asked.

'Sure.'

'Would you be able to drive me home after work so I can pick up my car? I know it's an imposition but I'm too scared to go there alone.'

'It's not an imposition. I'll meet you at the hotel after five. Take care this afternoon and ring me if you become suspicious of any character.'

'Thank you. To be honest, I'm suspicious of everyone.' The moment they parted at the café door, her gut wrenched. She searched the area for any sign of being watched the entire time it took her to reach the second estate agency.

The properties she visited were no more suitable than the three she had inspected earlier, so before returning to the hotel, she called in at a third agency to scroll through what they had available. Finding four possible places she organised a time the following day to be taken through them.

It appeared it wasn't going to be easy to find a rental, she thought while powerwalking towards the hotel. Being alone gave her the creeps. Should she reconsider the sale of her home and be strong enough to not let Rob turn her into a victim?

An uncanny sensation pervaded her senses. She stopped. On

the pretext of looking at the items in a shop window, she searched the reflections for any sign of a person with their eyes on her. It was difficult to make things out so she turned and walked to the edge of the path, scanned each way along the road. No-one stood out but the uncomfortable sensation remained while she crossed the road and entered a large department store, which had rear entries. Once inside, she made her way to the escalator, rode to the top floor backwards so she could scan the floor below as she rose. At the top, she strode to the elevator, rode down a floor, alighted, sped to the back steps and crossed the road to another shop.

Unnerved, she waited hidden behind a rack of women's dresses to observe the doorway through which she had entered. Satisfied she hadn't been followed she hurried to the other side before moving outside through a different door. She had crossed two blocks and prayed the pursuer had lost her. Using back streets, she returned to her hotel where she locked herself in the room unsure whether her imagination was overwrought.

Shot nerves and boredom had her pace around the room while waiting for Luke. At his phone-call, she grabbed her bag, ensuring she had car and house keys. Instead of riding the elevator, she ran down the two flights of stairs to the ground floor. Luke waited by the elevator, his back to her. He swore under his breath when she said 'hello' from behind his back.

'Don't scare me like that.' He paused. 'Where did you come from?'

'I used the stairs.' She smiled; amused at the way he had jumped.

'You have a bit of devil hidden underneath all your sweet innocence.' Grasping her elbow he guided her to his car.

As they neared her home, Jenna noticed the windows had been cleaned. 'I need to get all my belongings out of here fairly soon so I hope I find another house. If I can't find anything suitable to rent, I might look for a house to buy.'

'You can store your gear in my other spare room if you need to. Apart from a dozen boxes I haven't unpacked yet, it's pretty well empty. If you haven't found a place by the weekend, how about we spend Saturday moving. You haven't got a lot so wouldn't take many trips.'

'I'll keep it in mind. Let's see what tomorrow yields.'

'Will you join me for lunch again tomorrow?' He leant towards her but jerked back.

'Sure.' Mystified, she eased from the car. Why did he keep jerking away every time he got close to her? Did her barriers give off too much… she couldn't think of a word. Iciness? Primness?

'You take care. I look forward to lunch,' he said with a casual wave.

Does he? After the cold shoulder act? Miffed, she stalked inside, slammed the door with a huffed out breath. It was as though he wanted to kiss her but thought better of it whenever he did. What if her breath stank? To check, she blew into her cupped palm and sniffed hard. Didn't have a rotten odour. To make sure, she went into the bathroom, found a bottle of rarely used mouthwash. A good gargle and spit, she winced at the acidity and rinsed out her mouth with fresh water. How long had the bottle been there? Could be out of date. It went in the bin.

If she was going to be locked up, she needed activities to keep herself occupied, so collected her school files to plan for the next term's work. She also grabbed her laptop and a few novels she had never found the time to read. Well, she had the time but never the mood. After stowing the last armful in the car boot, she opened the garage door, anxious to get away. While driving, her thoughts were of Luke and how he always jerked away when she thought he was about to kiss her. Slow learner, Jenna Louise.

Too scared to sit in the hotel lounge or restaurant, let alone roam nearby streets, she ordered the evening meal from room service.

Next morning, despite her angst, she ate breakfast in the dining room before leaving for the first appointment. Her confident stride to the car park came to a grinding halt at the sight of her car. The hairs on her neck rose and nerves tightened while studying the surrounds. There were a dozen or so parked cars but no person watched from the shadows. Spinning on her heel she hurried back inside to call the police. At the officer's advice she spoke to the reception manager who returned with her to inspect her car. Each window had been scrawled on with white paint. *You can't hide. I'll catch you and give you what you deserve - bitch.*

Freaked out, she had the hotel call a taxi and stuck to the side of the concierge like a limpet while waiting. She still had the shakes when she arrived at the estate agency, leaving the hotel staff to deal with the police. With a frazzled mind not on the condition of a new home, she wished she hadn't made the appointments. But she was here and the agent had keys in hand.

He drove her to all four houses but they were as bad as the previous ones. It was no wonder they were empty. The downtown area appeared slum-like, dreary and unkempt. After inspecting the final house, she asked the estate agent to drop her off at Luke's office - too scared to walk alone. She was way too early but approached reception to inform them of her presence. Asked to wait, she settled in the chair with her arms wrapped around her body.

Luke read the message on his computer screen. *Your next appointment is early, but the client has arrived.* He wasn't told whom it was and was mystified for there were no more clients booked in and he didn't want any more appointments. He was looking forward to lunch with Jenna. He hurried through the questions with his client, took appropriate notes and when finished, stood to usher him out, striding out with the man to find who his unknown client was. A broad grin broke out when he spied Jenna in the chair across the foyer. The grin altered the moment he noticed the naked fear and desolation in her eyes and the way she sat huddled with her arms wrapped around her as though protecting herself from a ghastly ogre. Three long strides and he stood in front of her. Without saying a word he ushered her into his office.

'What's wrong?'

Jenna leant into him, her silence causing his unease to turn to alarm.

'What happened?'

'He found my car. He knows where I am,' she blurted against his shoulder.

He stiffened on a sucked in breath. Easing it out, he settled her in a chair and squatted in front of her. 'Tell me everything. Did you call the police?'

'When I went out to my car this morning there were messages scrawled over the windows. Yes, I called the police. I told the reception manager. He called me a taxi to go to the estate agent and I had the agent drop me off here. Which is why I'm so early. I'm too scared to walk by myself. I thought I was being followed yesterday after I left you but I couldn't be sure. I'm getting scared now.'

'What was written on your windows?'

'I can't remember the exact words, but they threatened to give me what I deserved. I've never done anything to hurt anybody. Why is this… animal doing this to me?'

He reached out, eased her into his arms and rested his chin on her head. What could he say? He had no idea what was going on. 'Give me a minute to find out what the police have to say.' He slid his mobile phone from the inside coat pocket and stabbed at the number now a permanent resident in his phone. He spoke with the officer in charge for a few minutes before returning to Jenna, who sat cowered in the chair.

'They have photographed your car and tested it for prints but again couldn't find any apart from yours. But they do have security footage they are going through now. No strangers went up to your floor during the night but they will move your belongings into another room on a higher level, which can't be reached by the stairs. Security cameras will monitor the elevator at all times. The police will call me after they have perused the films. They may want you to view them to see if you recognise anyone. Now, you and I will have lunch before I drive you back to the hotel and personally guide you to the door. I only have one client this afternoon so I can collect you to take you to the station. I'm certain no one will harm you in broad daylight. This creep is doing things under the cover of darkness but you need to tell the police about being followed yesterday.'

Luke chose a different eatery. The café was smaller but in a prominent part of a busy street. Not prepared to take any chances he sat them at the back so he could observe the entire room, especially the entrance. Jenna did nothing more than pick at her food. After paying the bill he drove her to the hotel where he asked the manager for the new room number. While they rode up in the lift he kept his arm around her waist. He opened her room door with the keycard he'd been given. Her eyes popped wide at the size of the apartment.

'It appears they have given you a bit of luxury.' Luke refused to comment on the size of the enormous bed but whistled when he walked into the bathroom. 'You should take advantage of this.'

When she sidled next to him, he pointed to the huge spa bath. Jenna went bright red.

'Much as I would like to join you in it right now, I have to go back to work. I have an important client, who no doubt, will keep my mind on dull, boring figures for a couple of hours and I don't mean gorgeous, curvaceous figures. I'll pick you up as soon as I'm finished, but you make sure you use the tub to help you relax.' He pointed to the spa again with a lascivious grin. Back at the door he gave Jenna a quick peck on her forehead before closing the door after him. Outside, he had to spend a few moments to take slow, deep breaths to convince his body he had no intimate thoughts of seduction involving an enormous spa tub built for two, nor of an equally sized bed. He was overawed by his traitorous hormones and the intense feelings he had for Jenna along with more stabs of guilt. Why now?

Bemused by the idea, Jenna decided to do as Luke suggested. Why not? While waiting for the bath to fill, she unpacked a few items and selected a book to read in the spa.

Enjoy it she did. She kept topping up the bath with warm water and every now and again turned on the jets to rejuvenate the bubbles but had to switch them off if she wanted to read for the water kept splashing, making the pages too wet to read and the bubbles from the over-liberal dose of bath-foam, rose over the edge and spilled onto the floor. So relaxed and engrossed in her book, it was a shock when a phone rang. It sounded close so she searched the wall and found a phone above her head. Talk about luxury.

'Let me picture you right now. Up to your eyeballs in bubbles, head back, soaking in warm water. The jets must be off because I can't hear them. Skin probably red as a beetroot or all wrinkled from wallowing so long. Your hair is tied up in a knot on top of your head. I've had trouble concentrating on my client's business report because my mind was centred on you in the bubbles.'

'Luke!'

'I'm right, aren't I? I'll be there in two minutes.' He laughed when she squealed in alarm.

Water splashed when she scrambled out of the bath, pulled the plug, grabbed a towel and dried her body while tearing into the bedroom to find fresh clothes – any clothes. She'd pulled on a pair of blue jeans when he knocked at the door. She yanked the zipper up while stumbling towards the door. The towel got flung into the bathroom as she walked past and closed the door on the mess. She forced a nonchalance when she opened the door to a grinning Luke.

He lifted her hand and grinned. 'As I thought, wrinkled and

red.' Next, he reached out and removed the pins from the hair she had forgotten to let down from the top of her head, not that she'd had time. He stepped past her, opened the bathroom door and dared to grin at the mess of bubbles, water and the towel over the toilet bowl.

'Messy little creature. You make Josh's bath time look meek and mild.' Luke closed the door again and grinned. 'Would you like a couple of minutes to clean up and finish getting dressed or are you coming to the police station like that?' His grin widened. 'Go and look in the mirror.'

Laughing, he sank into the sole armchair while she fled back to the bathroom, her cheeks blazing. She studied her reflection in the mirror and winced. Her shirt was on inside out, her hair bedraggled and there was a ring of soap bubbles around her ears. To regain composure, she took her darn time to put the bathroom and herself to rights.

Luke studied her when she returned. 'Next time I'll make sure I have my phone ready to take a photo.'

'Can we go?'

'We could or...' he pointed to her feet. 'Shoes? Are you going barefoot? I don't mind one way or the other.' Luke chortled at her continuing discomfiture.

She glared at him while searching for and put on shoes over wet feet. Still grinning, Luke stood, grasped her hand, flipped the keycard out of its receptacle and tugged her outside.

Less than fifteen minutes later they were seated in the office of the senior sergeant, waiting to view the security tape. The footage of the incident was clear. Luke scowled at the words painted on the car windows. 'I understand why you were so frightened.'

Unfortunately, the pictures of the culprit weren't so clear. The outline and shape indicated a man who wore baggy black and was hooded. The face was always in the dark shadows as if he knew where the cameras were.

'Do you recognise him? asked the officer.

'There's a vague familiarity about him but I can't place movement or shape with anyone I know.' She rubbed a hand down her face.

'Can you park your car in a space closer to the camera from now on?' the officer asked when he switched off the machine.

'Can I clean off the filth?' A wave of disgust rippled across her shoulders.

'Go ahead, we have all we need.'

'Sergeant, Jenna was certain she had been followed whilst in town yesterday.' Luke leant forwards and gave her hand a squeeze.

'You should have mentioned this, give me the details.' The sergeant settled into a chair, reached for a pad and pen.

After describing her escape tactics the sergeant smiled. 'I'll give those details to the officer who was tailing you and let him know how clever you were at losing him. He wasn't impressed, but congratulations. I must reprimand him for being sussed out to start with. Either you are perceptive or he slipped up. Now you know you have a tail, don't look for him or her.'

'Why are you guys following me?'

'Not to check on you. We hope to spot anyone who may be stalking you. It's obvious you have been followed or this person knows your movements fairly well. They didn't know you were at the hotel until you parked your car - so they must have known your car or followed when you drove it there. By the way, you are not booked in under your name, so if anybody asks, you aren't there.

'Except my car makes it pretty obvious.'

'True. All this activity happens at night, so we want you to go out in the evenings. Luke has agreed to work with us on this. You'll go to places open to the public and we'll keep watch. We're sure nothing will happen while you are with Luke. This person is a coward and Luke is too big to tackle but we may spot who is following you. If you do notice anyone you know, or don't know, who keeps turning up, phone us. You'll be safe in your room. We will catch this person. Have a good night.'

Unnerved, Jenna nodded, stood and left. Luke followed, caught her hand in his. 'Do you mind if we go to my place first? I need a shower and change of clothes.'

'Sure. I'm not keen on being live bait in a snare.'

Luke laughed. 'I'm a bigger piece of bait. I promise to protect you.' He opened the car door for her.

The entire way to Luke's house, Jenna couldn't prevent her eyes from scanning both sides of the road, nor the reflection in the side mirror for a dark figure intent on following her. An over-active mind caused by sheer terror, refused to calm.

Dressed in casual slacks and a collared knit shirt, Luke led her outside but stopped to chat with Stuart who had just arrived home. They were about to leave when Ryan pulled up.

'Hi folks. I was looking for Emily and thought she might be with you, Stuart.'

'No she's gone out for a girls' night with the terrible two and a couple of their friends. Come on in and have a beer.' Stuart indicated to all of them.

'Not for us, we have plans,' said Luke.

After parking his car Ryan speared Jenna with a stare before he turned away and followed Stuart.

A frisson of fear snaked across her shoulders before she followed Luke to his car, miffed at the news she hadn't been included in the girl's night out. Why no invite when they always went out together?

Buckled in, she racked her brain for something to say. 'Have you heard from Joshua?' Safe topic she thought.

'Every night. I miss the little tyke. My parents keep him busy.'

'Where are we going tonight?'

'Into town. The festival starts tonight. I was told there are stalls where we can grab tasty morsels while watching various activities. It should be fun. We'll need a jacket though as it might get cool. You can borrow one of mine or we can stop off at the hotel.' He returned inside and came out with a couple of jackets. 'Choose the one which fits best.'

The town centre was packed. They worked their way through knots of locals to an assortment of attractions. One end of the main street had a stage set up where various local groups put on short acts. All attracted large audiences who were appreciative of the efforts. As Luke had intimated, there were many interesting food stalls. By the time they had meandered along the main street and taken small titbits from various stalls they had eaten more than enough to satisfy their hunger.

At the last stall, Luke turned to her. 'Have you seen enough? It might be a good time to get you back to the hotel.'

'It has been a great night, thank you. I had fun.'

'You were more at ease.'

'I'm surprised, but yes. It's not far to the hotel, can we walk?'

'Are you sure?'

'Two blocks. I'm sure.' While they walked side-by-side, Jenna's thoughts centred on how much fun the night had been and how well they got on together. It was as though they read each other's mind to stop at the same stall, choose the same tasty treat, point out similar items that attracted them.

At the hotel, Luke nodded to the night manager who acknowledged them as they walked past. After opening her door, he pecked her cheek.

Even though she wanted a real kiss she pointed to the video camera above them so it didn't happen. The rejection would hurt too much. 'We are being filmed. You'd better behave if you don't want to give the police something to smile about tomorrow.'

He laughed. 'As long as it's only me in the replay and not your creepy admirer. Sleep tight. Lunch tomorrow? I'll be busy until one but after, I have a couple of free hours.'

'You don't have to spend all your free time as bodyguard. I can order room service.'

'And deprive me of the pleasure of your company? Not a chance. I'll be here a few minutes after one.'

'Okay.' She reached up to peck him on his cheek. Mortified, she closed the door and stood with her back to it, overwhelmed by the turmoil in her innards and the way her heart flip-flopped. How, when he touched her, warmth flooded and pooled in her core. They'd known each other mere weeks and he'd been able to tear to shreds the barriers she kept in place to prevent any man from destroying her emotions again. And yet, he was so aloof with her so it was obviously a one-way attraction.

In a brighter frame of mind than she had been for days, Jenna jogged to her car despite the exhaustion from the previous day. It had taken most of Saturday to empty her house except for the furniture left to show off the house. All the rest of her belongings had been jam-packed into boxes and sowed in Luke's spare room. Today she planned to catch up with a few friends at the squash courts after a week of being a virtual recluse apart from dinner with Luke each night.

She didn't notice the paper until she sat in the driver's seat. Her heart rocketed at the folded square lodged under the wiper. Too scared to move, she stared at the small insidious white shape. A glance in the rear vision mirror – she searched the shadows for any sign of life. The air in the car had evaporated. With a wildly palpitating heart, she dropped one foot onto the ground, eased up and reached out with shaking fingers to snag one corner of the paper. A quick yank – the wiper blade snapped against the glass. She flicked the paper open. Cut letters from a newspaper spelled out: *Soon you will be mine and will get everything you deserve – whore.*

With an ominous sense of foreboding she leapt from the car, slammed the door and ran full pelt to reception to report the incident.

'Ring the police,' the concierge said. 'We'll put the tape aside for them to view.'

Too scared to go far, she stood at the end of the reception desk to call the police on her mobile. Instructions given she slipped the note into an hotel envelope and dropped it off at the station on her way to squash.

Anger and frustration churned her stomach while she walked along the viewing alleyway that ran along the top of the row of courts. She stopped to watch Erin and Lily play against each other.

Sunday was their day. She called down to them between serves and smiled when they yelled back with their usual enthusiasm. She wondered what would happen if one of the pair met Mr Right as she moved along the walkway to the next court where two men she'd seen before but didn't know well, slogged it out. Intrigued by the standard, she sat on the wooden bench to watch. They were better than good.

'Looks like your boyfriend has given you the flick.' An arm snaked around her waist.

She froze. What was Ryan doing here on a Sunday?' He was so close, his breath fanned against her neck. By twisting her body to face him she was able to break his hold.

'How about a game, Jenna?'

'I don't have a boyfriend and I've got a match booked.'

'Make it a warm-up game.' He leant closer, put a hand on her knee.

She jerked upright to evade the unwelcome grasp. 'What court? I'll meet you there. I need to get rid of my bag.'

'Court four,' she heard as she turned away. Why, oh, why did she offer? Idiot.

After she'd lingered a tad too long in the locker room, she sped to the court but again had to dodge his hand by changing her racquet from one arm to the other. He was going to be an utter nuisance. Chastising herself for agreeing to the game, she decided to play him harder than ever. To give him a fighting chance she flicked the ball to him. 'You serve.'

From then on she was brutal. The first game was over in record time without her conceding a single point.

At the noticeable tension from Ryan she played softer in the second game to allow him to win a few points, but she still beat him. A glance at her watch told her she was due to play Luke. To get the third game over as quick as possible, she gave no mercy. Trounced, Ryan left the court without a word of acknowledgment or thanks. Good. Hopefully, he's now got the message and will be too embarrassed to play her again.

'Jenna.'

At Luke's call from above, she glanced up. He held up a two fingers to show which court they were on.

'That was cruel,' Luke said when he entered the court. The smile belied his words.

'I only played him so I didn't have to sit next to him. He couldn't keep his hands off me. I gave him seven points in the second game. I don't know why he wants to keep playing me.'

'Probably because you are a beautiful woman and he would like to have you as his lady.'

'He's never bothered to ask me out in all the time I've lived here. It's been close to two years. If he'd been interested in a relationship he would have made a move by now.'

'He might be too shy to ask you out.'

'Well he's not too shy to make a nuisance of himself and take unwelcome liberties with me. Anyway, enough of him, are you ready to receive the same treatment?'

'Not on your Nelly. Did you sleep well?'

'Extremely well, did you? You can serve.' She handed him the ball.

'Very well thank you. I didn't have Josh to wake me at sun-up which means I'm full of energy, so watch out.'

The first service was so good Jenna couldn't return it. She clapped her racquet to acknowledge the excellent shot. The rest of the game was hard and fast with Luke claiming victory. They took a short breather to sip on water before they began the second game.

'I had a visitor last night,' she said as an aside. 'He left me a note on my car. *Soon you will be mine.*

'You're taking it mildly. Aren't you alarmed?'

'Right now, I'm more fed up than afraid. I rang the police and dropped the note off on my way here. They'll probably want me to go through the security film again. I've worked out my friend is a weekend junky and I'm certain it's Rob. *Bitch* and *whore* were two of the not so nice words he called me and threatened I would get what I deserved. Those particular words were written on the note today. I'm heartily sick of the whole thing. Let's do something far more pleasant - my revenge on you.'

She forced a laugh as she readied to play more determined than ever: a determination that paid dividends when she beat Luke in the second game. She also won the third and deciding game. As the final ball was won, there was a shout from above. A female voice called her name. She smiled when she recognised an old friend.

'Michelle,' she called and turned to Luke. 'Come and meet an old friend of mine. We used to play on the same team.' Jenna grasped a puzzled Luke by the hand and led him up the stairs.

'You haven't lost your touch, Jenna. I feel sorry for you.' Michelle turned to Luke. 'Jenna never gave an inch to any of the men. She wasn't state champion for nothing.'

Embarrassed, Jenna dropped her head.

'So, she didn't tell you. Jenna was never one to big-note herself. I'm Michelle by the way.' Michelle held out her hand to Luke.

'Sorry, Luke, meet Michelle Williams. Michelle, Lucas Hunter.'

The two shook hands.

'Come into the cafeteria,' said Jenna.

They settled at the nearest vacant table. Luke sat back while the two women talked. Jenna noticed him call over a server. He didn't ask what they wanted to drink but ordered in any case and placed cold drinks in front of each when they arrived. When Michelle was called onto court for her club competition game the two women exchanged phone numbers. Jenna began to stand but a large hand grasped her wrist.

'Not so fast.'

She plonked down again but kept her eyes averted.

'State champion, eh? No wonder you play so well and are so hard to beat. How many times? You play too well for it to have been a fluke.'

'Three years. I gave up when I married.' Embarrassment prevented her from raising her eyes.

'Voluntarily or were you coerced into it? You don't need to answer. Your telltale blush has given me the right response. It wasn't long ago. Why don't you go back to competition playing?

You're still good enough.'

Surprised, she eyed Luke. 'If I wanted to, I would, but I'm not interested in putting in the hours needed to keep up to such a high level. I'd rather put my time into the kids at school. I enjoy playing as we do now; it's a lot more fun. But I would like to catch up with Michelle again. She was a great friend. Let's go. I promised I would call in at the police station on my way back. Have you got time to come with me?'

'All the time in the world. I'll meet you there. I don't want to leave my car around for your friend to tamper with. Let's shower first.'

In the change-rooms, Jenna pulled her bag close to grab towel and toiletries. Sliding the zipper open she stood back in alarm at the sight of a piece of paper on top of her belongings. Her fingers shook as she pinched the corner of the folded paper with the ends of two fingernails. *YOU'RE DEAD* was scrawled in biro. She dropped the paper, spun on her heel, tore the short way down the passage, banged on the men's room door and yelled for Luke.

Luke dropped his sodden T-shirt on the change-room bench. Jenna screamed his name. Two other men jerked, one with shorts around his ankles the other naked. Luke leapt over the low bench in the middle of the room and flung the door open. Jenna flew into his arms with such force she knocked him backwards into the room.

'What the devil is wrong?' He tried to peel her from his body to look into her face but she clung on tight. Waves of shivers ran up and down her body. To give the two men a chance to get decent, he shuffled her into the passageway and grasped her shoulders so he could step back far enough to look at her. 'What happened? Calm down. I won't let anything happen to you.'

The other two men, now decent, came to see what the commotion was about.

'My bag… he's… he's been in my bag,' Jenna stammered.

'What? Are you sure? Where is it?'

'In the change-room.' Since he doubted Jenna was game to return alone, Luke figured he needed to enter the ladies' change rooms.

'Are any other women in there?'

'No, I don't think so. Don't leave me,' she cried when he released her and began to stride down the passage.

Luke grasped her again and nodded to the two men in front of him. 'Jenna has received a number of threatening messages. Could you look after her a moment and keep any women away while I find her bag?' He handed her to the safekeeping of one of the other men. 'Keep her safe. She's pretty well scared out of wits.'

Both men crowded around her while Luke entered the ladies' change room and searched for her bag, which had fallen on the floor, upturned. He flipped it over, retrieved her belongings one-by-one, and placed each in the bag, searching for what had alarmed her. He spied a piece of paper under the bench. When he read it, his gut wrenched in anger. Re-folding the paper, he shoved it in the pocket of his shorts before grasping Jenna's bag and returning outside.

There was quite an audience gathered in the narrow passageway since the two men prevented the women from entering the change room. A few eyebrows lifted when he stepped out, chest bare.

'Sorry ladies.' A brief blush of embarrassment heated his neck when he realised the connotations people may think. He turned to the two men. 'Can you keep Jenna with you while I get my bag? I need to make a phone call.' Ignoring the looks, he went to retrieve his mobile phone from his bag. He spoke briefly with the officer in charge, threw his sweat-dampened shirt back on and shivered when the cold moisture hit hot skin. He picked up his belongings before returning to the passageway.

'Jenna, there's a plain clothes detective coming inside to talk to us. We're to meet in the cafeteria. Thanks guys, you've been a great help.' With both bags in one hand, he shook their hands. Slipping his arm around Jenna's waist, he guided her up the stairs to the cafeteria where he found a seat at the rear. A man, who surreptitiously held out his ID card as he neared, soon joined them.

'Good afternoon, I'm your tail for the day. I watched you play but went outside to wait for you. What happened?'

Luke removed the letter from his pocket. 'This was left in Jenna's bag in the ladies' change room.'

The officer opened it out and read the two words. 'He's getting brazen and careless. This has also become more serious – this is a death threat. It had to have been a person who was here today. We have photos of each person who entered or left since Jenna arrived. We'll ask questions of all the patrons and staff. The doors are locked. No-one can get out until we open them again, but a number have already left so we'll have to track them down, which will take time. Unfortunately, with the gymnasium and pool attached to this complex there were a lot of people in the vicinity. You two can go but we'll need you to go through the photos later this evening. Can I keep your bag, Jenna? Is there anything you need in it?'

'I need my car keys and purse.' She gingerly removed the items, treating the bag as if it was a live bomb about to explode. 'Luke, could you walk me to my car? I don't want to go out there by myself. I wasn't so afraid earlier, but I sure am now.'

'Of course. Come on, and I'll pick you up tonight.' He turned to the officer. 'Will one of your guys follow Jenna to the hotel?'

'Yes, but hopefully she won't notice him and give him the slip, like she did me.' The officer's smile was rueful as Luke picked up his bag and joined her. Together, all three walked to the barred front door where the officer indicated to a uniformed officer, the pair could leave.

Once outside, Jenna scrutinized the entire car park, her eyes darting from side-to-side, while Luke kept close to keep her shielded. After opening her car door, he used his body as a barrier while she eased inside. He leant in the window. 'Go straight back to your room and stay there. I'll go home to shower and change before I come over. I'm nervous about this person now there's a death threat.'

Upright, he slammed the door and waited until Jenna drove off before going to his car. He noted the unmarked police car pull out behind her, but it didn't ease the fear in his gut. The short distance to his home didn't take long. He pulled into his garage, ensured the door was shut before going through the connecting door into the house. It was ridiculous to be so jittery – this pervert wasn't after him.

As he passed through to the kitchen he noticed a white object out of the corner of his eye. Stopping short, he slowly turned and stared at the floor of the main entry passage. His heart missed a beat. He strode the few steps, stopped with his feet a few centimetres in front of the offensive folded sheet. He didn't want to read what instinct told him would be written. Ever so slow, he bent to retrieve what had been slipped under the front door. When he opened it out he noticed the similarity between his paper and the one from Jenna's bag. The same pen and lettering had been used. *BANG, BANG, YOUR WHORE IS DEAD.*

Luke shuddered on a huffed out breath. He refolded the letter with care before once again dialling the police number. Things had become a whole lot more serious and out of hand. They needed to catch this guy – soon. After a long discussion, he had a quick shower, changed into jeans and shirt, grabbed a jacket, along with the note and left. The tormentor knew where he lived which confirmed his suspicions they had been followed. His thoughts turned to his son. How safe was Josh?

He dropped the letter off at the police station before driving to the hotel where he parked next to Jenna's car. At least she had arrived back safe. As he passed them, he nodded to the reception staff and rode the elevator to Jenna's floor. Should he let her know about this new development?

When he knocked, Jenna took a long time to answer. The door opened only a crack; an eye appeared. She cried out, pulled the security latch off, opened the door wider and pulled him inside, slamming the door after him. She melted into his arms with her arms grasped tight around his waist, like an animal tick determined to stay put. He shuffled them over to the chair, sat and eased her onto his lap. With her so insecure and uptight, he wouldn't tell her about his note.

'I am so scared now,' she whispered, her voice breaking on the last word.

'I know you are. I hope the police can get the information they need from today's episode. If he wrote the note on the spur of the moment, he wouldn't have had gloves and may have left fingerprints.'

With her too scared to leave the room, they ordered a meal from room service for an early dinner, after which, he drove her to the police station where they were ushered into a different room than the previous time. Set up with a TV, there were a large number of photographs pinned to a wall. First, they were shown the security footage of the car park from the night before. Again it was difficult to make out any features, neither being able to identify the shadowy, well-camouflaged figure, this time wearing a clown mask.

'Could this be a woman?' Jenna asked. 'The note was in the women's locker room.'

'It would have been easy for a man to wait around and slip into the change rooms and your bag had been upstairs a while before you placed it in the change rooms. We had a man inside watching you. We also have a couple of fingerprints from the note in your bag and the one from Luke.'

Jenna gasped as she whipped her head around to stare at him. 'What note from you?'

'I didn't want to scare you again but there was a note under my door when I arrived home from the squash courts.'

'At your home? What did it say?'

'Much the same as yours.' He wasn't game to reveal more. She was frightened enough.

The officer stood. 'Study these photos.' He indicated the wall. 'Tell me who you recognise and any detail you think might be relevant.'

They recognised a lot of the players and all the staff from the courts but none from the other areas. Jenna dismissed most as not possible. All the pictures were sorted according to sex. The females were put on one side, the men on the other. One-by-one, they went through the men. Many Jenna didn't recognise, especially those from the other areas of the sporting complex so they were set on the *persons of interest* pile.

When they came to the photo of Ryan, the officer pointed to it? 'What about this person? Would he have a grudge against you? We noted how you mopped the floor with him and he wasn't happy when he came off the court.'

'Ryan! I don't think so. He's Emily's brother. She and I teach at the same school and we get on well. I've known them since I moved here. I admit I don't like him much, but apart from beating him at squash, I've never done anything to hurt him. Never rejected him when he wanted someone to play against.'

'Have you ever dated him?'

'No, because he's never asked me for a date but I've made up numbers at various group functions. Since I've never refused to partner up with him why would he hold a grudge. Surely you don't suspect him?'

'Right now, we suspect everyone who was at the squash courts today. He is a person of interest.'

'What about my ex-husband?'

'We have virtually discounted him on this issue and he wasn't at the courts today. Plus, he has confirmed alibis for most incidents but we can't disregard the fact he may have paid an associate to harass you, although we think it unlikely.'

'Do those alibis come from a lady called Nancy?' Jenna asked.

'Yes, why, do you know her?' The officer stiffened, suddenly alert.

'Oh, yes, I know her and I wouldn't trust even a smidgin. She's been lying to me for over two years.' Jenna winced. 'She was with Rob at the hotel the first night I spied him, which is odd because she's married to a different man and has young children.'

'That changes things. We'll have to investigate this further. I'm afraid this puts Mr Reynolds back high on our list. Is this Nancy in any of these photos?'

'No, I don't recognise her in any of them.'

The same questions were asked about each male person who had been in the courts, but Jenna didn't recognise most of them. 'I don't usually play on a Sunday. Only when I can't get there on Saturday. Why would any of these guys want to taunt me when I don't know them? I've never seen most of them.'

'It still could have been an offsider sent by the perpetrator.' The officer straightened the separated piles. 'It's going to take time to visit each of these people and seek fingerprints to match up with those on the two letters. But at least we now have fingerprints when we didn't before.'

'What about the red paint?' asked Jenna.

'A common brand available at almost every hardware store in the country. No local store has sold that particular colour in recent weeks.'

'Terrific.'

By the time they left Luke's innards had turned into a vacuum of nothingness, along with a brain full of fairy floss. On the drive back to the hotel, Jenna's eyes kept closing. He walked a robot to the hotel door where he tapped her on the shoulder. 'Give me your key. You look exhausted.'

'I am tired.' The key had fallen to the bottom of her handbag. She scrounged around but at last held it out. 'I'm sorry.'

'Sorry for what.' Luke opened the door.

'Getting you involved in my mess. You don't deserve this… this…'

'Nor do you. I can come in until you fall asleep if you like.'

'No. Go home. I'm safe in here and I'm so drained I can barely keep my eyes open.' She shut the door without a word.

Twice the following week Jenna found the courage to venture outside the hotel room in daylight hours. Both times she shadowed an unsuspecting person, too afraid to wander alone. Both times nerves were strung so tight the entire time she realised it wasn't worth the effort. Instead, she stayed in to plan the next term's programmes but it turned into a chore with neither her heart nor will in the mood. She read all the books she had brought with her and had secured three more on one of the forays to the nearby shops. The television became a constant background noise because the silence unnerved her as much as an amble outside.

The only brightness to the days were the regular phone calls from Luke – between clients, but he couldn't coerce her to join him for lunch, not only because of her fear but because she'd decided to take a step back from him. It didn't prevent the sheer joy of his presence for the evening meal in her room, where she maintained a polite distance. Chinese take-away one night, pizza the next, followed by Indian and two from room service. They were all delicious but she barely touched her food for hunger became a non-event.

'You need to eat.' Luke lifted the fork in her hand and aimed it at her mouth.

'Not hungry.' But she wrapped her lips around the piece of steak, eased it from the fork and chewed.

'You've barely eaten all week.'

'I'm fine.'

Luke snorted. 'Hardly. You have developed permanent frown lines on a pallid face. Your nerves are strung as tight as a piano wire and at a guess, I'd say you've lost weight. None of which will help you master this constant fear. I think you've given up to let this monster win. I figured you to be one who was strong enough to never become a victim again.'

Jenna scowled. 'You done with the psychoanalysis?'

He laughed. 'At least I got a response. I have an idea. How about you come for a drive with me tomorrow?'

'Where to? I'm not sure whether I'm game. It's the weekend. We'll probably be followed.'

'Come with me to collect Josh. You can meet my parents and Josh will be overjoyed. I ring him each afternoon before I leave work. The conversation starts with the same topic. Jenna, Jenna, Jenna.' His smile was wry.

'I don't believe you.'

'I swear.' He drew a cross over the region of his heart. 'The drive will do you good. A chance to get away from here. Come and see where I grew up. I can let the police know where we'll be. Which reminds me, have you heard from them?'

'They rang a few times.'

'And?'

'They tracked down most of the people who were at the complex. All agreed to be finger printed. A few were hard to trace. They were never home. The list is down to about a dozen.'

'I'm surprised they've got so far. There were a lot of people in the complex.'

'But not so many in the squash courts. Security cameras eliminated a lot.'

'Pity there aren't more security cameras, especially near change rooms.'

'Yes, well, they've never had incidents like this before and cameras in change rooms probably aren't appropriate. The police enquiries are a good thing.'

'Why?'

'There's been no more incidents, no threats, no nasty notes. With so much scrutiny he might have given up.'

'With you too scared to leave this room there hasn't been a chance for more incidents. So how about tomorrow. Come with me. Please?'

'Okay. But we have to inform the police.'

'I'll phone.' Luke stood, eased Jenna from her chair. 'Is eight too early? It's a two-hour drive. We can stay for lunch. I'll ring Mum. She'll be delighted to meet you.'

'She knows about me?'

Luke laughed. 'More than you could possibly think. Josh has been extolling your virtues for two weeks.'

'Excuse me? Why?'

'I had to spell out to Mum, how we've only been on one real date. How we barely know each other. How Joshua's vivid imagination is a tad over-exaggerated. Actually, it's a lot over-exaggerated.'

'Oh, Lord, what has he said?'

'Not going there. But I was able to quash a tornado.'

'I think it's better if I don't go with you.'

'I think it's better if you do.' Luke leant forwards, brushed her brow with his mouth. 'Not all of what Josh said is over-exaggerated.' He pecked the end of her nose. 'For two years I haven't been interested in women. But you? I have no idea why but you I am interested in. More than I believed possible.' He lifted his head, took a step back. 'For the first time since losing Lisa, I want more – with you. But it's hard because you have been hurt and these recent events have brought back your pain and your resistance to men. I know you have barriers and understand why. Trust is an issue with you. I don't blame you.'

Stunned, Jenna reeled backwards. 'I trust you.' It was all her addled mind could think of to say.

'You have no idea how much that pleases me.'

'But I'm scared.'

'Not half as scared as I am. Losing a person you love hurts – a lot. It tears you apart. It terrifies me to give my heart to another woman but it wouldn't be fair to Josh for me to live in a vacuum of grief. And right now, Josh is one of the most important things in my life.'

'Then why…?'

'Why what?'

I… A couple of times I've got the impression you wanted to…
um…'

'Kiss you?'

'Yes but you jerk away. God, this is so awkward.' She backed away, plonked on the end of the bed, thought better of it and returned to the small table where she sat on the other side – out of reach. There wasn't anywhere else to go unless she hid in the bathroom, which sounded like a fabulous idea. 'I thought there was something wrong with me especially since my husband walked out on me, and no man since I moved here, has ever shown any interest in me.

Luke sat opposite, reached out to take her hands but she clasped them in her lap. 'None of that is true. Ryan is desperate to have you in his life.'

She snorted at which Luke laughed.

'You have a secret admirer, stalking you, I am interested and Josh adores you. I suspect you have put up barriers because you're afraid of getting hurt again.'

Heat rose in her cheeks.

'As for me, the one time I kissed you guilt smacked me around the head.'

'Guilt, why?'

'I'm not a man who would ever cheat on a partner. When I kissed you it was as though I was cheating on Lisa which, I know, is illogical. She died. Two years ago. Do you feel guilty when we kiss?'

Jenna smiled. 'No, but my circumstances were different. Rob didn't want me. He was the one who walked away. I don't owe him an ounce of guilt, especially now.'

'And he left you desolated and with a sense of being unwanted or not good enough. Is this why you are so cautious?'

Jenna shrugged. 'I'm not sure I could stand being rejected again and you jerked away so many times, I thought you either didn't want more or I wasn't good enough.'

Luke leaned over the table. 'If there is one thing I've learned it's that there are no guarantees. Life can be tough but it can also be amazing. All we can do is give it our best shot and I'd like it if you and I could give whatever is between us, the best shot. Come with me tomorrow, meet my parents. Have a day out to relax and forget about this scumbag.'

'Okay.'

Luke leant back and smiled. 'Thank you. I'll pick you up at eight. Now go to bed and sleep. We'll need every ounce of energy to put up with the mini tornado named Joshua.'

The second he spotted the car, Joshua tore outside.

'Stop, young man!' Poppy yelled. 'Wait until the car stops.'

'Oops, sorry.' He stood shuffling his feet on the bottom step while he watched the car come along the drive, turn around the loop and park under a tree. It was taking forever.

'Daddy!' he screamed when the engine noise stopped. He ran full pelt around to the driver's door and reached it in time to be scooped up in Daddy's arms. He hugged – tight. The biggest ever bear hug. 'Daddy,' he whispered. He didn't care when a couple of tears escaped and dripped onto his face.

'Hi, I missed you,' Daddy whispered in his ear. 'And I brought you a surprise. Go have a look who is in the passenger seat.'

Joshua wriggled, skidded down to the ground and shot around the other side of the car. He tugged on the door handle. 'Jenna?' He scrambled up onto her lap and gave her another biggest bear hug ever.

'Hello, Joshua. How about you let me get out.'

He untangled his arms and legs, slid to the ground and grabbed Jenna's hand. 'Come on, come and meet Nanna and Poppy.' He jumped about while Jenna undid her seat belt. When her feet hit the ground, he grasped her hand again.

'Steady on, Son. Jenna has had a tough week and is tired. You take it easy and look after her. Walk slowly. Remember how we treat a special lady?'

'Yes, Daddy, I have to be gentle.' Joshua slowed, walked ever so carefully next to Jenna, one slow step at a time.

Nanna and Poppy stood on the landing in front of the veranda.

'This is Jenna,' said Joshua.

'We've heard all about you,' said Nanna.

'Now I'm worried,' said Jenna.

'All good, believe me. Joshua has spent two weeks talking about nothing else but you. Poor Lucas hardly cracked a mention. Welcome. You are prettier than Joshua told us. Come inside.'

Joshua kept his hand in Jenna's but she didn't move.

'You have such a fabulous garden. All these native plants.' She tugged her hand free. 'Those salmon gums over there with the ghost gum in the middle – gorgeous.' She turned halfway around, knocked Joshua who stumbled before regaining his balance. She reached down. 'Sorry, Josh. I bet you like playing amongst all these bushes.'

'Not really.'

She squatted in front of him. 'I would if I was lucky enough to have so many trees and bushes.'

'You've got lots.'

'Nowhere near as many as here. Look at those scribbly gums over there.' She turned him and pointed. 'Can you guess why they have such a funny name?'

He studied the trees and smiled. It was the first time he'd taken notice. 'They look like a baby has scribbled all up and down the bark.'

'That's right. You could research how those scribbles are made. A project for you when we get back to school. Maybe you should have a close look at the bark before you go home. It might give you a clue. Now, I guess we'd better go inside since your nanna invited me. Will you show me the way?'

'Okay.' But he couldn't figure out why she needed showing since the steps were right in front of her. With a shrug, he took her hand and tugged before remembering he had to be gentle so he slowed a bit.

J enna caught Luke's raised eyebrow when she was tugged across the veranda. Josh must have remembered to take it easy for he slowed a tad to lead her through the doorway and into the first room on the left. A long, tall buffet took up most of the opposite wall. A raft of family photographs sat in organised chaos in most nooks, along with what appeared to be treasured mementos. A long three-seater sofa sat opposite with two well-worn leather recliner rockers at an angle, facing a wall-mounted TV set. The room had a comfy aura. Joshua led her to the sofa, where she sat. It took two seconds for him to climb into her lap and snuggle in. Overcome with emotion to feel his small, warm body, she wrapped him in her arms and sent a smile to Luke's chagrined face.

'I might as well not be here,' said Luke with a deep frown.

His parents, who settled into the chairs, burst out laughing. It was obvious where Luke inherited his height, dark hair and eyes. He was a replica of his father. His mother was smaller, several inches shorter than Jenna, and an attractive woman in a pretty sense rather than beautiful. Her brown hair had grey streaks but the etched lines of a smile, along with twinkling grey eyes indicated a happy person.

'We're glad to see you again, Lucas.' His father laughed while Luke raised his eyebrows.

Embarrassed, Jenna lifted Joshua from her lap, stood and plonked him in Luke's arms. 'Your dad has been sad and lonely without you. Talk to him and make him happy again,' she instructed the boy. 'I need a bathroom,' she added to Mrs Hunter.

'This way.'

Jenna followed but noticed Luke had to grab Joshua to prevent him from following. With her back to them, she grinned.

'I need to thank you,' Mrs Hunter said with a hand indicating a door.

'Why?'

'I can't believe the change in both Josh and Lucas. Josh thinks the sun shines out of you and Lucas has a spark in him I haven't seen for a long time. I am forever grateful.'

Stunned by both her frankness and the words, Jenna eyed Mrs Hunter. 'I don't understand. I'm just Josh's teacher.'

'He's taken a shine to you, which is a blessing for he's been a sad young boy since the accident. And Lucas – he's more relaxed, more alive, more like the son we knew. Come to the kitchen and talk to me so I can find out for myself what it is about you my son and grandson have taken to so readily.'

Nerves fluttered when Jenna bypassed the lounge room in search of the kitchen. Mrs Hunter stood at a huge gas stove, stirring a pot.

She turned and smiled. 'Come in, my dear. We're having an early lunch so you can get back in plenty of time.'

'What can I do to help?'

'Talk to me.'

'Only if you give me a job to do.'

Mrs Hunter smiled and pointed to the end of the stone bench. 'Ingredients for a tossed salad need to be sliced, diced and chopped. I'm sure I don't need to tell you how.'

'I think I can manage a salad.'

'And the best chocolate brownies ever, according to Joshua.'

'Lord, now I'm worried. What else has he told you?'

'The bestest ever vegetable garden, the bestest ever teacher, the bestest ever babysitter and a few more bestest ever's Lucas ordered me to not mention.'

Jenna groaned, picked up a sharp knife and cut a tomato into wedges. 'Luke did mention a vivid imagination. I'm sorry. All I did was fill in when the original babysitter wasn't up to standard and it was a pleasure. Josh is a lovely child. Mature for his age.' Two more tomatoes went into the bowl.

'Awful circumstances forced him to grow up way too soon.'

'Luke is an amazing father. It's been tough for him as well.'

'Tough for us all. It was a good job Lucas and Joshua had each other. But I have to tell you, you have made a huge impact on them both.'

'Luke has been kind. He's helped me through a… um…' She stabbed the knife through a cucumber, cut off a hunk instead of a nice delicate slice.

'He told me the basics. He also told me not to bring it up so you can have a day of relief and peace.'

'Oops. My lips have been zipped.' With less vigour, the hunk got sliced, the pieces went into a crystal salad bowl. She broke up lettuce leaves from the already washed crisp, green ball.

Mrs Hunter stood by her side. 'I understand why my boys like you so much and all Joshua has said and all Lucas has either denied or not said. You have our blessing and our thanks.'

The knife fell from Jenna's fingers. 'Embarrassment 101 over here.'

Mrs Hunter picked up the knife and held it out. 'Don't be and I like your sense of humour. How about you round up the menfolk while I finish this?'

'Sounds good.' Glad to escape, Jenna went to round up the men. At the doorway she paused when she noticed Luke sprawled on the sofa with Joshua spreadeagled across him, his head on Luke's shoulder. Her heart did a somersault at the sweet sight.

'Lunch is ready,' she called softly. Three sets of identical eyes turned to her. It was a shock at how similar Joshua was to his father and grandfather. It wasn't hard to imagine he would grow to be more like them as he matured.

The meal was happy, despite Joshua taking centre stage with constant chitchat about all the things he'd done over the two weeks. There was a sudden silence when he mentioned he'd spent a day with his other grandparents.

'At their place?' Luke asked in a tone that sent up alarm bells.

'No, I invited them to spend the day here.' Mrs Hunter patted Luke's hand. 'They were fine. No hassles, no demands. I think they've learnt their lesson.'

Jenna eyed Luke with a raised eyebrow.

'I'll tell you later,' he said in an undertone.

While the men did the dishes Jenna found herself with Joshua curled in her lap while the ladies sipped on coffee and chatted with Joshua interrupting constantly.

Soon after lunch they had to leave for the return journey, which was nowhere near as silent as the morning's trip. Joshua was full of questions to both Jenna and his father until Luke demanded silence from him so Jenna could rest. Luke glanced at her. She grinned back.

'Nice quiet music will help me rest,' she suggested and reached over to turn on the CD player.

After another thirty minutes the music worked, for Joshua slept for the last part of the trip and was still asleep when Luke dropped her off at the hotel. He leant over and gave her a peck on her cheek before she alighted.

'I'll ring you tonight,' he murmured. 'I'll wait here until you are inside. Take care.'

It was after eight before Luke rang. 'Josh has finally gone to sleep. It's been chaos the past few hours. He hasn't shut up for more than thirty seconds. I miss him when he's not here but after this afternoon I have to wonder why.'

Jenna laughed. 'He missed you so much he has to make up for lost time.'

'All in one hit? I think he has rehashed every second he was away, about a zillion times.'

'What was that about the other grandparents?'

'Ah. It's a sorry saga. They blamed me for losing their daughter. If she hadn't married me she wouldn't have been picking Josh up from Kindy, wouldn't have been in the car at the same time a drugged up, drunk driver decided to speed.'

'I get the picture.'

'They were so upset they attempted to take Josh away from me.'

'What? Why?'

'Told the authorities I wasn't a fit father. Made up a lot of porky pies about my treatment of Lisa. I suspect they wanted control of his money.'

'His money?'

'Lisa and I both had life insurance policies. I was awarded the payout from Lisa, half of which bought me the new business partnership. Josh was awarded a large payout from the driver of the other car. It paid for his medical treatment, including the child psych, plus a substantial amount from the trauma he went through and the loss of the most important person in his life. The court took into consideration the cost of care he would need while I worked and it pays for a cleaning service one day a week to clean floors and bathrooms so I have some spare time each day to dedicate to Josh. It was when Lisa's parents heard the amount, they began their vendetta against me.

'It went to court. Fortunately I'd sent Josh to a child psych right from the get-go to lessen his trauma. And I'd taken a month off work to be with him 24/7. The psych was ordered to ask Josh subtle questions about our life prior to the accident to figure out if there was any truth in the allegations. I came out squeaky clean. It helped when Lisa's brother and sister denied the allegations. Her parents were ordered to undergo grief counselling and after they threatened to kidnap him, they could only spend time with him under supervision. I didn't like doing it to them but had no choice in the end. I figured it was their grief, and probably greed, that caused them to act this way but they are adults. Josh was a four-year-old kid who'd lost the most important person in his life while he watched on. The judge rebuked the grandparents. They don't much like me anymore but I have never denied them time with Josh. They are his grandparents. I think they may have come around but I can't take a chance they will carry out their threat.'

'Oh, Luke, I'm sorry.'

'It is what it is. Josh's welfare is number one priority and he's doing okay.'

'Thanks to you. You're a great dad. Pity a couple of my other students don't have a dad like you.'

'You know how to make a man blush in embarrassment. But Josh is my life. Everything I do is for him. I hate the idea of a kid not having good parents. Have you got many?'

'Only a couple.'

'Thanks for coming today. My folks were impressed. They like you. How about tomorrow? Can we spend the day with you?'

Jenna thought it was more important for father and son to have the next day together. 'School starts Monday so I need lessons for the kids. It will take most of the day.' She lied, for the entire term's lessons were planned. 'Tell Josh I'll see him Monday morning. I enjoyed today. Thank you.'

'So did I. Good night.'

'Good night.'

In an attempt to thrust the threats and scare tactics of her stalker to the back of her mind, Jenna threw all her energy into work. First thing Monday morning the children were full of renewed vigour after their break and were keen to impart their holiday experiences to both her and their friends in a cacophony of jabbers. To bring calm she suggested they write in their diaries the best thing about their holiday. There were lots of smiles as she helped each with their words and the sound of eager voices didn't cease much. It was a surprise when Joshua wanted to write about her coming to pick him up since his constant chattering had revealed lots of wonderful things he had done with his grandparents.

'This can't be the best thing of the holidays. You told me about so many other fabulous things you did with your grandparents. There was the picnic and…'

'It's my bestest.'

'Best. There's no such word as bestest.'

'Sorry.'

'No need to apologise. We learn when we make mistakes. You made a mistake. I gave you the correct word so you learned what the correct word is. It's why we go to school.'

'Okay.'

At story-time Joshua edged his way forward on the floor until he was at her feet with his head leant against her knee. It wasn't unusual for the younger children to creep as close as they could during these quiet times. There was often a child with their head rested against her. They also ran their fingers up and down her legs or played with her shoes while she read a fantasy. It amused her how often she was called Mummy, with the perpetrator going bright red.

No longer a silent member of the class, Joshua didn't mind reading aloud any more. He was a competent reader and adept at maths, which had Jenna constantly stretching him in this field, giving him more complex problems to solve, along with another five students who were in the top group.

The afternoon session consisted of a craft activity and ended with games outside in the sunshine. This term she wanted to increase their bat and ball skills – how to throw properly, to keep their eye on the ball, to catch by wrapping their hands around the ball and how to hit well. After a few shots practising each skill, she set up a game of rounders. Most of the children were competitive and they ended the day with much laughter and on a high which continued while she helped them gather their belongings and handed them over to their parents.

Instead of staying at school to tidy the room as she usually did, she had to leave straight away for a long put-off dental appointment. One she'd hoped to fit in during the holidays but every child in the entire town must have had dental appointments in the holidays for she couldn't gain one until school began.

The moment the last child disappeared she hurried to her car and drove off to get to the appointment on time. Joshua was on his way to the gate when she passed him and waved. There was no longer any need to worry about him for his new sitter was reliable and always arrived a few minutes before the siren. While driving she figured that, until the person responsible for the threats was caught, it might not be wise for her to remain at school after hours. Too easy to be caught unawares and too dangerous if she was alone, especially after the cleaners had gone. The realisation of how this had changed her life, hit. One thing she knew for sure – she didn't have the gumption to go back and live in her house.

Luke was in the middle of an interview with a client when the receptionist knocked on the door and entered without waiting for a response. This wasn't acceptable and both knew it. He sent her a scowl to let her know he didn't appreciate the interruption in the middle of an interview.

'I'm sorry, Mr Hunter, but there is an urgent phone call from your babysitter. She says it is vitally important – an emergency. Line four.'

Alarmed, Luke excused himself to his client, lifted the receiver and pressed four. His heart hammered when he heard the frantic message. 'Oh, God! Are you sure?' He replaced the receiver and stood. 'I'm sorry, Mr Fielding, but my six-year-old son has gone missing from school, I must go. I'll ask the receptionist to make another appointment. I hope you don't mind.'

'Of course not. Got young kids of my own. I'd do the same. You go.'

Luke garbled a message to the receptionist as he rushed out. He barely kept under the speed limit during the eternal drive to the school where a distraught babysitter paced outside the main gate.

'Oh, Mr Hunter, I got caught in a small traffic jam. There was an accident and I was only five minutes late but Joshua wasn't here. I can't find him anywhere. I've been to the office and the teachers have searched the school. I've searched along all the nearby streets but there is no sign of him. I don't know what else to do.'

'You did the right thing, Mrs Hamilton. Could he have gone back to his teacher's classroom? He often did before. Mrs Reynolds would look after him if the sitter didn't arrive. Let's go and have a look.'

'I've been there. Her room is locked. They said Mrs Reynolds left straight after school.'

Luke was at a loss as to what to do next. He rang the hotel to speak to Jenna but was told she hadn't come in yet. A ghastly thought shot into his mind. He pulled out his mobile phone and dialled the police number, asking to speak to the officer in charge of Jenna's investigation. Fear surged and gnawed while he waited an interminable two minutes to be connected. This was his worst nightmare.

'Sergeant, my young son has disappeared from school. My concern is that Jenna's unknown assailant knows about my son and me. He surely wouldn't have kidnapped Josh as a means of getting at Jenna would he? And I have no idea where Jenna is. She left school after the siren but hasn't arrived at the hotel yet.'

'Jenna informed us about a dental appointment she had this afternoon. I can contact my man to find out where she is. Your son wouldn't have gone with her would he? Have you checked your home to make sure he hasn't walked? This happens quite a lot with missing children. Try to keep calm, we'll find him. Give me a description and what he was wearing.'

Frantic, Luke garbled out the details and agreed to search the streets between the school and his home then wait for a phone call. He sent Mrs Hamilton on a similar search between the school and her place, suggesting she stay put in case Joshua turned up. His heart sat lodged in his throat while he drove, his eyes scanning all the nooks and objects along the way. Fear had turned into a serious bout of nausea.

Jenna's frustration at having to wait so long for a simple check-up eased when she was only in the surgery for less than fifteen minutes. It was always the same in medical and dental surgeries. The demand was too high, appointments went over time and patients always waited ridiculous times.

Alarm bells rang at the sight of a familiar police officer standing at the front desk when she approached to pay the bill.

'Mrs Reynolds, you wouldn't have taken young Joshua Hunter with you when you left school this afternoon?'

The hand holding out her credit card took on an uncontrollable shake. 'No, of course not, I waved to him as I left. He was walking towards the gate where he meets his babysitter. She is always on time waiting for him. What's happened?' Jenna turned between the receptionist and the officer while she spoke, willing the receptionist to hurry.

'He's gone missing. We needed to check with you first.'

When her legs turned to melted jelly she had to sit. Her mind spun with ideas, none of which made sense.

'Obviously Luke knows. He must be frantic. What can I do? We must find him. Oh, heavens.' Jenna dropped her head into her hands in an attempt to unscramble the maelstrom of thoughts. 'I'll go back to the school and search around there, go through the classrooms…' A sudden thought hit. 'You don't think… Oh no… He hasn't been taken by the pervert who… I'll never forgive myself.'

'Don't get alarmed. It's early days. He's only been gone a short while and it's possible he decided to walk home.'

'It's been over an hour.' She checked her watch. 'What happened with his sitter? She has always been reliable.'

'Apparently she was held up in a traffic jam and was a few

minutes late. Young kids often do these types of things. We've got people out looking now. You go back to the school and look there but remember to keep yourself safe. I want to know where you are at all times. Do you have a mobile?'

'Yes, but I don't often use it.' She scrabbled around in her handbag until she found the phone lying at the bottom. Every item you ever needed was always at the bottom. After switching it on to check battery strength, she wrote the number on the pad the officer held out.

They left the building together but each went their separate ways. Jenna drove back to the school, got out and ran to her room to ensure Joshua wasn't inside, although it was unlikely since she had locked her own door and had noticed him afterwards. Finding the cleaners still there, she spoke to each when she came across them while searching the school. They informed her they had been asked to keep an eye out for him but Joshua hadn't been seen. Dejected she returned to her car and rang Luke. 'Has he turned up?'

'No! Where are you? I've been trying to contact you.' He sounded frantic.

'I was at the dentist. I've searched the school. What can I do? We must find him soon before it gets dark.'

'Can you come here? I need someone to be here in case he comes home. I have to get out there and search for him. I can't sit here like a stuffed fish - I feel so utterly helpless.'

'I'm on my way. We'll find him.' She drove at the pace of a lumbering tortoise along the streets towards Luke's house, unable to believe Joshua would attempt to walk the distance. She also couldn't believe he wouldn't wait for his sitter. He was an intelligent young man - he would wait. He'd waited hours for the previous young girl. So where was he? The only logical conclusion she could come to, was her greatest fear - Joshua had been taken, unwillingly and if that had happened it would be her fault. By the time she reached Luke's house guilt had taken hold, along with terror. She sat in the car, not wanting to face Luke but he was already stalking towards her. He opened her door.

'This is my fault. I'm so sorry, I'll never forgive myself if anything happens to Josh.'

Luke eased her out of the car. 'None of this is your fault. You have done nothing wrong. Now I need you to come inside and stay here while I go out searching. I'm going to walk - go down driveways and back lanes where I can't go in my car. I'll take my mobile. I can't sit here and wait. He could be lying hurt in a ditch or a bush.'

'Luke, I can't imagine Josh would ever attempt to walk here. He's too smart…' She stopped short when an idea came. 'I have an idea.' She climbed back into her car. 'Wait here. I'll ring you in a few minutes.'

Not waiting for Luke's response she reversed out of the drive, turned onto the road and sped off with a squeal of tyres when she planted her foot a tad too hard. She sped back the way she had come, miscalculated one corner, jolted over the kerb and screeched around another, incurring the verbal wrath of a pedestrian whom she barely missed. It was beginning to get dark and if she was right, Joshua would be terrified. She reached the school in record time, sped straight past, spun her wheels as she rounded the next corner and raced along the two blocks to her house. Joshua didn't know she had moved out. It could be the one place he would go where they hadn't thought to look.

Jamming on the brakes, she pulled up on the verge outside her front gate. A slam of fear returned the moment she alighted. Now she regretted the hasty decision to come alone. What if her stalker was here – with Josh? Dear Lord, she should have brought Luke with her. The thought of walking around the house by herself sent paroxysms of fear through her innards. The place was locked so it was unlikely Joshua would be inside but her predatory pursuer could have broken in again to make her life more miserable than it already was.

Creeping to the front door, she placed her ear against the wood and listened. There was no sound coming from inside but plenty of subtle noises outside. Birds were happy, distant traffic hummed; kids laughed in backyards. Inside was a heavy silence.

She slipped the key in the lock and turned it slow so there was no noise. Now she regretted being so hasty in having the power turned off. The only light she had was from the remains of a sun lying low on the horizon. It was difficult to make out shapes in the shadowed gloom. Nerves tense, she crept along the passage, opened each door, peered into the dim darkness of the curtained rooms. The furniture gave off sinister shapes. Her nerves were on the verge of shattering, afraid she might be attacked at any moment. A fear she knew was unfounded because the house had been locked, but she couldn't help the ghastly apprehension.

Satisfied the house was empty she crept back to the front door, secured it and pocketed the keys while she began the search of the front yard. There weren't any real hiding places at the front but she scouted around in any case, her heart in her mouth. Happy he wasn't there she opened the side gate and tip-toed along the path she had kept clear of dense shrubbery but the shadows from the neighbour's taller overgrown shrubs scared her.

With the large back garden a haven of hiding spots, a shiver took hold and wove across her shoulders. One step up onto the back veranda from where she searched the murky darkness with her eyes for any signs of a frightened young boy. She had no desire to go wandering around the tall shrubs looking for him so she called out his name.

'Joshua, it's Jenna, I'm here by myself.' At a muffled sound, all the hairs on her body stood on end. A spurt of adrenalin surged through her veins. Was he being held back?

She paused to listen, head turned in the directions of the sound, ears alert for the slightest noise. 'Josh,' she called again and dared to step off the veranda and creep along the path towards the vegie patch hidden behind the dense bushes and tall trees.

'I'm really, really scared, Josh.'

A muffled squeal came from the forest of peas.

'Josh?'

A dark form hurtled out from behind the tallest plants straight into her arms. Even though she half expected him to be there, his sudden movement startled her enough, a scream escaped. She had to steady herself from the force when Joshua flung his arms around her waist and gripped so tight his fingers pressed into her flesh.

'Sweetheart, are you all right?' She knelt down and held him close. 'Why were you hiding behind the peas?'

He put his mouth next to her ear. 'So the man wouldn't see me.'

A cannon ball bounced in her gut. 'What man?'

'Shh,' whispered Josh. 'The man was looking in all of your windows.'

The cannon ball yo-yoed. 'When? Did you recognise him?'

'No. He had a big black hoodie over his head.'

So not the police was he first thought. The second thought sent the cannon ball on a free-fall. The third thought eased her mind.

'There's nobody there now,' she whispered to Joshua.

'Are you sure?' His voice quivered.

'Yes. I've been inside and there's nobody there. And now I need to ring your dad to tell him you are safe. He's worried about you.'

'He'll be mad at me. I had to find you, Jenna, but you weren't here,' he mumbled between wracking sobs.

'Your dad won't be cross. He loves you too much to be angry with you. He'll be overjoyed you have been found and are safe. Let me tell him you aren't hurt so he can stop worrying.'

Jenna released her tight hold but he still gripped his arms around her waist while she dialled Luke's number. He must have been waiting right next to his phone for it only rang once before his worried voice barked, 'Hello.'

'I found him and he's unharmed. He's frightened, cold but unhurt. He's afraid you are going to be mad at him, can I tell him you're not? I'll be there in a few minutes. You'd better let the search parties know.' Closing down her phone, Jenna turned to Joshua and placed her arms around him again. 'Sweetheart, Daddy isn't angry. Let's go home so you can give him a great big cuddle.'

He still trembled when she picked him up, bag still on his back, and hoisted him high on one hip. Overcome with relief, she planted a kiss on his hot, sweaty forehead. While she carried him to her car his arms choked her with a tight grip around her neck. With no booster seat, she settled him in the passenger seat and secured the seatbelt before lifting the corner of her blouse to wipe the worst of the moisture from his face. Since he was still upset she hugged him a while longer until he calmed. While she drove at a far safer speed she explained how she didn't live in her house anymore because she was going to sell it.

'Are you too scared after the bad man broke in?'

'Yes, that's why I don't want to live there anymore. You are a brave young man.' Glancing at him, she noticed the serious look of concern on his tear-streaked face. 'The most important thing is that you are safe and I will tell the police officer about the man in the hoodie. It might be the same man who knows I don't live there anymore. It could be a homeless person who wanted to steal food. He could be a hungry person.' As if, but she couldn't let Joshua think the worst.

After coming to a halt in Luke's drive she reached over to open Joshua's door and noticed how Luke stepped outside, ran and dropped to his knees when Joshua neared and pelted into his father's wide-open arms and was lifted up high in a tight embrace.

'Oh, Josh, I love you to bits. I'm so glad Jenna found you.'

Jenna sat watching before she alighted with Josh's bag to join the two. Luke released one arm from his son, placed it around her shoulder. Once they were inside Luke threw a questioning glance in her direction.

'We'll talk later. Joshua needs to have a shower, get warm and be fed. You get him cleaned up while I raid your fridge. He's frozen and right now needs his dad more than anything else.'

After shooing the two into the bathroom she opened the fridge, pulled out eggs and vegetables to whip up omelettes filled with grated vegetables and cheese. She found a loaf of bread and opened cupboards until she located the toaster. She was serving up the light, nourishing meal when Joshua ran in, followed by a more subdued and shaken Luke. She could tell Joshua had told him where he had been. She settled Joshua at the bench and slid his plate in front of him. 'Eat it all. You too, Lucas.'

Luke gave her a wry look but tucked in, whispering to Joshua. 'Jenna only calls me Lucas when I'm in trouble and she means business. It means I'd better do as I'm told.'

Joshua's giggle twisted Jenna's heart.

'Your mother calls you Lucas all the time,' she retorted.

'I don't dare disobey her either.'

'A huge man like you, afraid of your sweet little mother?'

Joshua giggled again. 'I'm not scared of Nanna.'

'No, you are a brave boy.' She ruffled Joshua's hair. He grinned before shovelling in another mouthful of food.

She didn't miss Luke leave a small amount of food on his plate before he nudged Joshua and pointed to the morsel, placed his knife and fork together and pushed his plate away.

Joshua laughed out loud when her hand shot out and pushed the plate back. Luke shrugged and finished off the last bite with a big grin on his face.

She poured Joshua a drink of milk and cleared up the dishes while he drank it down. She waited until he was finished. 'If you go and clean your teeth and hop into bed, I'll come to read you a story. You find three stories and let me choose which one I would like to read.'

Joshua sped off with a wide grin.

'He usually moans and groans and picks the longest story he can find to delay having to go to bed,' Luke said.

'Which is why I gave him three. I choose the shortest. You have to use reverse psychology with smart kids like him. I'll be back in a few minutes.'

Tossing the dishcloth at Luke, she followed Joshua and left Luke to finish the dishes. When she returned the last dish was being put in the cupboard. 'I must have chosen the right book. Dishes are done and Joshua is asleep.' Her grin was supercilious as she took the cup of coffee he handed her.

Luke followed her into the lounge room. 'How did you know where to look?' He settled into a chair.

'It suddenly dawned on me it was the one place he knew, where we hadn't searched. He didn't know I had moved out. He's too smart to walk this far. He thought I had gone home when I waved to him as I left school. When his babysitter didn't arrive, he knew

I wasn't at school. Once at my place he didn't know what else to do, so he waited for me to come home. I can tell you I was mighty relieved when I spotted him. He's not the type of child who would wander off by himself. Under normal circumstances he did the logical thing.'

'I'm so relieved he's safe. I've never been so scared in my life. I couldn't bear it if I lost him as well. Thank you.'

'I noticed Josh doesn't have any electronic devices.'

'No. Before he was born, Lisa and I agreed our children would never be babysat by TV, devices or phones. He knows how to amuse himself by being creative. I built him a computer – deleted all games. I teach him all he needs to know about how they work. He can create word documents, knows how to search for information – but only under my guidance. As he gets older, I'll loosen the reins bit-by-bit until he can handle a computer with competence. I won't allow him to become addicted to games and social media. I do have a personal email account as well as one for work but I don't have pages on any social media platforms. Not interested, nor do I have the time. Josh does send emails to his grandparents and other relatives on occasion. He knows how. I limit and supervise what he does.'

'Pity there aren't more parents like you. I can't be bothered with social media. My brother sends me regular emails and I keep in contact with old friends the same way. I refuse to give parents my email address. If they want to discuss their child, they can – in person and in school hours.' She swallowed the last of her coffee and stood. 'I have to go.'

'Really?'

'It's been a hectic day and I'm tired.'

Luke stood, drew her into his arms and held her. 'Much as I would love you to stay, I understand.' He walked her outside. 'Will you be okay by yourself?'

'Yes. Go inside and give your son a kiss and cuddle. Good night.' The second she stood outside a quick shiver started at her head and wove down her body. She fled to her car, leapt in, slammed the door and drove off. Luke hadn't mentioned the man so Josh might not have told him, which she couldn't believe. Instead of going to the hotel, she detoured via the police station to let them know.

Every day for two whole weeks, Joshua stood on the end of the veranda with his eyes glued to the gate, too scared to leave until the babysitter arrived. Every day she turned up and came into the playground to meet him while he ran towards the gate. He gripped her hand so he didn't get left behind and whenever they passed a man he made sure his side touched hers and dropped his head down so the man wouldn't recognise him.

Every night when Daddy picked him up, they played a new game – what if. What if the babysitter was late again? He was to find a teacher and stay with them. Any teacher and not only Jenna because she may not always be there. And she wasn't. Every day she left in her car as soon as he met with the babysitter. It was kinda good she waited until the babysitter came. A warm fuzzy settled in his tummy when she waited. He liked warm fuzzies.

What if there were no teachers left at school? Find one of the cleaners. What if there were no cleaners? He was to hide between the fence and the shed where all the sport's gear was kept. Daddy would know where to look for him and there was a roof hanging over to the fence to keep him protected if it rained or it was too hot. He'd checked it out. It wasn't too scary and was a good hiding place.

They also talked about Jenna, resulting in them making a pact. A better secret than he'd had before. Joshua crossed his heart and hoped to die to promise he would keep it a secret, especially from Jenna. This was a *men's business only* game. No women allowed.

Step one. Daddy was going to take Jenna out on a date. Joshua agreed to be babysat on Saturday night.

Step two. Daddy was going to get Jenna to like him – a lot. Joshua promised, cross his heart to not do anything bad so Jenna wouldn't like either of them. Daddy didn't like the *hope to die* bit.

He said it wasn't a good idea to say such a thing. Joshua agreed when he thought about it. He didn't ever want anyone else to die. It hurt way too much.

Step three. Josh promised, cross his heart, he wouldn't let out any secrets by writing them in his diary at school. He didn't, but he shoved his hands over the sentence when Jenna wanted to read, *Daddy and I have the bestest ever secret about Jenna.* Oops, he forgot and to cross it out would make the page messy and Jenna, oops, Mrs Reynolds didn't like the kids to have messy work. They always had to try their hardest to do their neatest work. He tried hard but the letters didn't always come out right.

The next day he forgot again and wrote, *Daddy is going to ask Jenna to go on a date.* When she came towards his desk he slammed the diary shut and shoved it in his desk. Oh, oh, almost got caught.

'What are you up to, young man?' she asked.

'I've finished. Nothing much happened. Can I read?' He didn't like the way she put her finger on her cheek with a frowny face.

'Okay.' He did like the smile and nod but not as much as he liked Jenna. Phew.

When he took out his library book he hid the diary underneath all the other books in his desk. For the rest of the day he made sure he didn't mess up because he wanted Jenna to like him – a lot.

Curious about his antics, Jenna waited until Joshua had left with the babysitter before she went to his desk and searched for his diary, amused when it was hidden. 'Oh, my,' she whispered with a smile when she read the entries. The smile stayed in place while she made sure the diary went back where she'd found it.

Wise enough to leave it alone and not ask questions, she couldn't help but grin when she had a phone call from Luke that evening, asking if she would care to join him for a meal on Saturday night.

'I would be delighted.' She had to squeeze her nose shut to prevent a giggle from escaping. 'What time?' she managed to get out in a sort of normal voice.

'How about I pick you up at seven? How's the house hunting going?'

A much safer topic. 'I've inspected a few homes for sale. None suitable but I had a call earlier from an agent. A house has come up for rental in the past few days. I'm going to inspect it tomorrow after school. This one is in a better area and not too far from school.'

'And your stalker? Any news?'

A shudder wove itself across her shoulders. 'The latest info is - they have narrowed down their short list of suspects and only have a few more people to catch up with. They are keeping their eye on Rob who is still high on the list. Three have refused to give fingerprints and a couple have been impossible to track down. Never home. I hope they find him soon for I'm tired of living the life of a recluse in a hotel room.'

'Why don't you return to the squash courts? How about a game on the weekend? Make it Sunday since we're dining out Saturday night.'

'No way.'

'What if I pick you up so we only have the one car? We can leave all our gear locked in the boot and I promise to keep you by my side. If we arrive already dressed, play and leave without showering or changing there shouldn't be any problem. Come on, I need the exercise to get fit again and this time I'm determined to thrash you.'

'Give me a minute to think.'

'While you think, add this to your thoughts. Are you going to let this maniac control your life? At the moment you don't have a real life because of him. This man has got you too scared to breathe, let alone leave your room. Don't let him. Show him you're not a victim. I promise to keep you safe.'

Luke was right. She was acting like a victim. 'Okay, I'll go, but any sign of the nutcase and it will be the last time.'

'Thank you – get ready to be beaten.'

'In your dreams, Lucas Hunter.'

He was laughing when he hung up.

After school Thursday, Jenna ensured Josh had been picked up before she left to drive to the address of the new rental where she was to meet the agent. At first sight of the house, her pulse quickened. Built of pale orange brick with a cute, neat front garden full of a mass of greenery and every colour bloom possible, it had a welcoming aura. She pulled up behind the agent's car and alighted. The agent stepped through the front doorway.

'I already like it,' she said as she mounted the two solid long steps onto the wide, covered veranda, big enough for a couple of comfy seats and a table.

'I thought you might. It's a nice, well-kept home. Basic, but good furniture. The only problem is, it's only a month-by-month lease.'

'In case I wreck the place?'

'The owners have been caught before. Not this last tenant but the one prior.'

'I understand. It might be a good thing for I'm putting my house on the market. I need to sell it before I can afford to buy another. So a month-by-month lease could be beneficial. I wouldn't be stuck with a six month or annual contract.'

After a thorough inspection of the property, Jenna signed the lease without hesitation. It was perfect for her immediate needs and would fill the gap until she could find a more permanent home.

Saturday morning, she spent with her head in schoolbooks before packing up the belongings she wouldn't need the following week. Her new home would be ready next weekend. The relief at being able to leave the hotel had made Friday in class light-hearted and fun. With a new spring in her step, after a snack for lunch, she folded into a taxi at the front entry of the hotel to take her to a salon where she'd booked to get her hair cut and styled for her date with Luke. A real date. The taxi would drop her off at the door leaving no chance for creepy morons to spoil the day. Nothing was going to spoil it.

While waiting for the taxi to arrive to take her back to the hotel, Jenna dared a peek in the next-door dress shop. An outfit in the window caught her eye: one she had to try on. It cost more than she was usually prepared to pay for a dress but it suited her well and her new determination about enjoying life had her walk out of the shop with the dress neatly folded in tissue paper in a flash carry-bag. To add to her exhilaration the taxi pulled up as she stepped from the shop.

Back in the hotel she dared a soak in the tub, without too many bubbles or the over-steaming of the hot jets to spoil the new hairdo. Once she'd dried off she took more care than normal in applying make-up. A shiver of anticipation took hold when she eased the new dress over her head, zipped up the hidden side zipper and stood in front of the mirrored door of the narrow wardrobe. 'Oh, my goodness.' The dress was mostly white with large red swirls. The soft fabric was cut perfectly so the pattern matched each side of a seam. Heat rose at how the fabric clung to her curves showing off her figure too well for her liking. She shrugged. Luke had seen her in less at the squash courts, but a sports outfit didn't cling quite so well. What she liked most about the dress was how the skirt was cut on the bias with layers hanging down so the hemline appeared jagged. The short parts ended at the knee while the longer sections reached mid-calf. Was this too much? Had she gone overboard?

A knock at the door sent her nerves so tense she was too scared to move. Another knock. Blowing out her cheeks, she ran, opened the door and gasped. Luke was dressed in black. Black trousers with a black skivvy and a black leather jacket.

'Turn around.' He spun the fingers of one hand around.

She turned on a held breath.

'You look exquisite.' He reached out, caught a strand of her hair. 'You've had it cut.'

'Just a trim.'

'More than a trim. At a guess, I'd say you treated yourself to a couple of hours being pampered. Which you deserve.' He entwined the fingers of one hand in hers. 'Are you ready?'

Too overwhelmed to utter a word she nodded, lifted the sparkly evening bag she'd left on the chair next to the door, removed the keycard from the slot and pulled the door shut.

Thank goodness his car was right outside the main door. Luke walked her around the passenger side, opened the door and bent to help her sit. Overcome, she smiled and whispered, 'Thank you.' Any more words defied her until Luke had driven around the curved driveway and onto the road.

'What's wrong?' Luke asked with a quick grip on her knee.

'Nothing, why do you ask?'

'You're a little – tense.'

'I'm terrified.'

He glanced at her with a small frown. 'Of what?''

'All this – a date – it's so…'

'Terrifying?'

'So new.'

'We've been on a date before.'

'I know. This is scarier. But amazing,' she added. 'It's been so long.'

'For me as well. Could be I'm equally afraid. What if I stuff up?' He patted her knee. 'Let's enjoy the night. Forget about everything else. We're going to enjoy a meal together. We've shared meals before so this shouldn't be any different. Tell me about the house you found.'

God, she was glad of the change in topic. 'I can move in next weekend. It's nice. Three bedrooms and two bathrooms this time, not that I will ever use one of them. Roomier than my house. Enough furniture for one. No vegies in the garden though. I've signed to put my house on the market. The agent said it would be snapped up in this housing crisis. I was shocked at the asking price he suggested but to buy another home there'll be a high price as well.'

'I can help you shift next weekend.'

'I'd appreciate it. Thank you.'

'Any news from the police? Oh, sorry, I promised myself we wouldn't go there tonight.'

'It's okay. I made a pact with myself while I was having my hair done. I refuse to let this nutcase control my life a moment longer. To answer your question. No. And I will still take care and not walk alone.'

Luke grinned. 'Reading my mind now, are you?'

'No, but I'm not stupid enough to put myself in harm's way. How's Josh?'

'Not quite as excitable, thank goodness. School has settled him. How's he been in class?'

Did she dare mention the diary? Better not in case Luke mentions it to him. Josh would know she'd snuck a look. 'Josh is Josh.'

When Luke escorted her to the table in the restaurant, the pressure of eyes staring at them, stabbed in her back.

'I told you how beautiful you look tonight. All these people have eyes only for you,' Luke said as he pulled out her chair.

'Don't sell yourself short. I'm certain none of the women are looking at me. If they are it's with daggers, wishing they were in my place.' She studied the room. 'I've never been in here before. I've heard people talk about it but have never had the opportunity. It looks special.'

'I was told it is and they have an excellent chef.' Luke sat opposite. The waiter hovered with held out menus. Luke took one. 'What would you like to drink?'

'Tonight I have a new lease on life so make it a sparkling wine.'

'Sparkling wine for a sparkling lady it is.' Luke leant towards the waiter, 'How about this one?'

'Good choice, sir. And for you?'

'I'll share a bottle with my sparkling guest.'

She rolled her eyes. 'Please.' She picked up the food menu and opened it out to hide her embarrassment.

Luke laughed and did the same.

They spent a few minutes selecting their dishes and after the wine had been poured, Luke lifted his glass to make a toast. 'We've known each other for about two months now. We've both been scared witless on more than one occasion, we've spent countless hours with police officers, young Josh has ruled our lives and, I suspect, manipulated it to a certain extent. We've been the main attraction at the squash courts - thanks to your brilliance - and hardly had time to be alone. Tonight is only our second true date together. A toast to a less traumatic and far more pleasant next two months.'

Lifting her glass with a coy smile, Jenna saluted, her thoughts running around in her head. She yearned for the day they were free to go out and enjoy themselves without all the unsavoury interruptions. 'A more pleasant two months,' she added as they chinked glasses and took a sip. 'Wow, this is better than nice.'

When their main course was served Luke sat in silence, watching her, as he took up his knife and fork.

'What's wrong, Luke, cat got your tongue? I've never known you to be so quiet.'

'Only if you class yourself as a cat. Soft, warm and cuddly, purrs with contentment. The claws came out when you whitewashed Ryan on the squash court. It would have to be a Persian cat with your long, thick hair. Yeah, I could say a cat has got my tongue.'

'I do not purr,' she spat back.

'You sighed with contentment - that's pretty much the same,' he countered with a grin. 'Although, I've never seen a cat blush the way you do.'

'Lucas!'

'Oh, oh, I'm in trouble.' His grin belied his words.

Jenna managed a smile as they went back to enjoying their food.

They opted for a small cheese platter and coffee, rather than sweets. While waiting for them to be served, Jenna stood. 'I need a visit to the ladies. Please excuse me.' She wove between the table to the discreet sign in the far corner. It was a surprise the rest room was as swish as the restaurant. 'Nice,' she said with grin.

After washing her hands and a quick check in the mirror, she smiled again and stepped into the small passage. The grin vanished in an instant.

Rob stood leant up against the wall.

'What do you want?' she stammered when her pulse rate shot to an unhealthy speed.

'To talk.'

'After what you did to me, you expect me to talk? You're not allowed anywhere near me. Why are you tormenting me like this?'

'I was here first. You came in after me. You surely don't expect me to leave halfway through my meal, do you?'

'Even if you were here first, you aren't allowed to approach me. Yet you have. I'd appreciate it if you disappear and leave me alone.' When she went to step past him he straightened and reached out.

'Luke,' she yelled as she backed away.

'I only want to discuss things.' He stepped closer.

Jenna backed up further until the wall prevented another step. 'No. Go away.'

'Please?' He jumped when a door hit the wall.

'Where the hell did you come from?' Luke roared. 'Get out.' Luke moved around him and placed a protective arm around Jenna, moving his large frame closer to Rob while edging her away. 'If you have trouble understanding any part of the word no, I don't mind explaining it to you. Please respect Jenna's decision and leave her alone. As far as I can figure out with my limited legal knowledge, you have breached the terms of your restraining order so I don't mind calling the police to have you physically removed if you would like to make an exhibition of yourself. You decide but make it quick because the manager heard Jenna scream and is on his way.'

It was a relief when Luke used his body to shield her as he guided her along the passage, around the chairs and tables back to their seats. A wave of shivers ran up and down the length of her body. When she plonked into her seat he squatted next to her. 'Are you all right? We can go if you prefer.'

It took a few moments to gain composure. 'No, we'll stay. I don't think he'll come over. I made my pact today - I won't allow him to rule my life anymore. I lost two years because of him and now I've lost the past two months because of him. Please, can we enjoy our cheese and coffee?'

'If you're sure.' He rose and returned to his seat.

'I'm sure. I will not allow him to ruin a wonderful evening.'

It was later than usual for her regular squash game for the last session at four was the only vacant spot Luke could book. To fill in time before she was picked up Jenna became absorbed in an interesting mystery saga. She reached a scary scene when loud bangs on the door caused her to jump and swear. With her hand pressed against her heart she opened the door to be assailed by a small bundle of energy when Joshua leapt in for his customary hug.

'Hello, young man,' she managed to get out in a normal voice, even though her innards weren't quite so co-operative. 'Did you bring your dad with you or are you going to play squash with me today?'

Joshua giggled as Luke stepped into the room behind them.

'I trust you slept well,' said Luke.

'Extremely well, I slept until lunchtime.' She laughed at Luke's growl.

'Remind me to lend you Josh next time we go out. He was up not long after the sun, which means you are full of energy and I don't have a hope of beating you today.'

To hide another laugh she slapped a hand over her mouth, bent to pick up her bag and led the way outside. 'I promise to take it easy on you.'

'With such a grin, I doubt it.'

Unable to suppress it, laughter gurgled out. There was no choice but to hold Joshua's hand while they made their way to the car. He chatted non-stop all the way to the squash courts. Once there, despite her determination to not be a victim, her heart hadn't received the message for it began a hard tattoo against her ribs before the car drew to a stop. She shouldn't be scared. Luke was with her. She was safe. And it was late Sunday, not her normal appearance at the courts. Her innards didn't obey her thoughts.

Before alighting she scanned the area for any sign of an unwelcome person, though she couldn't be sure who to search for.

Luke opened her door, took one look at her. 'We're on court four today. I'll be with you to ensure nothing unsavoury happens. You go straight down to the court and warm up while I settle Josh and find an adult to keep an eye on him.'

Oh, sure. As if she wanted to walk anywhere without his big body to protect her. But she pulled on her big girl pants and walked beside him across the car park, Joshua skipping next to her. She glued herself to Luke's side while they moved into the building. It sure felt good when he slung his arm around her waist and it stayed there until he opened the door of the vacant court to let her in. He set his racquet and a couple of balls against the back wall.

'I'll be back as soon as I get Josh settled. Even though he'll be above us where I can keep an eye on him, I don't dare leave him without supervision.' He took Josh's hand, smiled and thank goodness, shut the door behind him with a decided *snick*.

To fill in time, Jenna had a few hits against the wall. The door opened. Expecting Luke she turned with a smile, which vanished at the sight of Ryan.

'Oh, I'm sorry, but I don't have time to play against you today? I'm about to start a match with Luke.'

Ryan glared. Her stomach wrenched. Why, oh why did he appear? Especially when the game was two hours later than normal. Had he hung around waiting for her? And it was a Sunday. Hmm, maybe he spent both days of the weekend at the courts because he'd been here the last time she played on a Sunday.

'No, you wouldn't play with me, would you, bitch?' The door slammed behind his back.

'What did you say?' A sudden rise of bile burnt her oesophagus at the same time a cold sweat swamped her brow.

'I said you're a bitch,' Ryan repeated a tad louder with his face screwing into fierce scowl.

'What are you on about?'

'You wouldn't go out with me, but as soon as the Hunter bastard turns up - you go on a date with him. You're my girl, not his.' Ryan's face reddened. He stepped closer, racquet raised.

A light globe sparked to life in her brain. 'It was you who trashed my house. You wrote those notes. Why?' It was a fight to keep her voice calm. It was more difficult to keep alert and maintain a safe distance between them. Luke would be back soon. In the meantime she needed to keep talking despite her brain cells getting all muddled up.

'I'm nobody's girl. Nobody owns me. And I'm not a girl.' With a brain refusing to find the right words, she paused, took another step back. The word date, registered. 'How could I go out with you when you never asked me to go on a date?'

Her back hit the wall. She stepped forward. 'If you wanted to date me, why didn't you ask?' She swallowed her panic with a gulp. 'If you had asked me out ages ago, I probably would have agreed. But now I wouldn't consider it for you have shown me what kind of a person you are. A self-centred, egotistical bully. I went out with Luke for one simple reason - he asked me. So nick off and leave me alone,' she spat, puncturing the air with one finger at each word.

As Luke carried Josh upstairs he couldn't rid his mind of their date. Pictures of the evening had flashed through his mind most of the night and he hadn't had much sleep. Josh had leapt on him way too early demanding to know all about his date with Jenna, most of the details he kept to himself. He settled Josh on the front bench overlooking their court. 'I'll get you a drink and snack. Don't move from that spot.' He went to the cafeteria to purchase a bottle of water and sausage roll and searched the area for a person he could trust to keep an eye on Josh, although he was aware at least one plain-clothed officer was roaming around.

'Daddy, come quickly,' came from his side.

'I thought I told you to stay put.'

'But, Daddy, the bad man is talking to Jenna and he said a naughty word.'

'What?' Luke grabbed the food in one hand and Josh's arm in the other. He shot back to the bench and peered over the balcony. Ryan? What's going on?

'Leave me alone,' Jenna squealed loud enough to have the few people still there, stop and listen.

'Stay here.' Luke plonked Josh on the bench and dropped the food next to him. He turned, shot towards the staircase but was stopped by a man who held out his police ID badge.

'This is the man who has been stalking and threatening Jenna.'

'Ryan? Why would he?'

'Only he can tell us. There's an officer outside the court door. We won't let anything happen to her. Keep back so you're out of sight and keep your son quiet.'

The last thing he wanted to do was move back and do nothing. He picked up the food and hustled Josh from the bench to the back of the spectator gallery. To keep the unfolding scene from Josh's eyes, he turned his son to face his stomach and held him there. All he could see was the top of Ryan's head. Being the last session of the day, there were far fewer people around than normal. The court next door was still playing, which was a good thing to create a sense of normalcy in the area.

'You think you're in love with him,' Ryan screeched.

'I like Luke a great deal. He's a good man. A fantastic father to his son.'

'He's a bastard with a brat. Comes here to steal my girl.' The tone had become maniacal.

'I'm not a girl. I'm a mature woman with a mind of my own. I thought of you as a friend and have never had any romantic feelings towards you.' Jenna's sounded calm but there was a quiver to her words. 'Right now, I don't like you. How can you treat me like this when I've never done anything to hurt you?'

At a loud masculine roar, Luke edged closer, peered over the rail. The words must have fired Ryan up for he stepped towards her, his cheeks suffused with angry colour.

'You never went out with me,' he screamed.

'Like I said – you never asked me to go out with you.'

'I thought you were a nice girl, but you're nothing but a whore.' Ryan screeched.

'I beg your pardon?'

'I saw you, bitch, sleeping with Hunter. You stayed the night in his house.' Ryan moved towards her again, one arm held high, his fist clenched so tight his knuckles were white.

Jenna stepped away, edged closer towards the door. Luke's gut had twisted itself into a tight ball. He was desperate to get to her, to take the bastard out.

'You've been stalking me? Get one thing straight, Ryan. I have never slept with any man outside of marriage. Yes, I stayed in Luke's guest bedroom…'

'Liar!' Ryan yelled so loud Luke jumped and Josh whimpered. His fingers gripped tight into Luke's waist.

He twisted Josh behind his back. 'Stay there,' he said and

stepped forward. 'Jenna isn't lying.'

Ryan spun around, peered up while Jenna took advantage and sidled around the wall towards the door. Ryan must have noticed for he spun back and planted his body closer to the door to block any escape.

'Calm down and listen.' Luke placed both hands on top of the glass partition. If he had to, he would leap over. 'When a prowler broke into Jenna's home in the middle of the night, her house became a crime scene. To give her a safe place to stay for what was left of the night I offered my guest room. Not that she got much sleep because she was too scared to close her eyes.'

'You slept with my girl!' Ryan screeched.

'No. I would never take advantage of anyone who had been terrorised and was in a state of shock. Jenna is an adult and only she has the right to say who she will go out with. I don't have that right, nor do you.'

'She's mine!' The scream echoed.

'If Jenna chooses to date you it's fine by me. If she doesn't, it's her choice to make.'

'Why have you spent every freaking minute with her over the past four weeks if you're not interested?'

Luke scoffed. 'To keep her safe from the maniac who trashed her house, painted disgusting graffiti on all of her house and car windows and sent her death threats. You.'

'I love her. She's mine.'

'If you truly love a person you do everything in your power to ensure they are happy and safe. It certainly isn't a power trip of demands and threats to make the person too scared to step outside her room, which Jenna has been unless I've been with her. All I've done, at the request of the police, is to be her security guard. Nothing more.'

'You took her out on a fancy date.'

'I took her out for a pleasant meal as a thank you for the care she took of my son when his after school care arrangements fell through. I heard her say you never actually asked her to go on a date, so how could she agree? As far as I can figure out an unattached woman is the only person to decide with whom and when she socialises and goes on dates.'

'She's mine!' Ryan turned around, racquet high and stormed towards Jenna who squealed and backed away, her hands over her head.

The door opened. A man barged in and grabbed Ryan from behind in a headlock. Ryan screamed, bucked and kicked. The officer used one foot to sweep Ryan's legs from under him. Both thumped to the floor with Ryan underneath. His arms were tugged down and around and handcuffs slammed on before he could catch his breath.

The other officer joined them. Between them, both officers dragged Ryan to his feet and shoved him through the doorway.

Jenna folded like a concertina suddenly devoid of air - down the wall to the floor.

Luke bolted down the steps, three at a time - yanked the door open. Jenna was leant up against the back wall of the court, her head on her forearms, which rested on bent knees. Spasms rolled along every part of her body.

'Jenna, it's okay, he's gone. The police arrested him.' Unsure of her reaction, he eased against her, aped her pose. Game to rest one hand on her knee, he waited for her reaction.

When she shuddered at his touch he removed his hand.

'It's over now. He's gone and won't hurt you again.' An idea came. 'Josh?'

'Daddy?'

'Can you come down here? Bring the bottle of water with you.' Footsteps pounded down the steps. Josh crept in with eyes wide and a worried frown.

'Daddy?' He tiptoed across the floor.

'You know how big cuddles make your tummy better when you're scared.'

Joshua nodded.

'One of your super cuddles might help Jenna feel better because she is really scared right now.' Luke nodded and pointed towards Jenna. 'Go on.' His heart flip-flopped at the way Josh shuffled on his knees towards Jenna, leant over her huddled form and wrapped his arms around her shoulders. The sweet kiss on the only exposed part off her cheek, brought moisture to Luke's eyes. When Jenna's arm came out and tugged Josh close, Luke lost the ability to breathe.

They didn't move for a for a good minute until Jenna raised her head and caught his eye. 'Sneaky, Lucas Hunter.'

He grinned. 'As long as it worked.' He humped closer, handed her the open bottle. 'Have a sip. Wish it was stronger. Do you still want to play squash?'

'Huh, no. I… I can't… no.'

'Nor do I. At a guess, I'd say shock has set in. Let's go home where it is quiet.' He helped her up and caught her when she swayed. 'Easy. Josh, hold her other hand.'

'Okay.'

Jenna kept her head down while those few still there, ogled, but they stepped aside to let them through. She didn't say a word until Luke reached the roadway.

'Can you take me back to the hotel?'

'Uh, are you sure?'

'I need to be alone – to process – to think – to… please.'

'I'm not sure you should be alone. You're in shock.'

She lifted her head, stared at him. The blank eyes scared him.

'I need to be alone.'

He paused, sighed. 'Okay.'

Able to collect the keys to her new home a couple of days earlier than planned, Jenna spent the time after school on Thursday, moving most of her belongings out of the hotel, only keeping her toilet bag and a change of clothes with her. The number of smallish boxes was a shock. How was it possible to accumulate so much in mere weeks? Although they all fitted into her car.

Luxurious as the hotel room was, she was overjoyed to leave when she checked out after breakfast on Saturday morning. It took only three minutes to drive to the new house where she gazed at the front, still unable to believe this was hers for the next month at least. The house was as close to the school as her previous one but in the opposite direction. Inside there was the lingering scent of cleaning fluids to indicate it had been under the ministrations of a vacate clean. She had the doors and windows open to let in fresh air when Luke pulled up, a trailer laden with boxes of her gear. Joshua was out of the car, prancing around within seconds.

It didn't take long for the trailer to be emptied and Jenna was left with a pile of boxes to unpack while Luke and Joshua returned home to load up again.

First task was to make the bed in the master bedroom. Even though the hotel bed had been comfortable she was keen to spend her first night in what was to be her own bed for the interim. While they were gone, she walked the few houses to the local store to purchase enough provisions for their lunch. Having a general grocery store so close to home was a welcome bonus. By the time Luke and Joshua arrived back there was a generous pile of sandwiches waiting to be consumed. All three sat on the edge of the back veranda in the glorious sunshine, demolishing the pile before attempting to unpack the last load.

By mid-afternoon there was a neat pile of boxes stacked in the third bedroom, many of which wouldn't be unpacked in case the stay was short-lived. They were enjoying a much-needed cup of coffee when Luke asked if she had enough energy to go out that night. 'I have the baby sitter booked, so how about we take in an early movie with supper afterwards. We can have an early night. But if you are too tired, don't be afraid to say so.'

With a shiver of anticipation she smiled. 'Thank you, but no. I'm tired.' She wasn't but after so much anguish during the week she'd decided the heartache was too much. A shiver beset her at the memory, one she'd tried in vain to shove into the dark recesses of her mind since the incident at the courts. Hours she'd filled with activity to keep the memories at bay.

'What's wrong, Jenna?'

'What do you mean?'

'I've rung each day, more than once. My calls have gone to your answering machine but you haven't called back except for the one about today.'

'I've been busy.' It was a lame excuse in one sense but the truth in another. She'd been busy sorting out her thoughts, wondering why the torture Ryan had put her through paled into insignificance compared to the torture of knowing Luke had only spent time with her to act as a personal security guard at the behest of the police. His words at the squash courts had replayed over and over. It had taken many sleepless hours at night to figure out why it hurt so much. She'd lost her heart to the wrong man – again. One who didn't, or couldn't, return the level of love she needed. So who was the idiot? Hadn't he told her guilt hit whenever he kissed her? Hadn't he indicated all he wanted was friendship? Did she listen? Oh, she heard but didn't take note.

'I miss you. So does Josh.'

'Hardly. I've seen Josh every day at school.' She ruffled Josh's hair.

'You know what I mean.'

Embarrassed, she stood, collected the mugs and Josh's glass and took them inside, desperate to escape.

Luke followed; minus Josh. Jenna busied herself at the sink, spied Josh exploring the back yard. Damn, she could do with his presence. This was going to get awkward.

'Jenna?'

She scrubbed a mug. 'Yes.'

'What's going on?'

'Nothing.'

'Why have you gone *incommunicado?*'

'I haven't.'

Luke scoffed. 'Then why no call backs?'

'I've been busy.'

'Doing what?'

'School work mostly. After school I went on long walks to enjoy the freedom without the fear of being attacked. I spent Thursday and Friday after school moving odds and ends here. I've relished a meal in a café without looking over my shoulder. I went to work early to prepare each day and have been writing end of year reports at night. It takes at least thirty minutes to write each one. More for the strugglers. Satisfied?' She plonked the mug on the sink, grabbed the other one, scrubbed, rinsed and plonked. Her hand was grasped.

'No, I'm not satisfied. Granted, you deserve the freedom to do all of those but you didn't answer my question. Why no call backs?' He turned her around, lifted her chin.

'I needed time alone to come to grips with everything. Pictures flash in my mind – scary pictures. And now I need time to unpack boxes, sort through my things and find homes for them.'

'I can stay to help.'

'First I'm going to catch a few hours of shuteye. I'm exhausted and not just physically.'

Luke's shoulders rose on a sigh. 'Okay. Are you up for a squash game tomorrow?'

'Not tomorrow. I'm working on a concert item for the kids. We start rehearsals on Monday. At the moment we'll be rehearsing one line.'

'The concert isn't for weeks.'

'You have no idea how long it takes to get it right. Especially with the younger children. And there are costumes to figure out, actions, music. It takes an entire term and we are already half-way through.'

'Okay, but I have to wonder why I think there is another reason for this non-contact. I'll get Josh.' He turned away, went to the back door and called Josh.

Although she regretted the lame excuses, she knew it was right to take a step back. She followed them to the front door, hugged Joshua. Her ready smile for the boy changed to more of a forced one for Luke. 'I appreciate the help you gave me today. Thank you. When I get settled I would like to cook you both a thank you dinner.'

'Yay,' Joshua yelled while Luke nodded. 'Sounds good.'

With a stab of pain in the region of her heart, she waved until the car and trailer were out of sight.

At school Jenna forced a positive attitude. No longer did she withdraw in isolation during the breaks but joined in and often instigated conversation. It was forced because she was desperate to bring normalcy to her life. During a chat with Emily, who said she'd been horrified about her brother's obsessive behaviour, Jenna discovered Ryan had been admitted to a psychiatric hospital for assessment and treatment, which meant any court proceedings were to be put on hold until a report had been finalised. After all the anguish Ryan had put her through, she couldn't help but be sorry for the man who had virtually wrecked his life through obsessive behaviour. Not only his life. It surprised her how often pictures of his antics centred in her mind and set up internal anguish. Now she looked back at his behaviour over the past months and could see it for what it was. Obsession. Too bad she hadn't realised sooner. A decent sleep at night had become a non-event.

Rehearsals for the concert started. She selected an amusing action song all her students could participate in one way or another and put her own stamp on it by adding percussion sounds, little jingles and twisting words with cute innuendos. Percussion instruments banged and dinged in a cacophony of pure noise until the children learned how to harmonise. Each afternoon peals of laughter emanated from her room while the children practised. She prayed by the time the concert came around the class would be so sick of practising they wouldn't fall about laughing when they came to certain parts. But they were only six, and their parents would think them cute no matter how they performed - well it's what she hoped.

Luke rang most nights. To pretend everything was hunky-dory, she took his calls, kept the conversation casual and was too busy to catch-up whenever he asked. Even too busy to play squash. She didn't tell him the courts gave her the heebie-jeebies or how the pleasure had gone out of the game, or how it hurt to be with him when she wanted more than he could give her. Instead she took up a regular jog to maintain a decent level of fitness, although she hated running. At the moment it was more of a fast walk most of the way. Each day she jogged a few extra metres. By the end of next year, she might be able to actually run a few kilometres.

It was her pupils who eased the constant nervous tension. She couldn't deny her love for each child, especially Josh, which made her aware she had to make sure he didn't receive preferential treatment. In fact, it probably went too far the other way. Like today, so far she had given one-on-one attention to each child while they wrote their diary and had ignored Josh. A quick glance at him had her alarmed.

He was scoring thick black lines through his words. Stunned, she moved behind him.

'What are you doing?'

Josh jerked his head up and slammed his hands over the page. 'Uh, nothing.'

She lifted his hands. 'It doesn't look like nothing to me.' When she tried to make out what was under the scrawl it was a shock to see he'd scrubbed over a prior entry. *The bestest secret ever.* She knelt next to him. 'Care to tell me what this is about?'

'Uh, no.' He sniffed. A tear dropped.

Her heart melted. 'Hey, what's wrong?' She draped an arm around his shoulder and gave a hug.

'You don't like Daddy 'n me anymore,' cracked out before more tears fell.

'Sweetie, that's not true. You are an amazing young man. And so is your dad. Why do you think that?'

'You never come any more.' He dropped his head on the desk and sobbed.

She whooped a tissue from the box between the desks. 'I want to. Do you think we could talk about this while we eat our playlunch? Where it's just you and me. How about you go and clean your face, work hard until playtime and I promise I'll explain. Okay?'

He scrubbed his face, sniffed and blew his nose. 'Okay.'

She stood. 'You have permission to go to the toilets so you can wash your face.' She pulled his chair out as he stood. It was obvious he was embarrassed by the way he ran with his head down. Her heart leapt into her throat where it got jammed until she swallowed and slammed on a smile for the other children.

Joshua rubbed water over his face, filled cupped hands and slurped a long drink. With a paper towel, he wiped his face dry. Still too upset to go back to class, he decided to pee. Another wash of his hands, another splash on his face, he scrubbed the water away with a second paper towel. He didn't want to go back. The kids knew he'd been a cry-baby. But if he didn't return he'd be in trouble. To waste time he dawdled, looked at everything across the bitumen, counted the bags on the hooks until he reached his classroom. He huffed, grabbed the handle and ever so carefully, so as to not make a noise, opened the door. The kids were on the floor huddled around Jenna who had a big book on the wooden stand. Sophie was reading the page aloud. He snuck up behind the others and slowly sank down, crossed his legs and gripped fingers together in his lap. Everything inside tingled when Jenna smiled at him. Boy was he glad none of the other kids turned around to stare.

Sophie sat. Jenna turned the page. 'Who would like to read this page?'

Lots of hands shot up but Josh stared at the floor. If he said nothing the others wouldn't look at him. He was glad when Jenna wrote the new words on the board and explained what they meant because it gave him more time to hide. When she sounded the words out all the kids copied. He didn't.

After reading they did maths. There were sheets to fill in. Easy take away sums. He made sure the numbers were the neatest ever and checked the answers two times, using his fingers to take away in case he got one wrong. Daddy said it was why we were given ten fingers – so we could use them to do maths. And if we ran out of fingers we had ten more toes to use. Money worked in tens. Ten cents times ten made a hundred cents which was a dollar. Daddy showed him how to count money. He passed his sheet along to the end of the row. The kid on the end took the piles to Jenna's desk at the same time the siren went. Phew.

'Josh, go and get your playlunch,' said Jenna when all the kids stood, pushed in their chairs and filed out in a neat line. They weren't allowed to run or push. If they did they had to go to the end of the line to be last one out.

By the time he opened his school bag and took out the banana, Jenna stood next to him.

'Let's sit on the bench here to enjoy the fresh air.'

'Okay.' He sat, tugged the thick, black end of the banana until it snapped and he peeled a strip downwards.

Jenna sat next to him. 'You're lucky to have a nice banana. I've got grapes. Would you like one?' She held out a bunch of huge black grapes.

'I don't like the pips.'

'This variety is seedless. Go on, try one.'

He picked one off, bit off a tiny piece and chewed. It was juicy and sweet.

'Do you like it?'

'Yes, thank you.' He tugged the other pieces of peel down until they hung from the end.

'We can share if you like. There are too many for me. Now, let me explain what we were talking about in class. I heard your dad mention the scary feeling you get in your tummy when you are frightened. Did you get a scary tummy when you saw what happened at the squash courts? Were you scared?'

'Yes. Ryan was going to hurt you.'

'I was scared. Adults get as scared as kids but we learn to not show how scared we are. Like your dad when he couldn't find you. You remember?' Jenna held out the grapes.

'Yes.' He tugged a grape from the bunch but two fell off so he shoved one in his mouth and held the other.

'He was scared because he loves you to bits and was terrified something bad had happened to you. You occasionally have bad dreams that scare you, don't you?'

'Yes.' He ate the other grape and took a bite of the banana. They tasted nice together. He could ask for grapes as his fruit. Daddy makes him mooshed up egg sandwiches one day a week now.

'My dreams haven't been so good after what happened at the squash courts. They scare me so much I'm too afraid to go back to sleep. I haven't got a nice daddy like you to give me cuddles to make the bad dreams go away.'

'I'll give you a cuddle.' He gave a tiny smile.

Jenna patted his hand. 'I know you would. Like you gave me the bestest ever cuddle after Ryan was taken away.'

He grinned. 'You said bestest when it isn't a real word.'

Jenna laughed. 'It isn't a real word but it sounds good. Maybe it should be a real word. You could give me cuddles but you don't live with me and aren't there when I wake up scared. I haven't been back to the squash courts because it's a place where I get the scary feeling in my tummy when I think about it.'

'Like your house because of the bad man who broke the window?'

'Exactly.'

'Was it the same man?'

'No, it wasn't Ryan.'

'I don't like Ryan.'

'Nor do I, but I feel sorry for him.'

'Why? He was mean. Daddy said you should walk away when people are mean to you.' He bit off another piece of banana and chewed.

'I would have if I could have got out but Ryan was too close to the door and I knew other people were there to help me. You know how you get sick when a part of your body doesn't work properly. Like when your tummy gets sick and you throw up. Or a cold when your nose gets all runny and stuffy.'

'I've had a bad cold.'

'Well, Ryan's brain wasn't working so well. He's in hospital now where the doctors are giving him tests and treatment to get his brain better.'

'Okay. Daddy said we can't make you like us.'

'Oh, Josh, I love you to bits. You are an amazing young man.'

'But you don't like Daddy.'

'Yes I do.'

'Why won't you visit him anymore?'

'It's taken me a while to stop being so scared. And your dad only spent time with me to keep me safe from Ryan because we didn't know who was making threats against me. He was a fabulous guard and he is a fantastic dad to you. He's a busy man who has to work during the day after which he has to carry out chores like wash the clothes, and cook, and shop, clean the house at night. He only has the nights and weekends to spend time with you. I took up too much of his time.'

'But he wants to see you and so do I.'

'Remember when you moved all the boxes into my new house?'

'Yes.'

'I promised I would cook you a meal when I settled in. I was going to invite you and your dad this Saturday. Would you like to come?'

'Yes.'

'How about I write a proper invitation and you take it home this afternoon to give to your dad? You can bring the answer back tomorrow.'

'Super. Can I give you a hug now so your scary tummy goes away?'

'Oh, Josh, I would love a hug.'

He stood, wrapped his arms around Jenna and squeezed tight.

'Thank you. I'm heaps better. Now you've got enough time to go to the toilet and play for about five minutes. Thank you for talking to me.'

'I love you, Jenna.' He skipped away, tossed the peel in the bin and leapt off the veranda.

When the kids walked back into the classroom after playtime, Jenna gave him an envelope. Mr Hunter was written on the front. When he was supposed to take his phonics pad out of the desk he snuck a peek in the envelope. *Luke and Joshua Hunter are cor… di… ally invited to dinner at the home of Jenna Reynolds. Saturday night at 6 p.m.*

R.S.V.P via Joshua. He didn't know what R.S.V.P meant, nor the long word but would ask Daddy.

'Joshua, the class is waiting for you.'

Oops. He grabbed his pad, shut the desk and sat up straight with his arms folded. He couldn't mess it up now.

The rest of the day took F-O-R-E-V-E-R before he spotted Daddy's car at the end of the babysitter's drive. 'Daddy's here.' He grabbed his bag and ran to the door. 'Thank you for looking after me,' he called over his shoulder. The door slammed. 'Oops.' He remembered to not run down the drive until the engine stopped. The moment it did he bolted, yanked the back door open and scrambled up onto the booster seat, snapped the safety belt into place and rummaged in his bag.

'You're wrong, Daddy.'

'Wrong about what and what happened to hello?'

'Sorry. Hello. About Jenna. She loves me. Here.' He thrust the envelope over Daddy's shoulder. 'And she does like you. She's been too scared to visit us.'

'Excuse me? What is she scared about? And how do you know?'

'We had a talk 'n she gets a scary tummy like I do. The squash courts scare her and you only spent so much time with her because you were guarding her and we are having dinner with her on Saturday.'

Joshua didn't like the way Daddy made such a long groan before he shook his head and, at last, started the engine.

'Aren't you going to read the invitation?'

'As soon as we get home.'

All Luke could do was drive although it was impossible to concentrate. He didn't want to know how such a conversation came about but he bet his son was the instigator. What had he said? Dear, God. And what was Jenna still scared about? Surely Rob hadn't turned up again. She never mentioned him during their phone conversations: civil, polite conversations. Never anything personal. She'd hidden her concerns from him again, said she was fine. Such an inane word which usually meant the opposite when a person said it.

As soon as they arrived home he sent Joshua ahead to open the door while he scanned the note. Such a formal invitation. What was wrong with a plain old phone call amongst friends? There was something not right about it. On a sigh, he eased from the car. A call to sort out what was going on wouldn't happen until the evening chores were done. Joshua needed a decent meal, a bath and the usual hour spent together: an important hour he did his best to never miss.

After changing from business suit to jeans and a polo shirt, he went to the kitchen. Josh had unpacked his bag without a reminder. A miracle. 'Read your pages while I get dinner ready.'

'Okay.' When Josh opened the current reader and sat at the bench, Luke raised his eyebrows. Another miracle. No arguments, no hassle, no urging.

With leftover meat from last night, Luke took out salad ingredients to add to the plates.

'Can we get grapes for playlunch?' Josh asked mid-sentence.

'Since when did you like grapes?'

'Jenna gave me some. Purple with no pips.'

Luke rolled his eyes. 'We'll buy a small bunch. Test them out to make sure you like them.'

'You'll like them too.'

'I do, but you never ate any so it was a waste to buy them.' He pointed the knife towards the book. 'Keep reading.'

'What does R.S.V.P mean?'

'You read a note addressed to me?'

'Sorry.'

'*Repondez s'il vous plait.* It's French for please answer the invitation.'

'Okay. Jenna said I was to give her the answer tomorrow. What's cor… er… cor-di… it's a long word. What does it mean?'

'Cordially. It means friendly. It's a friendly invitation.'

'Told you she likes you.'

'Read.'

After a faultless two pages, Josh shut the book and shoved it back in the bag.

'Any other homework?'

'No.'

'Anything happen at school you want to talk about?'

Joshua shrugged. 'No.'

'Thought you said you had a talk with Jenna.' Luke so wanted to know what went on. 'You want to tell me about it?'

'The squash courts give her a scary tummy. Bad dreams wake her up like they do me but she hasn't got a daddy to give her cuddles to make the dreams go away. She loves me and likes you and you don't have time because you have to do the housework and cook and clean and wash and… I forget.'

Now Luke was sorry he asked. What had Joshua said to start such a conversation? He wasn't sure he wanted to know.

'Go wash your hands. Dinner is ready.'

Dinner, bath and together time seemed to take twice as long as normal. It was well after eight before Joshua fell asleep and Luke had a chance to sit on the sofa to dial Jenna's number. A call he dreaded in one sense but it could finally give him answers as to why Jenna had been so unavailable over the past few weeks.

There were too many rings before a click. 'Hello, Jenna

Reynolds speaking.'

'I thought we were past the Mr Hunter stage.'

'Luke?'

'It appears it's Mr Hunter to you.'

'If another teacher, parent or student sees the envelope it would look like a normal teacher/parent missive.'

'Fair enough. Sorry. But why such a formal invitation? A friendly phone call would have been easier.'

'Josh was upset.'

'Upset? Why?'

'He had a melt-down in class.'

Alarmed, Luke straightened. 'As in? What happened?'

'I caught him scouring out past entries in his diary. Big, black angry lines.'

'Now, I'm worried. Has he ever done this before?'

'No. There were quite a few tears.'

'He cried? In class?'

'Accused me of not liking either him or you.'

Luke groaned. 'He's been on to me about why we never get together away from school. Blames me. How about enlightening me? Mind you, he did mention how scared you are about the squash courts and a few nightmares yet each time I've asked how you were you never mentioned any of these concerns. Has your ex been back?'

'No.'

'You have stubborn teeth.'

'Excuse me?'

'The old saying – it's like trying to pull teeth, as in getting you to tell me the truth about what's going on. Hang on, I've just recalled something else Josh gabbled to me. So many words came out of his mouth in two seconds flat it was hard to catch them all. How I only spent time with you to guard you. What did he mean?' He grinned at Jenna's whispered epithets.

'Josh has a big mouth.'

'You only now learning this?'

'And he's too smart for his age.'

Luke laughed. 'Right at this moment I'm glad he's so smart. Talk to me. Let's start with - what did he scrub out?'

'He scrubbed out an old entry about his bestest ever secret.'

'He wrote that in his diary? Dear, God. He didn't happen to mention what the secret was, did he?'

'No.'

'Thank goodness for small mercies.'

'What was it?'

'Not going there.'

'It can't matter if he was so determined to scrub it out.'

'It matters. He's angry with me, not you. I'll deal with it.' Although he had no idea how unless Jenna softened her current stance on staying away. 'Now tell me about the bad dreams.'

'Recurrence of what happened at the courts and pictures of what happened before.'

'I understand. What I don't understand is why you never mentioned this to me.'

'My problem. I'm dealing with it. You've done enough for me.'

'Which leads me to the next issue. Please explain what you meant about only spending time to guard you.' He smiled at Jenna's groan.

'You made it clear to Ryan you only spent time with me, at the police request, to protect me from him. You only took me out to dinner to say thank you. I figured…'

'You figured wrong. I thought you would be smart enough to realise I was doing my best to placate the idiot. I glassed over the reasons for us being together to calm him down. Kept his attention focussed on me rather than you. At the time he was in such a state he had no control over his emotions so how do you think he would have reacted if I mentioned how much I like you, how much I enjoy your company, how amazing it was to spend time with you over a nice meal, how you went on a date with me. I didn't dare use the word date. Or how much pleasure you gave me when we spent the lunchtimes and evenings together. He was already so manic you wouldn't have stood a chance of escaping without being harmed.'

'Oh, I thought… thank you.'

'My pleasure and you thought wrong. How about we discuss this further Saturday night. Josh and I would love to dine with you although my nose will probably get put out of joint with my six-year-old son ensuring he is the centre of attention.'

'He's going to be a lady-killer.'

'I think he already is. I might have to ask him for advice. Sweet dreams. We'll be there Saturday at six.'

'S low down or you'll crush those flowers.' Luke grasped his son's shoulder to stop him belting along the path to Jenna's door.

'Sorry, Dad.'

'You took so long choosing the perfect bunch, you don't want them to end up all ragged and falling apart. Here, give me your hand.' He gripped the small fingers tight to maintain at least a smidgen of control over his hyper son.

'You chose them too. They're from both of us.'

'Another reason to take more care. I want the pink roses to look like roses when we give them to Jenna.'

'The yellow daisies are the best.'

'What makes you think that?'

'They are a happy colour because Jenna has been sad.'

Unable to answer, Luke was pleased they'd reached the door. He knocked.

'Coming,' came from inside.

When Joshua bounced, Luke gripped his hand tighter. The day had been horrendous with Joshua so hyped up about visiting Jenna, Luke had wanted to ring his mother to come and save him. A mere thirty minutes of relative calm would have been welcome.

The door opened. Joshua wriggled his hand free and leapt upwards. The flowers got crushed between the two bodies.

'Hello, young man,' Jenna managed to get out between a laugh and a grimace aimed at Luke.

'Flowers, Son.'

'Oops.' Joshua slithered down and held out a bunch of sad blooms in crushed cellophane. 'Sorry.'

'Are these for me?' Jenna's lips quivered. 'Thank you. They are beautiful.'

Luke quirked up one eyebrow. 'They were about ten seconds ago.'

'Sorry.' Joshua dared to look chastened.

'Come on in.'

The chastened face changed to delight in the split second before Josh charged inside leaving Jenna at the door and Luke still on the doorstep.

'Someone's excited,' said Jenna.

'You have no idea. It started before six this morning. He hasn't taken a breath the entire day. Driven me insane. Now we have a few seconds of peace you can tell me what's wrong.'

'What do you mean?'

He tapped under both of her eyes. 'Traces of tears aren't hidden well enough.'

'Oh.' She dropped her head. 'I went to my house today to harvest as many vegetables as I could. There was a letter in the mailbox.'

'Obviously not of the good kind.' Luke put his hands on her shoulders, turned her to face him when she turned away.

'No. It was from Rob's lawyers. Rob wants to talk to me. It brought back ghastly memories.' Jenna's voice faded so much Luke had trouble making out her words.

'Let's get inside or the tornado will be back. We'll talk about it later. I hope he crash lands soon. He should because the amount of energy he's expended today would get a spaceship into space. Make that outer space: way, way out beyond the galaxy.' At least he managed to get Jenna to crack a smile.

The tornado was fingering items on the already set table. 'I want to sit next to Jenna.'

Jenna ran her hand through Josh's hair. 'You can for I will sit on the end where I can get to the kitchen easy. Your dad will sit opposite you.'

Josh thought for a second, eyed the table and shrugged. 'Okay.'

'How about a drink? There's fruit juice or a traffic light for little boys and wine for big boys, either with or without alcohol.'

'What's a traffic light?'

'Like a traffic light it has three colours – one on top of the other.'

'No way?'

'It's my secret magic recipe. Would you like to try it?'

'Sure do.'

'You'd better sit at the table and be ever so quiet while I create magic in the kitchen. No peeking.'

'Why not?'

'It's a secret. And I need to put these flowers in water. They need a drink.' Jenna turned away but turned back when Luke went to follow. 'Big boys aren't allowed to know my secret either. You have to sit and be quiet as well.' She sent him a smirk.

When he sat he could still see what she was up to while Joshua couldn't. 'Bet she can't make three different colours sit on top of each other. They would all mix together.'

'Even if it's magic?' Joshua leant sideways and skewed his head around towards the kitchen.

'I see a head. Someone doesn't want a traffic light. White, red or bubbly, big boy?'

Joshua straightened with a cheeky grin. Luke had to stifle his laughter before he could answer. 'Red. Non-al since I'm driving.'

Water gushed. 'Who knew I love yellow daisies?'

'Me.' Joshua's grinned widened.

'They are beautiful and the pink roses have a gorgeous scent. Thank you.'

The fridge door whooshed open. Shelves rattled. The door closed. Ice tinkled into a glass followed by relative silence.

'One traffic light coming up.' Jenna settled a large tumbler with a straw in front of Joshua whose eyes boggled. 'And a red for the big boy.'

'How did you do that?' Joshua ran a finger up and down the glass.

'Magic. Be careful when you drink it. Don't swish the straw around. Let it rest on the bottom and sip slowly so you can make out each flavour as it goes down. Let me get my glass.' She was back in a second but only sat only long enough to take a sip of her own wine. 'Dinner is ready. Give me five minutes.'

'I'll help.' Luke stood and followed to see Jenna take three alfoil covered dishes from the oven. The alfoil was removed to reveal a variety of roast vegetables in one, cauliflower, broccoli, corn and beans in the second and sliced meat in the third. A sauce boat fill to the brim with gravy sat on the edge of the stove top. Two oven mitts appeared before his eyes.

'I thought we'd serve ourselves at the table. You know how much Josh can eat.' She lifted the gravy and meat while he carried the other two huge dishes.

'I had to use my magic spells to tell me your favourite food,' she said when she placed the roast lamb slices on the table in front of Josh.

'Roast lamb? Yum. Bet you told her, Dad.'

'No. Cross my heart.' Luke settled the other dishes on the waiting place mats. He might have mentioned it but couldn't recall.

'Wow, the potatoes are all chopped up.'

'Diced into cubes to make square chips. They roast quicker. Vegetables from my garden. I picked them all today. Let's eat before it gets cold.'

'Smells delicious.' Luke scooped a small pile of diced root vegetables onto Josh's plate, doubtful he would try any other than potato. He added two baby carrots, a piece of corn cob and two florets of broccoli and cauliflower. 'You want any gravy?'

'Yes.'

'Yes, what?'

'Please, Daddy.'

'Boys who can't remember their manners miss out on sweets, which would be a pity because it is so cute.' Jenna picked up the tongs and placed a slice of meat with crisp skin on Joshua's plate. 'How many slices would you like?'

'One… uh, please. What's for sweets?'

'Secret. You only find out after you've eaten all your vegies.'

It was hard for Luke to keep a straight face when Josh hoed into his meal. Not once did he question what each cube was, but forked each piece into his mouth, barely chewed and swallowed. The yellow sweet potato which, until now, he hated, went in and down without a comment. Josh always had a healthy appetite but tonight he gave the impression he hadn't eaten for a week. Thank goodness it took longer for him to chew each mouthful of meat, giving the adults time to eat at a more leisurely rate.

Food finished; Jenna stood to clear the table but left Joshua's empty plate in front of him. He sent Luke a puzzled frown.

'How do you leave your knife and fork to show you have finished eating?' Luke whispered.

'Oops.' There was a mad scramble to straighten the cutlery after which, Josh sat back in the chair and folded his arms as he would in school.

Jenna grinned from the kitchen, returned to the table and stood behind Joshua. 'Oh, you have finished eating. Looks like we can all have a swan for sweets.'

'A swan? We gonna eat a swan?' Josh screwed his face.

Still behind Josh, Jenna grinned at Luke. 'A white swan. Who wants a swan?'

Luke shot his hand up. 'Yes, please.'

Josh turned to Jenna. 'Can I see what it looks like?'

'Sure.' She returned to the kitchen, opened the freezer, lifted out a plate and settled it in front of Luke. The swan's body was a long scoop of vanilla ice-cream while the wings, neck and head had been formed from baked meringue. It swam in a freshly poured pink pool of coulis.

'Oh, wow,' said Josh, his eyes wide.

'Would you like one?' asked Jenna.

'Yes, please.'

Jenna returned with two more. 'It might need a minute to thaw a bit.'

Josh didn't wait but snapped off the top of a wing and popped it in his mouth. 'Yum. Did you make these?' he asked Jenna.

'Yes.'

'How?'

'With meringue and a piping bag. Baked them in the oven. One day I might show you. I have a few extra wings and necks you could take home so you can build your own swans. If you have ice-cream at home.'

'Can we, Daddy?'

Luke laughed. 'Sure. I think there's still ice-cream left in the freezer.'

It didn't take long for Josh's swan to vanish, followed by an enormous yawn. About time, thought Luke as he stood. 'Is there a place I can put Josh to bed?'

'Second door on the left along the passage. There's a single bed already made up. Bathroom is the next door along.'

It took less than ten minutes for Josh to go to the toilet, wash his hands and face and close his eyes. After turning off the light, Luke returned to the dining room to find the table cleared.

'In here.'

He turned towards the voice to find Jenna curled in a lounge chair with a mug of coffee in her lap. A second mug sat on a low table in front of the other lounge chair. So, no sofa. He sat. 'You went to a lot of trouble to make a little boy happy. I appreciate it. Thank you.'

'It was a pleasure. It gave me positive activities to concentrate on.' She flipped an envelope across the table. 'You can read it. Tell me what you think.'

After scanning the typed words Luke studied them again. Rob wanted to talk to her and since she had a restraining order against him, would she agree to meet with him in the lawyer's office? She could have anyone she liked to be present. It also detailed the charges laid against him and date of his court hearing. He glanced at Jenna. 'Aggravated assault causing injury, attempted rape, breaking and entering. Nasty.'

'But true. The police had informed me. I didn't know the date of the hearing. It's the first bit I'm concerned about. Why?'

'I can't give you an answer. How do you think meeting him will affect you? You don't have to, you know? It's only a request.'

'My initial reaction? I want nothing to do with him. The thought of being in the same room sends waves of shivers through my innards.'

'It could be a way to finalise things between you. My guess is, he probably wants to apologise for his attack. The fact he's doing it through a lawyer and inviting you to have whoever you want present indicates he's going through the right channels. You do have unfinished business with him, you know.'

'He wanted nothing to do with me.'

'He has a right to know about your daughter, despite abrogating any responsibility. He was still her biological father.'

'I know.' On a long sigh Jenna hunched back in the cushions, drawing her knees up to her chin and the coffee to her mouth, which she sniffed and sipped.

'It won't be easy but it's not such a bad idea. You still have to give evidence when he goes to court and this may make it easier for you.'

'Would you come with me if I agreed? Would you be able to get a few hours off? I don't think I can handle facing him by myself, not after… The mere thought gives me the creeps. I'd like to get it finished before Christmas.' Jenna settled back further, one arm wrapping tight around her bent legs while the other balanced the coffee on her knees.

'I can arrange my clients around any date if you're sure it's what you want. Set a day, let me know and I'll make sure I have no client interviews. Do you want a legal representative there as well? You are entitled to one.'

'I don't have a lawyer and it would be expensive. For what? A chat? I'll insist on his lawyer being present and if things get out of hand I'll walk out.' A long groan rumbled out. 'The thought scares me.'

Jenna sounded sad. Tough as it was going to be, Luke was certain it needed to be done to bring closure to her past. But right now she needed friendship and company. 'There are a couple of other things I wanted to clear up.'

Jenna frowned but said nothing.

'Why the cold shoulder over the past few weeks?'

'I thought we already discussed this and there was no cold shoulder.'

Luke snorted. 'What do you call it?'

'Time to come to grips with all that happened: to process…'

'You never told me you were too scared to go to the squash courts.'

'I'm not scared to go.'

'Then what?'

'It's… my mind, I guess. What happened plays on my mind.'

'You could have PTSD.'

'I wouldn't go so far as to say I suffer from PTSD.'

'You underwent a traumatic situation after weeks of stress about the unknown. Even though Ryan was arrested you still replay it in your mind. Sounds like a form of PTSD to me.'

'Maybe.'

'There are the bad dreams, if what you said to Josh is true.'

'Big mouth.'

Luke laughed. 'He's never afraid to say it how it is. Are you still waking from bad dreams?'

'It's not so bad now I know he's locked away. But that is also a problem.'

'What problem?'

'I think Emily blames me.'

'Emily? What do you mean?'

'She's only spoken to me once since the incident at the courts. In the past she came to my room for a catch up each morning. I go into the staffroom now and there is instant silence. They all stare at me as though I've committed a gross sin. It's so uncomfortable I only stay long enough to make a hot drink. The talking starts again as soon as I leave.'

'Have you tried speaking to Emily?'

'There's no point. She knows I did nothing wrong, knows I never wanted a relationship with Ryan.'

'What about the other teachers? Speak to one you trust. Ask the question. What about Erin and Lily?'

She shrugged. 'They turn away from me.'

'Do you want me to ask?'

Jenna straightened, swung her legs over the edge and plonked the coffee on the table. 'No way. My problem. I'll deal with it. I needed time to get my head together.'

'Okay but how do I stand with you?'

'What do you mean?'

'I miss the time we spent together.'

'We're together now and I took up too much of your time. Sure, most of it was in the holidays when Josh wasn't here but he needs every spare minute you have.'

'Josh misses you, too, which is why he had a meltdown.'

'He spends seven hours a day with me.'

Luke shook his head. 'Why do I get the sense I'm being given the right royal brush off?'

Jenna stared at him. 'No. God, I'm so confused. I'm not brushing you off. You're about the only friend I have at the moment and I adore Josh. I guess I'm not in such a good place at the moment.'

'How about next weekend? A day out with Josh and me. I'll sound Josh out for ideas.'

Jenna smiled. 'Sounds lovely. Thank you.'

By the end of the week, every time Jenna entered the staffroom to make a hot drink, the tension had been so overwhelming she didn't bother at lunchtime. Instead she walked three blocks to a local deli, purchased a take-away of fresh brew and took her time to wander back. The far better taste and aroma of real coffee instead of the bulk powdered variety, brought a smile to her face by the time she reached the gate. 'Should have thought of this before,' she said to gate after closing it and heading for her classroom where a salad sandwich and a peach waited. For once she had an entire day free of yard duty.

After rounding the corner of her building she stepped onto the veranda and paused at the sight of her boss seated on the bench outside her classroom. When he stood as she neared, her heart beat a tattoo of drums.

'Jenna, could you please come to the office?'

'Now?'

'Yes.'

'The siren will be going in a few minutes.'

'This won't take long. I'll send another teacher to look after your class if needed.' He turned away and strode along the veranda so fast her gut twisted into a tight ball of suspense.

As she followed thoughts were so wild and fast they all got tangled up in her brain. Her hand shook when she pushed the door to the office block open. When the school secretary dropped her head instead of the usual cheery hello, serious trepidation took a firm hold of Jenna's innards.

She knocked on the principal's door.

'Come.'

The single command sent a shiver across her shoulders. She gripped the coffee mug, opened the door and stepped inside. Two men sat on the other side of the desk.

'Mrs Reynolds, please take a seat. This is Mr Doherty, our regional...'

'Superintendent, I know and I'd prefer stand.' She lied for her legs had turned into limp, overcooked spaghetti. She locked her knees into position to keep her upright while sweeping her eyes between the two men in an attempt to figure out what was going on. Two serious faces stared back.

'This is an awkward situation, Mrs Reynolds, one of your making,' the super began while John Mortimer stabbed the end of a biro on a yellow pad.

'Excuse me?'

'We require you to tender your resignation.'

Shocked, Jenna stumbled, found the chair and plonked into it. Coffee spilled over the top of the crushed mug. 'Why?' she squeaked before searching for a bin where she tossed the remainder of the coffee, not caring about how much spilt. 'If my standard of teaching isn't what you require, why haven't you mentioned it?' It was the only reason she could think of.

'You are an excellent teacher,' John said without lifting his head.

'Then why?'

'It's your morals we have an issue with.'

Jenna shot up. 'Excuse me?' Anger caused her to gasp before her lungs could breathe properly.

'It has been brought to our attention you have been having an affair with a parent of one of the children in your class.' The super folded his arms while John kept his head down.

'An affair? As in having sex with a parent?'

'Since you put it so crudely – yes.'

A light bulb flashed on in Jenna's head. Like a slinky where all the rings follow each other, all the incidents of the past couple of weeks fell into place. She sat, leant forwards. 'Am I to know with whom I've been having hot sex?'

The two men glanced at each other with quizzical frowns. 'Mr Hunter, of course.'

'Interesting. And what, exactly, leads you to believe this?'

'You were seen moving your furniture into his house. Your house is on the market,' said John.

'How do you know my house is on the market?'

'I went by to speak with you. Your house is empty.'

'No it's not.' She paused for effect. 'All of my furniture is there. So, whoever told you I moved my furniture into Mr Hunter's house was lying. Yes, my house is on the market but I fail to understand how it is a crime or slip in morality standards for a person to sell the house they own. Or are teachers a unique bunch where it is a crime.'

'No need to be facetious.' John dared to waggle his finger at her.

'There's every need after such ludicrous claims and I can't believe we are having this conversation in the middle of a school day. Surely such matters should be discussed outside school hours. And surely I should have been given prior notice of such a meeting.'

Both men glanced at each other and blushed.

'If I was having an affair with Lucas Hunter, it's not a crime worthy of being sacked since both he and I are single adults of legal age. And why is it any of your business what I do in my private time when I am not at school?'

'It is inappropriate for a teacher to have an affair with one of their parents.'

'Both of my parents are dead.' Jenna had to bite her lip at the startled looks on both their faces. It took several seconds before either man caught on. Idiots. She understood how easy it was for them to be duped into believing gossip made up to discredit her, and she bet she knew who was responsible.

'Enough of your insolence.' John stood and leant over the desk.

Jenna laughed. 'And I find your ludicrous claims to be insolent. Give me a second.' She reached over the desk, took the landline phone out of its stand and dialled Luke's private mobile number. As soon as he answered, she pressed the button to put it on speaker.

'Jenna?'

'Mr Hunter, you are on speaker phone. My principal and superintendent are listening to this conversation. Are you free to talk?'

'Yes, I'm on my lunch break, is there a problem?'

'A major one. I've been sacked from my job.'

'Excuse me? Why?'

'I'll hand you over to these two men to ask questions otherwise I will be accused of priming you up to lie.'

'What? I don't understand.'

'Here.' She handed the phone to John Mortimer. 'Ask away while I return to my classroom to carry out the duties I was employed to do – educate and care for twenty-six young children. I'll have my resignation on your desk after school but I will outline how and why I have been sacked and keep a copy on file for when I take you to court for unfair dismissal.' She stood, went to the door. 'It wasn't a pleasure.'

As she fled she remembered it was early closing for the kids because they had the monthly staff meeting. Just dandy.

It was a relief when the siren sounded at two. It had been a difficult hour trying to maintain a happy teacher attitude while holding back simmering rage. Now she had to face the staff who must all believe Emily's lies. Jenna didn't want to know the extent of the lies but she bet the embellishments weren't held back.

After the hubbub of packing away the children settled in their seats, ready to be dismissed. One-by-one, they ceased their chatter, folded their arms and eyed her. Jenna forced a smile. 'Good afternoon. Have a great weekend.'

'Good afternoon, Mrs Reynolds,' they chanted as they stood and pushed in their chairs.

Jenna opened the door to find both John Mortimer and Luke standing outside, along with a group of parents.

John stepped forward. 'A word please.'

'Wait inside. It's my duty to ensure the kids get off safely.' She stepped aside and shut the door on him after he'd entered.

Luke came forward. 'Are you okay?'

Jenna shrugged. 'Sort of if you count a mixture of fury and disbelief. Why are you here?'

'I cancelled my afternoon appointments and spent the last hour with your boss and his superior. Where I outlined a few home truths.'

'Daddy!' squealed Joshua as he flung himself at Luke's chest.

Luke laughed. 'Hi, Mate. Thought I would pick you up today so we can hang out together.' He turned to Jenna. 'Are we still on for tomorrow?'

'I'll ring you later. Got the staff meeting from hell to face first. What did you tell them?'

'All the details from when and how we met, through all the traumas until today. You never told your boss about any of these incidents.'

'My private life is none of his business. I'm not one to carry on about personal issues in the public arena.'

'No, you are a private person, which I pointed out to these idiots. Emily got hauled in while I was there. I'm not sure if she was chastened or pretended to be. Vindictive nastiness must run in the family.'

'And now I've got to face her in the meeting.'

'No, she was sent home.'

'Thank God.'

'Call me.'

'Will do.' Jenna hauled in a long breath, turned around to check all the children were with an adult and opened the door. John jerked away making it obvious he'd been eavesdropping.

'John?' She wasn't going to make it easy for him.

'I owe you an apology.'

She tilted her head to one side.

'You never mentioned the troubles you'd been having.'

'As long as what happens in my personal life does not affect my work it can't be anybody's business but mine.'

'It would have helped if I'd known about Emily's brother.'

'I doubt it.'

'Pardon?'

'Emily came to you with a pack of lies to discredit me and my reputation and it's obvious she spread those same rumours amongst the entire staff. Not once in the past few weeks did you,' she pointed to his chest, 'have the courtesy to come to me about those accusations to find out if they were true or not but went directly to the super without proof. Now. if you will excuse me, I have a staff meeting to attend. Part of my duties as a teacher.' She picked up her bag and stood by the door, staring at the back of the room. With shoulders shoved back she followed John to the staff room and sat slap bang in the middle, amused at the looks she received while the entire staff sought out seats as far away from her as they could get. Unfortunately for a small group, they had to sit at her table.

As soon as John called the meeting to order she stood. 'Before we begin, I wish to speak to the entire staff.' She held out an envelope and handed it to John. 'You asked for my resignation. Here it is.'

'No. There's no need. We sorted it out.'

'I cannot work in such a toxic environment where the entire staff take for granted the slanderous comments made by one person, whose brother was arrested because of his evil actions towards me. Not one of you came to me to ask if what Emily said was true. None of it is. Not one of you gave me any support or trust. You all shunned me for the past few weeks, treated me as vermin. Today I was humiliated, shocked, disappointed and am furious about the treatment I received. I am not having an affair with Lucas Hunter. I have not shared any man's bed since my marriage ended and I haven't moved into any man's house. Granted, Lucas has become a friend who gave me assistance when I was terrorised by a stalker who broke into my house, tipped all the items I own onto the floor, wrote graffiti on my car and house windows, sent me death threats and stalked me continually. For weeks I was so scared I wouldn't leave the security of a hotel room the police suggested I live in for my safety. The only time I was game to leave was when Lucas accompanied me, at the request of the police, I might add. The stalker was Emily's brother, Ryan. I have no doubt you have been led to believe I treated him badly by never going on a date with him. How could I when he never asked me to go on a date. But none of this is any of your business. My personal life is mine to keep private. It has nothing to do with how I carry out my job as a teacher. I will finish the year to prevent my students from having the turmoil of a new teacher so near the end of the year. During the Christmas break I will seek a position in a school where I am welcome and are treated with honesty, respect and friendship. Now, if you will excuse me, I'm not in the space to sit here for two hours under the scrutiny of each one of you. I'm going home – to the house I have rented until my desecrated by Ryan Johnson, home, has been sold. The rental where I live *all by myself.* I have never been a big drinker of alcohol but I am going to open a bottle of wine and hopefully drink enough to numb my mind.

When tears threatened, she grabbed her bag and ran.

'**S**low down and be gentle with Jenna. She's had a tough day.' Josh ignored his father and banged on Jenna's door. Head down, he waited. When there was no sound from inside he banged again. 'She's not here, Dad.'

'Her car is in the garage. Wait here, I'll go around the back.'

'Jenna?' Josh yelled with another bang on the door. The door opened a tiny bit. He spied one eye.

'What are you doing here?'

'We brung you dinner. Daddy, she's here! Chinese.'

'Brought not brung.'

'Oops, sorry. Honey chicken and noodles and beef and cashews and garlic… er… something and prawn crackers and… I forget. Daddy!'

'I'm here. Hi.' When Daddy stood behind Josh the two big paper bags crinkled against his back. 'Joshua decided you needed company tonight so he suggested we bring you take-away.'

'Joshus did, did he?' The door opened. Jenna looked funny with messy hair and tracky-daks with a huge hole at one knee.

'Well, it was a joint decision. Care to share Chinese with us?'

Jenna smiled. 'Come in.'

Josh followed but slowed when Daddy grabbed his shoulder. 'Take care. I think Jenna might need one of your super-dooper cuddles while I set out the food.'

'Okay.' He followed Jenna into the lounge room where there was an empty glass on its side on the small square table in front of the sofa. A wine bottle was not quite empty. Jenna grabbed them and went to the kitchen.

'Drowning your sorrows,' he heard Daddy say but didn't know what it meant. You drowned in deep water.

'Doing my best.'

Daddy laughed. 'I figured you wouldn't call.'

'But you came instead.'

'When a friend is in need…'

'Well you're about the only friend I have these days.'

Joshua ran to the kitchen. 'I'm your bestest ever friend.' He wrapped his arms around Jenna's waist and hugged tight.

Her arms looped down his back. 'Yes, you are. Thank you.' She squatted in front of him and hugged him tight. 'How about you help your father serve the food while I get cleaned up?'

'Okay.' He let go and watched Jenna walk along the passage. She bumped against the wall. 'She's been crying, Dad. Why is she sad? She was happy at school. Did you make her sad?'

'Not me. I told you Jenna had a tough day.'

'Why?'

'It's not my place to discuss Jenna's private things with you. It's adult talk. We need to be extra nice so she is happy again. So how about we use our best manners and talk about happy things? Here, you put the food on the table while I find plates, forks and spoons.'

Josh carried one container at a time and spread them out along the table. Daddy took off the lids, shoved a spoon in each container and put empty plates on the table with forks next to them. Steam swirled from the food. It all smelt yummy, except for the prawns. He re-arranged the plastic dishes so the prawns weren't near his nose. The tap went. Daddy came in with three full glasses of water held in his big hands and put one in front of each plate.

Jenna came back wearing black slacks with no hole, and a pink T-shirt. Her hair was all neat in a pony tail. He liked how her hair was so white. Nobody in his family had white hair. Well, Nanna had a grey streak but she was old and Poppy's whiskers were grey when he didn't shave them away. It was scary quiet while they sat and scooped food onto their plates. Josh bit his lip when a few noodles slipped from the spoon onto the table. He peeked at Daddy. Oh, oh. Daddy lifted one of his eyebrows.

'Oops, sorry.' Josh scraped up the noodles with his fork and plonked them on his plate. Too scared he might make more mess with the other food he twirled the fork around the noodles but couldn't get them to swirl like Daddy could so he used two fingers to put the end in his mouth and slurped it like a worm into his mouth. Sauce splattered onto his nose. A paper napkin landed on his hand. Daring a peek, he smiled at Jenna and wiped away the sauce. Daddy scooped small mounds of the other dishes onto Joshua's plate. All except the garlic prawns. He didn't like garlic but he sure loved the honey chicken. It was his favourite – and the noodles. Then he remembered he had to make Jenna happy.

'Why wasn't the teddy bear hungry? he asked Jenna.

The food fell off Jenna's fork. 'Are you asking me?'

'Yes.'

'Let me think.' She scooped up her food, put it in her mouth and chewed. 'I don't know.'

'Because he was stuffed.' Josh grinned and Jenna smiled. More jokes might make her happy.

'What type of music doesn't a balloon like?'

'A balloon?'

Josh nodded.

Jenna turned to Daddy. 'Do you know?'

Alarmed, Joshua shook his head at Daddy because he knew all of Josh's jokes.

'I do, but I'm not telling you.'

Josh blew out a long breath.

'You'll have to tell me,' said Jenna when she turned back.

Josh grinned. 'Pop.'

This time Jenna laughed. 'Do you know a lot of jokes?'

'Hundreds,' said Daddy with his fork pointed at Josh, 'Eat first.' He frowned when his phone rang. 'Excuse me.' He took his phone from his shirt pocket, glanced at it and stood. 'I have to go. It's my house alarm.' He swiped at the phone. 'Oh, God, no.'

'What is it?' asked Jenna.

'Are you sober enough to look after Josh for a while?'

'Sure. The bottle wasn't full. I only had two glasses. What's the problem?'

'I'll tell you later.' Daddy took big fast steps to the door. 'I'll ring as soon as I can,' he called after he'd disappeared.

Luke had an itch to speed but didn't dare. After Lisa's accident it was rare for him to go over the limit, especially with Josh. And he couldn't show Jenna the picture on his phone. It would destroy her already eroded self-confidence. On occasion modern technology scared him. Being able to log onto the cameras of his home security system was a good thing – until you didn't want to see what it showed.

He slowed to a crawl at the final corner, eased around to find the street bare of humans, which was a wonder since the security alarm shrieked and a blue light flashed from over the front door of his home. Closer, he noticed a gaping hole in the loungeroom window. He swore, pulled into the drive and turned off the engine. As he eased from the car the flashing blue light highlighted two bricks that had bounced off the front wall and one in front of the large crack on the front door.

After switching off the alarm he turned around and strode towards Stuart's house, glad Emily's car was in the driveway. He knocked, stood back and waited. The door opened.

'Luke, good to see you, mate,' said Stuart.

'Is Emily in?'

'Sure, come on in.' Stuart led the way along the passage and into the kitchen that overlooked the back garden and pool. Emily sat at the central bench with her back to him.

'Why, Emily?' Luke asked trying to keep his anger at bay.

'Why what?' asked Stuart.

'Emily knows.'

She half-turned. 'Knows what?' She couldn't look Luke in the eye.

'Why the bricks?'

'I don't know what you are talking about?'

Luke rounded the bench. 'Does telling so many lies sit well with you? A bad habit of yours.'

'Hey, come on.' Stuart pressed one hand into Luke's shoulder. 'What's with the aggro?'

'Emily hasn't told you?' Luke stepped sideways, took out his phone and brought up the video of Emily hurling bricks at his house. 'I would like to know why there is a dirty great hole in my front window, why there's a huge crack in the front door.'

'Holy sh… Em. What's going on?' Stuart held the phone in front of Emily's eyes. 'Why would you wreck his house?'

Emily stood so fast the stool legs squealed on the tiles. 'It's his fault,' she screeched.

'What is my fault?'

'I got transferred. Not to another school. To another flaming district. Out woop-woop. All because of him.' She pointed one finger at Luke's head.

'What? Why? What's going on?' Stuart pulled out a stool and sat.

'She hasn't told you?' Luke sat next to him.

'Told me what?'

'Thanks to Emily, Jenna lost her job today?'

'Excuse me?' Stuart shook his head. 'I'm confused.'

'I spent an hour this afternoon with John Mortimer and the school superintendent detailing how Jenna is *not* an immoral whore who sleeps around with a different man every week…'

'Jenna? She avoids men; never goes on a date.' Stuart screwed his face in amazement.

'Pity Emily couldn't have told the entire staff at school those details instead of the regaling about Jenna's regular drug taking, and drunkenness every night and…'

'Em?' Stuart turned to her but her head hung too low to catch her eye. 'Why would you? And what is Luke's fault?'

'Because he came here, Ryan has been locked away in a psycho ward. It's all his fault,' Emily spat with a glob of spittle flying from her mouth. 'She wouldn't go out with Ryan, but as soon as Luke turns up she moves in with him.'

'What? Jenna hasn't moved in with Luke. Why would you suggest such a thing.' Stuart stood and stepped back.

'Sure she did when they carried all those boxes inside.'

'Luke only stored her books and things for a week or two while Jenna searched for a new home. And Ryan has been locked away because of his appalling behaviour. Hell, Em, he stalked her, trashed her house, threatened her life.'

'She should have gone out with him!' Emily yelled.

'Why? She hasn't gone out with any man since she moved here. How many times did she say she wasn't interested?'

'She went on a date with Luke.'

'Luke took her out for a meal to say thank you for her looking after Josh. You knew this. And why shouldn't she go? It's about time she got back to socialising.' Stuart paced across the room and back with his head shaking. 'What other porky pies did you tell the staff?'

'Nothing,' Emily whispered with her head hung low.

'Not true. John Mortimer had a list of the numerous sins you claimed Jenna had committed. None of it is true. And you were supposed to be Jenna's friend. Some friend. You're no better than your scumbag brother.' Luke stood. 'About my house. You have two choices. You either pay for all the repairs or I go to the police.'

'You have insurance.' The tone was snarky.

'With an excess I have to fork out but why should my insurance company pay for deliberate vandalism and I lose my no-claim bonus. Like I said – two choices.'

'You've got no proof.'

'Yes I have. There was already a good security system on my house when I bought it. I upgraded it to the latest on the market. There are camera's covering the entire outside. You smiled for the camera. The system is connected to my mobile phone, which sent me an alarm. I have saved the footage I showed Stuart. The police will have no doubts. Your choice. I'll get quotes for a new window and door tomorrow. If you don't pay, I visit the police.' Too angry to stay, he headed for the passage, Stuart on his heels.

'Sorry, Stuart. Jenna is already suffering from PTSD because of

Ryan. Apart from turning up for work each day since the incident, she holed herself in her home – too scared to visit the squash courts for a game on the weekend. Add on today's treachery and, well, she would have drunk herself into oblivion if Josh and I hadn't turned up with a take-away meal. She knows about Emily's betrayal. Well, actually she doesn't know the extent of the lies, which were beyond nasty, and I'm not going to tell her. Nor about tonight's incident. I don't think she could handle it.'

'Jenna was sacked?'

'Asked to hand in her resignation. I'm not sure if she did since I resolved the accusations. The super was pissed and did say they had got it wrong. He wasn't impressed when Mortimer hadn't investigated the claims properly before involving the department. I'm surprised Emily only received a transfer. Doesn't seem fair. And none of this is fair on you. I'm sorry I brought it to your front door but I was furious.'

'Don't blame you. Since this Ryan incident we've had a few arguments, which has shown me a side to Emily I'm not sure I can live with. After tonight, well, there isn't a future with her.'

'Hell, I'm sorry.'

'No need. Better I find out before… well, I was going to do the proposal thing at Christmas. It won't happen now. Ryan has always been an odd fish but I didn't realise how odd. He gave me the creeps a few times. I don't know why Jenna put up with him so long. She was always polite but you could tell she was hesitant whenever he was around. Her gut instinct is astute.' Stuart glanced up and smiled. 'Think she likes you quite a lot.'

'How can you tell?'

'I think she trusts you and she's got closer to you in the short time you've been here than she has with anyone else since I've known her. You could do a lot worse.'

Luke couldn't hold back a grin. 'Good to know. Josh adores her.'

'And you?'

'I'm attracted to her but at the moment I'm sure all Jenna needs is a friend to believe in and support her. It's early days. Got to go and cover a gaping hole in my front room before I pick up Josh.'

'Where is he?'

'With Jenna. We had not long begun to eat. I couldn't let him see this. Nor Jenna. I'm certain she was tipped over the edge today. Sorry about this. We'll catch up soon.' Luke left with a wave over his shoulder and jogged towards his house with a long sigh.

Nerves had Jenna on edge. While waiting for Luke to pick her up for the drive to the lawyer's office, she forced calmness until she ended up pacing backwards and forwards, eyes downcast, fingers twisting the edge of her jacket into a knot.

The past couple of weeks had been tough. Most of the staff had taken her aside, apologetic and begged forgiveness. She was polite to each, smiled and accepted their apologies but couldn't get over how they had all believed the outlandish lies and snubbed her. A couple had let out snippets. She had slept with different men each week: men she had never heard of. She went to night clubs wearing such scanty clothes her boobs hung out and her knickers were on show. As if. Not one of her items of clothing, except underwear, could be called scanty. Even her squash outfits covered more than many others she'd seen. She was drunk most nights and snorted white powder of at least three varieties she'd been told about. There was the fact she had moved in with Luke and slept with more than one father of the kids in her class. It was difficult to believe a so-called friend could make up so many lies. Emily had vanished. Since the day all hell broke loose, she hadn't seen or heard from Emily. It had been rumoured she'd been transferred to a bush school. Jenna didn't know if it was true, nor did she care. According to Luke, Stuart had broken off the relationship. She couldn't blame him.

At school she still kept to herself, carried out her duties and occasionally stayed in the staffroom to eat lunch to pretend all was forgiven. But it wasn't. John had asked her to take back her resignation and said he wouldn't send it in until the end of the year. She still hadn't decided.

Knock, knock.

She jerked at the noise, stood and wobbled to the door, the reason for Luke being here sent her nerves into overdrive again.

Rob. She had to meet with Rob.

It took two attempts to get the door open where she stood too scared to move.

Luke studied her face. 'You will be fine. I won't let things get out of hand. We can walk out anytime you've had enough.' He gave her a quick hug, which she sure needed but it wasn't long enough. To be held until security settled jittery nerves would be far better. It wasn't going to happen with Luke.

For the entire drive of fifteen minutes she wrapped her arms around her body to hold herself together. It was a relief when Luke slid his arm around her waist and held her close while they walked from the parking lot into the lawyer's office. The pressure of his arm ensured she took steps forward and not turn around to flee. Words were beyond her.

They were ushered into a small conference room and handed a cardboard cup of coffee to drink while they waited. The coffee tasted like the cardboard so she didn't drink any beyond the first sip. Instead, she huddled as close to Luke as she could. A warm fuzzy settled around her when he reached out and his long fingers settled over her cold hand clenched tight in her lap.

When a door opened behind them, she froze. Luke squeezed her hand before politely standing to acknowledge the two men who entered.

Jenna dared a glance. Rob's face was ashen. Her hand took on a mind of its own and trembled. Too late, she wished she hadn't agreed to this stupid meeting.

The lawyer introduced himself, pulled out the chair opposite her and Rob sat in it. Bad, cruel move, she thought. They intended to put pressure on her. Dread settled in the pit of her stomach.

'Thank you for coming,' said the lawyer who stood next to Rob. 'My client is desperate to clear up matters. We sought the permission of the court for this meeting since there is a restraining order against Mr Reynolds. Mrs Reynolds, you are under no obligation whatsoever and can call a halt to the proceedings and leave any time you want. I pray you will hear what Mr Reynolds has to say after which, you have the opportunity to say whatever you want to discuss. I'll leave it to my client to begin.'

Jenna couldn't look up but sensed an overbearing presence when Rob stood.

'Jenna, first I want to apologise for what happened at your place. I'm sorry about the whole episode and can assure you it will never happen again. I didn't mean for things to get so out of hand.'

Disbelief punched her in the gut. Her top teeth clamped over her bottom lip to prevent shouting abuse at him. Luke must have sensed her tension for he placed one hand over her tight fist.

'I've messed up your life as well as my own and you didn't deserve any of it. I took my annual leave from work and came to town after I found out where you were. I guess I've done a lot of growing up since we parted. I now realise I wasn't ready for marriage or commitment but I did love you.'

Her teeth clamped tighter to prevent a cynical laugh from escaping. He has a strong commitment to Nancy. And you don't rape and abuse a person you love.

'I sought you out because I want to build a relationship with our child and I guess I was pretty angry when I discovered you had given him or her up for adoption.'

A gasp whooshed from her mouth. Tears plopped down her face. Luke's arm wrapped around her shoulders. She so wanted to sink against him and bury herself inside his chest. There was a *whoop* and two tissues landed in her other hand.

'Despite what has gone on between you, he has a right to know about your daughter. You need to get it out,' Luke whispered in her ear.

'I might point out you have broken the law for you cannot sign away your child without the agreement of the other parent.' The lawyer's voice was officious.

She glared at the man. 'What makes you think I had my child adopted?'

'There's no indication of a child in your life,' said Rob. 'No small clothes on the line, no toys in the backyard. There's never a child with you at the squash courts.'

Startled by the admission, Jenna jerked upright. She swept a clenched fist across her eyes in a defiant move to brush the moisture away. 'You bastard! You've been spying on me. It's obvious you knew where I lived but you didn't bother contacting me. Why couldn't you have got your lawyer to write to me or phone? No, instead you sneak around, follow me and spy!' She paused. 'I didn't have her adopted out. Unlike you, who ordered me to have an abortion or the marriage was over, I could never give my child away.'

She jerked her head towards the smarmy lawyer who thought he was so damn smart. 'You are not the same jerk of a lawyer he had last time. Have you read the demands this… this…' she jabbed a finger in Rob's direction, 'arrogant rapist made me sign? *Never* was I to contact him. *Never* did he want any communication about *my* child. Even though he abrogated all responsibility I knew he would have to pay child support. Did he ever get any demands for child support from the authorities?'

'Well did you?' She glared at Rob.

'Err… no.'

'I wonder why.'

'You had it adopted, or worse. Did you put it in foster care?'

'You are such an arrogant arsehole.'

Luke sniggered beside her at the same time the lawyer sputtered, 'Now, now, there's no need for such language. We want to know where the child is so Mr Reynolds can have access and build a relationship.'

'Well good luck. You need to dig a six foot hole.'

The gasps echoed, followed by a heavy silence.

'I'm sorry… I didn't know… I assumed. What happened?' Rob sounded genuinely concerned.

Jenna didn't care. 'What the hell do you care? You don't have a child you have to support - you should be thankful.'

'Jenna, I had no idea, you never told me,' Rob stammered.

She was so furious she stood and leant over the table. 'I never bloody well told you because you insisted, through your lawyer, that I was never to contact you. You damn well walk out on me the day I find out I'm pregnant and I never hear from you again. All I get are letters from a flaming lawyer making ridiculous demands. You got far more than your fair share at settlement leaving me with barely enough to buy a tiny place. Not once did you show any concern for me, or our child. You weren't there when I struggled through a pregnancy with no financial support from you or anyone else. I'd given up my job because you demanded it and wasn't about to get another teaching position being pregnant. You weren't there when my daughter died inside me. Nor were you there offering support when I had to go through twenty-four hours of labour knowing that at the end of it my baby was going to be born dead. No one was there to support me except for the few hospital nurses who checked how I was progressing. You weren't there when I held her lifeless body in my arms or when I had to bury her tiny casket in the ground.'

She squirmed and fell back into her seat. 'She was so beautiful and so perfect. I held her for a few minutes… they took her away from me.' Jenna dropped her head in her hands, leant on the desk and the tears came. They wouldn't stop when Luke dragged both their chairs around, gathered her against his chest and held her tight. Every atom in her body was in agony.

'We'll give you a few minutes,' she heard from the lawyer before there was a scraping of chairs and shuffle of feet.

Jenna jerked up, swept a fist over her face. 'No.'

'Excuse me?' The lawyer paused in the doorway; Rob next to him.

'You leave, so do I, so if you want this finished you stay.'

Both men returned but neither sat. It was a good job Rob stopped a few metres away for she wanted to reach over and thump him. Instead she eyed him. 'I'm sorry for you. You have no concept about loving anyone other than yourself. You are nothing but a self-centred pig. You had an affair behind my back with one of my best friends. I assume it was going on right through our marriage.'

The sudden flush of embarrassment on Rob's face confirmed her suspicions. 'You come here, break into my house and try to rape me. Rape me!' she screeched. 'You physically belt me up, terrorise me and now have the audacity to come in here and say you are sorry. You certainly weren't sorry at the time. You enjoyed calling me disgusting names. You took pleasure in outlining all the gruesome things you were going to do to me to pay me back. Pay me back for what? What the hell did I ever do to you to deserve such appalling treatment? You know what? I don't believe for one moment you are sorry for anything. What I do believe is you set this up so you would look good in court so they will be lenient with you. You don't give a stuff about me. I hope you rot in gaol, because I sure as hell will say nothing good about you when they ask me to testify. I will tell them the truth.'

Jenna shoved her chair back with so much force it fell against the wall with a resounding thump. Spinning around, she stalked outside with head held high. Luke must have scrambled after her for he slid his arm around her shoulder and ushered her outside, across the road into a small park.

'Let's sit.' He led her to a park bench. Dropping down, he kept his arm around her shoulder and drew her close. Her head fell onto his already damp shirt.

'I'm sorry,' she said. 'I've never been so angry.'

'Don't be sorry. He deserved your anger and a lot more. If you want to talk about it I'm all ears, but if you don't, it's fine. When you walked out it prevented me from reaching over, dragging the smug bastard over the table and doing him an injury - a severe injury and I think you were too meek and mild in what you called him. Mind you, I sincerely hope I'm never on the receiving end of a tongue lashing from you. This cute Persian cat has got sharp claws.'

Jenna couldn't help but smile at Luke's teasing words. 'I wasn't too harsh?'

'Nowhere near harsh enough. But you were honest - which was a good thing. You needed to get your anger out. I actually think his lawyer might regret having him as a client. It's not often lawyers are at a loss for words, but you certainly silenced that one. Are you okay now?'

'Sort of. I'm glad it's over and I never have to have contact with him again.'

'We have the rest of the day to ourselves so how about we get a bite to eat?

'You don't have to get back to work?'

'No, I took the day off in lieu of all the hours I've put in at night, and since I own half the business I can take the occasional day off when needed, without having to be accountable to anyone other than my partner. So let's enjoy what is left of the day.'

'Okay, anything to get my mind off unpleasant things.'

The classroom was abuzz with excited chatter by the time the last of Jenna's pupils arrived, the parents leaving them in her care while they found a seat in front of the stage in the covered assembly area. She tried to calm the animated youngsters by handing out items needed by each child before lining them up in the correct order. Her class was the first item and she wasn't sure who was the most nervous, she or the children. Many hours had been spent rehearsing with the children still dissolving into giggles in certain parts but at least they didn't roll around the floor laughing any more. It should be a fun filled opening to the night's performances. She had watched other classes at the dress rehearsal earlier and had been impressed with the standard. The parents were in for a treat.

The siren sounded for the classes to make their way to their allotted places. 'One single line,' Jenna called. 'Remember your order and make sure you have all you need.' After much wriggling and swapping of places, a single line snaked around the desks. Jenna put her finger to her mouth. 'No talking from now on. Lead the way, Simon.'

A hush went over the expectant audience when they arrived. It took ten minutes before all classes were seated on rolls of carpet in the front, the chairs needed for the parents. John Mortimer welcomed the parents and made the first announcements. From then on the children were to run the show with the Year Six's making the introductions and changing the stage for each class.

After Jenna's class was announced, the children made an almost orderly entrance onto the stage. Two boys tripping on the steps created a few seconds of humorous chaos before they stood ready. The children performed to perfection despite breaking up in giggles in the funny parts and when a costume fell apart, but it all added to the involvement of the audience. Warm pleasure rippled through her innards at the genuine laughter and thunderous applause. The kids were so excited a quiet orderly return to their seats was impossible. There were sneaky waves to parents and bright grins resulting in a few trips and not so hushed whispers and giggles.

The entire concert was well received before a brief graduation ceremony for the Year Sixes, after which the children carried the chairs back to their classrooms to remain under their teacher's care until each child was collected.

Having offered to drive Jenna home, Luke browsed through Joshua's workbooks while he waited. Jenna noticed his look of alarm when he read Joshua's diary. She smiled at his glance to her.

Luke approached. 'Are you sure no-one else reads this?'

'Only Josh, you and me.' She laughed at Luke's chagrined face. 'He's an eloquent writer.'

'Too damned eloquent. And you knew, before I had a chance to ask that I was taking you out on our date. I hope they don't write diaries in Year Two. Are the other kids this open and honest?'

'Oh, yes but Joshua is more advanced than most. They're not quite as expressive as he is. I only ask Joshua to read his to the class when I know it's safe.'

'Thank God for small mercies.' Luke returned to his son and replaced all the books in his desk.

As soon as they were settled in the car Joshua emitted a loud yawn and was asleep by the time they reached Jenna's house. It had been a long day for him. Luke left him in the back while he walked Jenna to her door.

'I'm too scared to kiss or hug you goodnight in case Inspector Clouseau is watching, ready to write his in-depth action replay,' Luke commented with sarcasm.

She laughed.

'Goodnight, sleep well.' He strode away.

Unable to get the past couple of weeks out of her mind, Jenna lay awake too long. Since the ordeal in the lawyer's office, Luke had been in the background offering support and positivity. There had been regular phone calls, a few meals with Joshua, which had been fun filled, but deep down it rankled how it wasn't enough. She wanted more – a lot more. It would never happen because Luke hadn't laid Lisa to rest. Why, oh, why did she allow herself to fall in love with a man who couldn't love her back?

The alarm jerked her awake. She shot upright then flopped back onto the pillow. It was the last day of school and she was already exhausted from lack of sleep. It was a struggle to get up, shower and dress. Needing a boost of energy, she made porridge, sliced a banana on top and drizzled it with honey. A mug of hot tea washed it down. Since she had to bring home the rest of her personal belongings, she drove to school. For a boost of energy, she made a strong mug of coffee in the hope a caffeine hit would help start the day. She got the children to pack up their belongings to take home, followed by a cleaning session of benches and desks. She gave the children a pile of activities they could do at their own rate while she took work from the pin-up boards and cleaned as she went. A few children at a time returned each item to its owner. By home time it was difficult to find the energy to drive home. The minute she walked in the door she continued to the bedroom, kicked off her shoes and fell onto the bed.

The phone's strident ring woke her. She fumbled for the receiver while trying to get her brain to function.

'Good evening, how was your day?'

'Overlong. You woke me. How was your day?'

'Hectic. All our clients are desperate to clear their financial problems before Christmas. By the way, I've hidden a certain diary so it can't be passed on to grandparents. I rang to ask if you wanted to share dinner with us.'

'To be honest I would love to but am exhausted. I'd probably fall asleep at the table. How about tomorrow?'

'No go. Josh and I haven't finished our Christmas shopping. For the first time since meeting you, he doesn't want you around and I'm not allowed to tell you why. He says it's a big secret.'

'Another secret. He's big on these secrets.'

'Only between him and me. If anyone else asks him to keep a secret he is under strict instructions to tell me. It was a difficult but necessary conversation. Hard to explain to a six-year-old. The other thing I wanted to ask is what your plans are for Christmas Day? I know I should have asked before.'

'No plans for Christmas Day is not my favourite day.'

'Why?'

'It was Christmas Day, two years ago, when I gave birth.'

'Oh, hell, I'm sorry and I understand. Mum and Dad invited you to their place. Since our office will be shut for two weeks, Josh and I plan on going late on the 24th and stay until New year's Day. I was hoping you would agree to join us. Josh will be devastated if you aren't with us on Christmas Day and so will I.'

'Can I think about it and let you know in a couple of days?'

'Sure. When I told Mum I intended spending the day with you she made this suggestion. While you think, consider this: no matter which way you decide, Josh and I will spend the day with you.'

'You can't miss Christmas with your parents.'

'I can when a person important to me needs company. After the trauma you've been through these past few months, spending Christmas alone isn't about to happen.'

'Oh, I don't know how to respond,' she said while a warm fuzzy rushed through her innards. Important to him, echoed through her mind.

'Say yes.'

'Okay. I probably need to go to stop me from dwelling, although I don't suppose Joshua will allow me to dwell.' She smiled at the thought. She so adored the young boy. And his father, her inner voice added.

'I'm sure he will do his best to keep your mind totally focussed on him and I'll have to fight him off to have time with you to myself. I'll ring Mum to let her know. They will be pleased.'

'Thank her for the invitation.'

'Will do.'

'Happy Christmas, Jenna!' Josh ran across the room and knelt by the side of the bed. 'Come on, wake up,' he added when she groaned and turned over. He shook her shoulder.

'Huh, what?' She opened one eye and peered at him.

'Wake up. It's Christmas.'

Her other eye opened. 'It's still dark.'

'But it's morning.'

'Not sun-up morning which means it's still night. Go wake your father.'

'I did. He's grumpy, too.'

'I'm not surprised. What time is it?'

'Time to get up.'

Jenna lifted her head, eyed the clock, groaned and flopped back onto the pillow.

'I swear that at birth, they feed kids a magic potion to make them all wake up at the crack of dawn every Christmas Day and birthday. Happy Christmas, Jenna.' Daddy stood at the doorway. He'd put on shorts and a bright red T-shirt but his hair was still messy.

'I don't think dawn has cracked yet,' said Jenna as she turned over and tugged the sheet over her head. One shoulder lifted. 'Your son so why am I missing out on half a night's sleep?'

Daddy laughed. ''Tea or coffee?'

'You can't be serious.'

'Come on, it's Christmas and I'm certain there is no way Josh will let you linger. I got jumped on half an hour ago. Did my best to keep him amused.'

'Obviously didn't work. I'm awake now in any case - so much for a nice leisurely lie-in. You two scoot while I get dressed and make it tea - hot and black.'

With a grin, Joshua leapt up and ran to his father. 'Told you. Can I open my presents now?'

'No. We have to wait for Nanna and Poppy and don't you dare wake them.'

'Why not?'

'Because they don't wake up until the sun is up. How about you help me make the tea, and maybe toast and jam will make Jenna happy?'

'Okay.' He skipped to the kitchen but had to wait, wait, wait for Daddy to come. Jam. He could get the jam from the pantry. And bread. It was on the bench in the bread box but he wasn't allowed to turn on the toaster. But he could get the butter. He opened the fridge door, searched with his eyes. Top shelf. On tippy toes he reached up. Too high. 'Oops.' The cheese fell on the floor.

'What are you doing?' Daddy bent over and picked up the cheese.

'I couldn't reach the butter.'

Daddy's eyebrows went up high and his face crinkled. 'You can get knives and spoons while I make the toast.'

'Okay.' He opened the drawer, took out three knives, dropped one on the floor. 'Oops, sorry.'

'Slow down. Put the dropped knife on the sink – quietly,' he added when it clattered.

'Who's making so much noise?' Jenna had dressed in a skirt and bright green top with a white Christmas tree that had red baubles. Her white hair was tied back with a big red ribbon. Josh grinned at her. Oh, oh. Nanna was with her. Daddy's gonna be cross. 'Hi Nanna, Happy Christmas.'

'Sorry, Mum. Did my best to keep him quiet.' Daddy gave Nanna a big cuddle and kiss.

'He's no different than you were at the same age.' Nanna laughed. She always laughed. 'Let me help.' She filled the kettle and turned it on.

'Can we open the presents now?' Josh asked.

'Breakfast first,' said Nanna and Daddy at the same time. 'And we have to wait for Poppy to get up,' added Daddy.

To hurry, he gobbled his toast and milo, and Poppy got up, but breakfast took F-O-R-E-V-E-R.

'Is anyone interested in a certain Christmas tree and what's under it?' Poppy asked after he'd put his mug in the dishwasher.

'Yay,' yelled Josh a split second before he ran. 'I'm Santa.' He dived for the first present, read the label but had to wait for Poppy to sit in his chair before he dropped it in Poppy's lap.

'Only the presents in front of the tree,' said Nanna.

'Why?'

'The others are for tonight when your cousins come.'

'Casey and Sophie?' Josh asked.

'Both your aunties, uncles and all the kids,' said Daddy.

'Yay!' Josh yelled and picked up the next present. The label said Mrs Hunter so he dropped it in Nanna's lap 'cos she was the only Mrs Hunter now. She grabbed him a gave him a kiss. He grinned and ran back to the tree. After finding six presents which all said to Joshua from Santa, he searched for the one he had wrapped for Jenna. All of a sudden his tummy squirmed when he held it in front of her. 'You have to open this one first.'

She smiled, read the tag. 'You bought this for me?'

Unsure what to say, he shrugged. 'Daddy helped.'

Jenna slowly slid off the silver ribbon, unwrapped the red Christmas paper and shook the small box. Joshua watched her face. What if she didn't like it? She took the lid off the box. Inside was the gold locket on a chain.

'Open it up, there's a secret inside.' Joshua helped until their fingers got mixed up. 'There's a secret tiny catch on the side.'

'You show me.' Jenna took her fingers away.

He clicked the weeny lever, opened out the locket and grinned. There was a picture of him on one side and Daddy on the other side.

'Oh, Joshua, it's beautiful, please put it on me.' She knelt on the floor in front of him.

'You have to help me, Daddy,' Josh said when he couldn't figure out how to work the tiny clip. He loved it when Jenna gave him a big hug and kiss.

'Thank you, Josh, it's gorgeous.' Now how about you open this present. She leant over to the floor and picked up a green parcel. He unwrapped it to find a large notebook. On the front was the word diary. He grinned.

'This is your own private diary which nobody but you can read. It has a special lock and you can hide the key so only you can open it.'

Daddy groaned.

'Cool,' said Josh as he flicked through. There was a whole page for each day of the year. Now he could write about all his secrets and no-one would know.

'It starts on New Year's Day, which is a week away.' Jenna smiled as she leant over to the pile of presents. 'And this present is for your dad.' When she handed it to Josh he turned and dropped it in Daddy's lap then grabbed another handful of presents, read the tags to give them to the right people but stopped when he figured he couldn't open his own presents at the same time.

'I don't want to be Santa anymore.' He sat on the floor and ripped paper from those in his pile. This was much more fun.

'Hey, Son, slow down. Make sure you read the tags and thank the person who gave you the gift.'

'Okay,' he said and yelled, 'thank you, Santa.' The super-dooper rocket had a switch. He pressed it. Coloured lights flashed when it roared.

'Not inside, Josh. Only outside,' said Daddy. 'Turn it off.'

'Okay.' He tore the paper from a big square present. 'Oh, wow, space Lego. Can I make it now?'

'How about open your presents first. And what happened to you being Santa?'

'You can be Santa now.' Josh ripped the paper from another present.

Daddy laughed.

With held breath Jenna watched Luke open her gift. Would he like it? Relief surged when he grinned.

'I love it. Is the cat for real?'

'Of course, you don't think I'd drape a dead one over me do you?'

'Where did you find it?'

'It wasn't easy. Not a single pet shop within driving distance of town had a Persian cat. I resorted to visiting vets to find out if they had any regular customers with a white cat. I now have new friends in town, Mr and Mrs Ridley and Thomas – a.k.a. Tomcat, who is no longer a Tom.'

'The perfect gift. I love the single claw.'

'Amazing what you can do with Photoshop.'

'Thank you.' He turned the silver-framed photo around to his parents. 'You two will never know the significance of this photo but enjoy the beauty of the subject.' Luke bent to brush against her ear. 'Yes, you do purr.'

He laughed when she jabbed him in the ribs. 'And this is for you.' He handed her a small gold-wrapped oblong.

Her fingers fumbled until she got the box open to reveal two exquisite, jewelled hair grips, one decorated with red stones and the other deep green to match the two dresses she'd worn on their dates.'

'Oh, Luke, they're beautiful.'

As she fingered the curved clips, Luke reached up and slipped the elastic from her ponytail. 'Put one in for me now,' he whispered as he drew a lock over her shoulder.

Flustered, she swept two thick strands to the top of her head and caught them in place with the emerald grip to match her Christmas shirt.

Luke stared. His chest heaved 'Perfect. You have the most amazing hair.' He lowered his head, cupped his hands around her face and settled his mouth over hers.

Her heart stalled until a flood of warmth settled in her core. When he lifted his head she was reluctant to lose the sensation of his mouth. Unsure what to do, she turned to watch Josh tear paper from his gifts. It was a shock when his joy jerked darkness from her subconscious. A picture of a tiny lifeless body centred in her mind. It should be her daughter delighted in discovering hidden surprises under the bright paper.

A tear rolled down her cheek. Mortified, she dropped her head and scrambled from the sofa. 'Excuse me a minute,' she managed to mumble as she fled to the kitchen.

'Jenna?' came from behind a split second before her shoulders were gripped. 'Are you okay?' Luke's concerned face appeared as she was turned. 'Hey, what is it?' One thumb swept the moisture from under her eyes.

'Sorry.' Embarrassed, she shut her eyes but it didn't prevent more moisture leaking.

'Let's get out of here for a while so we can talk.' He called out to his parents that he was taking her for a walk. When there was a scuffle and muffled voices she figured they had to hold Josh back.

Her insides quivered when Luke grasped her hand and led her through the garden to the rear of the block. He stopped suddenly and twisted in front of her. 'Please tell me what's wrong.'

'Lily would have been two today.' She couldn't add how jealous she was of Joshua.

'Hell, I'm sorry.' He wrapped his arms around her and drew her head against his shoulder. 'I understand the pain. To me it was as though a lump of lead pressed into my chest while at the same time a vacuum had sucked out everything inside me.'

'Same for me.' She sniffed back more tears.

'It was worse in the middle of the night when I didn't have work or Josh to keep my mind away. I would lie next to Josh and draw him into my arms, simply because I needed the closeness. I can't count the number of middle-of-the-night cuddles he got. But you had no-one. I can't imagine how tough that was.' He stepped back a fraction and tipped her chin up. 'Do you want to know when my pain eased?'

'When?'

'When I saw you caring for Josh after school.' His smile was wide but gentle.

'Huh?'

'Meeting you eased my pain and just so you know, I've wanted to kiss you for weeks.'

'Weeks?' Her innards did a few somersaults.

'More like months.'

'But… the guilt… you only wanted friendship.'

'No more guilt and the friendship bit was all you needed, not what I wanted. Sometimes I'm so overwhelmed by my feelings for you I don't know what to say. That's how I am right now.' He moved his hands to the side of her face and drew it up. His kiss started off slow and gentle but soon turned into one of deep passion.

Every atom in her body did jiggles and quivers while her heart exploded with warmth. They drew apart and stood with foreheads together, eyes closed, holding each other's hands.

When she regained her equilibrium she stepped back a fraction to study him. 'I… gosh, I'm confused. I don't understand.'

'At first I was equally confused even though I knew I was in love with you. I ring my parents several times a week. On one of those calls I had a long chat with Dad when I asked how it was possible to give my heart to two different women?'

'There's another woman?' A bomb exploded in the pit of her stomach as she took a step back.

Luke reached out, tugged her back, looped his arms around her back. 'No. I was referring to Lisa. I have never and will never cheat on a woman. Dad emphasised how the vows we make on our wedding day include the words, *until death do us part*. How there is a reason those words are included. Lisa died. Her death parted us but just because a person dies it doesn't mean your love for that person dies at the same time. He also pointed out how, if it had been the other way around, I would have wanted Lisa to find happiness with another man. Bells clanged; neon lights flashed. Of course I would. It was then I wrapped my love for Lisa into a small package and stowed it away in a corner of my heart for safe keeping. You can never forget your love for a person who has passed – the same way you will always love the daughter you lost and your parents. But we can open our hearts to new love. You can let things go and still hold them close to your heart. I have laid Lisa to rest. And now I can honestly say, I love you and want you in my life on a permanent basis.' He shook his head. 'I've gone about this wrong, haven't I?'

'It's a bit sudden. You've given no indication this was how you felt. I'm in shock.'

'Good shock or bad shock?' His grin was wry.

'The best.'

The grin widened. 'I held off because after what you've been through the past couple of months, the last thing you needed was another guy pressuring you for romance or a relationship. You said once you trusted me. I figured it was a huge thing for you to trust a man when men had done nothing but abuse you and were off the agenda. Josh adores you, and so do I and I know you love my son, so I was hoping you could learn to love me the same.'

Overwhelmed, Jenna shook her head. 'I already love you. Have done for ages but thought it was one-sided.'

'You do? So why did you step back with the *incommunicado* stance?'

'It hurt to be with you but at the same time it hurt to not see you. I don't know how to explain. I wanted to spend time with you but you insisted you only wanted friendship and I wanted more than you could give me. It was easier to not see you.'

'I think Josh had his first taste of a broken heart when you took a step back. Hence the melt-down in class. He was angry with me because I couldn't fulfill my side of our bargain.'

'What bargain?'

Luke smiled. 'The big secret he wrote about. I can't reveal all the details – yet.'

'I'm intrigued.' She reached up with one hand and ran it down the side of his face. 'I missed you but didn't know how to make things better. My mind was kind of skewed with all the… you know.'

He grasped her hand, turned it over and planted a kiss in her palm. 'And now?'

'Now, I'm beyond happy.'

'Happy enough to take on both me and Josh? Although Josh can be a handful.'

'If I can manipulate a class full of six-year-olds into being civilised human beings, I think I can handle one sweet little boy.'

'Sweet is not a word I would use to describe Josh. Manipulative – definitely.'

'He's amazing and has your caring nature. When he sees a kid in class is upset or needs help, he's the first one there. I adore him.'

'Good, because there's a surprise waiting for you inside.' He turned her around, swung his arm around her waist and guided her towards the house.

'What?'

'The big secret Josh wrote about. Now is the time to reveal all the details.'

'That was ages ago.'

'About the time both Josh and I knew we were in love with you. I would appreciate it if you went along with what is going to happen next.'

He left her seated on the sofa in a room devoid of piles of wrapping paper and new gifts. 'Please wait there.'

Joshua sat in the middle of the bedroom floor, already engrossed in building the space Lego. Luke squatted next to him. 'Do you remember all the details of our secret?'

'Yes, why?'

'You can ask Jenna now.'

His eyes lit up. 'Really?'

'Yes, she's on the sofa.' Luke grinned when Josh shot from the room. He followed, grabbed his mum's hand and beckoned his dad. 'You two will want to see this. Hurry.'

They reached the doorway in time to see Joshua drop to one knee in front of Jenna who glanced at them with curiosity. Luke nodded.

Joshua took one of her hands in his. 'Jenna, will you marry Daddy and be my new mummy?'

A gasp came from his mother, a grunt from his father. Scratchy moisture spread across Luke's eyes.

'Oh, Josh.' When she bit a quivering lip it was obvious Jenna was overcome. She sniffed, frowned and then smiled. 'Why do I have to marry your dad. I could marry you,' she said with a quick wink at Luke.

Josh baulked and turned to Luke. 'Dad?'

'You have to be an adult before you are allowed to get married and if you marry Jenna you still won't have a mother.' It was hard to keep a straight face, not from laughter but the scene had him choked up with emotion.

'Oh, okay.' Josh turned back to Jenna. 'You have to marry Daddy 'cos I want you to be my mummy.'

'In that case, yes, I would love to marry your dad so I can be your new mother.'

Josh gaped. 'Really?' He spun his head around. 'She said, yes,

Daddy.' He flung himself against Jenna who wrapped her arms around him.

Overcome, Luke couldn't stand there any longer. He crossed the room, knelt next to Josh. 'You have to seal the deal with a kiss.'

'So sweet,' whispered his mother when Josh reached up and pressed his mouth against Jenna's. It was obvious she was close to tears.

'Can I call you Mummy,' Josh asked as he fisted his eyes.

'Lisa was your real mummy so how about you call me Mum instead so you always remember who your mummy was?' Jenna ruffled Josh's hair.

'Okay – Mum.' He twisted towards Luke. 'You have to kiss her too.'

Luke grinned. 'I intend to.' He stood, reached down, levered Jenna up and cradled her face in his hands. 'Thank you.' His kiss was a lot longer than Josh's brief peck. Before it got out of control he drew away. 'There's one more thing we men have to do,' he said to Josh as he reached into his shirt pocket. 'When we ask a beautiful woman to marry us and she says yes, we give her one of these.' He held out the ring he'd bought, not sure he'd need it yet but certain it was going to happen. He lifted Jenna's left hand and slid the ring into place.

She gasped. Tears flooded her eyes as she studied the ring. 'Oh, Luke, it's gorgeous.' She plastered her body against him and gripped him tight around the waist.

'Now Jenna has to sleep in your bed.'

Startled, Luke stared at his son. 'Why?' slipped out before he realised it wasn't the best question to ask, especially after a few of Josh's previous revelations.

'Poppy said mummies and daddies always sleep in the same bed so the daddy can keep the mummy safe.'

Luke turned to his father, who wore a slightly pink tinge on his face.

His dad shrugged. 'Josh asked.'

A stifled gasp came from behind.

With his arms around Jenna he pressed his mouth against her

ear. 'I can't wait,' he whispered at the same time he heard his mother herd the other two from the room.

'Nor can I,' she said as she pressed her hips against his.

'Sweet mercy, Jenna, you know how to bring a man to his knees. Maybe we'll need an afternoon nap because we were up so early this morning and need the rest before my sisters and their families turn up for tonight's party.' He pressed his mouth against her ear. 'Maybe next Christmas, we can enjoy it with a sibling for Josh. That is, if you want another child.'

She pressed her face into his chest and gripped her arms tight around him. It took a few seconds before she drew in a huge breath, tipped up her face and smiled. 'Can we sneak away now?'

He laughed. 'If you're sure I know just the place.'

'Where?'

'Behind the shed is a long lean-to under which sits the family caravan. It has all the mod cons including shower and toilet and has been set up for my sister and her husband to use tonight. I'm going to be the kind little brother and slum it so they can use my room. If you are serious, pack your bag and meet me there in half an hour.'

'Really? What about Josh?'

'He'll be too engrossed in building a ginormous space Lego until his cousins arrive when we won't see him till dinner time. I'll get Mum to keep him occupied. Your decision. I will never pressure you.'

She turned and ran. 'I'll beat you there.'